HALF
YEAR

A NOVEL

HALF
LIGHT

JANET SARJEANT

ISBN: 978-1-966343-34-9 (hard cover)
       978-1-966343-35-6 (soft cover)
Sarjeant. Janet
Edited by: Amy Klein

Warren Publishing
Charlotte, NC
www.warrenpublishing.net
Printed in the United States

This story is dedicated to my classmates of 1969 who
continue to inspire through their creativity and steadfastness.
And to those classmates we've lost along the way, *requiescat in pace*.

"With humor, Sarjeant created vivid, likable characters who deal with confusing feelings, conflict, and serious crucial issues. Music is always front and center ... I heartily recommend this one."
— Mary Kratt, author of *Watch Where You Walk*

"Janet Vass Sarjeant takes us on a journey through growing up in a small town. ... She brings to life friendships and experiences that let us reframe our own days of teenage awkwardness and insight ... [and] shares the highs and lows of growing up in an authentic and endearing way."
— Michael C. Maxey, President Emeritus, Roanoke College

"*Half Year, Half Light* is a winner! With this novel, Janet Sarjeant proves she is a capable storyteller. Her prose sparkles. The experiences of her characters feel thoroughly authentic. This novel reveals the vital place that adolescence occupies in every person's life journey. I was totally captivated. You will be too."
–Judy Goldman, author of *Child* and *The Rest of Our Lives*

"*Half Year, Half Light,* as seen by music-loving high school senior Eddy Walters, reminds us what it feels like to ponder leaving home while still dancing to our favorite teenage songs, where the angst of growing up is balanced against the fun and curiosities of young life. Set in a small town in the late 1960s, Eddy's story is eager and questioning, a split-screen of activity: both carefree and searching, serious and adventurous, and loving and dispiriting. And best of all, we can feel the tempo, pulse, pace, and rhythm of Eddy's journey in the 45s she plays on her record player, with the crescendo rising to what life will bring."
–Landis Wade, Charlotte Readers Podcast founder and author of *Deadly Declarations*

THE ANCIENT DRUIDS are said to have taken a special interest in in-between things like mistletoe, which is neither quite a plant nor quite a tree, and mist, which is neither quite rain nor quite air, and dreams, which are neither quite waking nor quite sleep. They believed that in such things as those they were able to glimpse the mystery of two worlds at once. Adolescents can have the same glimpse by looking in the full-length mirror [...]. The opaque glance and the pimples. The fancy new nakedness they're all dressed up in with no place to go. The eyes full of secrets they have a hunch everybody is on to. The shadowed brow. Being not quite a child and not quite a grown-up either is hard work, and they look it. Living in two worlds is no picnic. One of the worlds, of course, is innocence, self-forgetfulness, openness, playing for fun. The other is experience, self-consciousness, guardedness, playing for keeps. Some of us go on straddling them both for years.

—Fred Buechner, *Whistling in the Dark*

PART 1

JANUARY 1969

CHAPTER 1

I really like January.

She stands with her cart of books during her fourth-period library shift, looking at the spine of the book in her left hand while sliding her index finger along the books lining the shelf. She finds the place where *Great Expectations* by Charles Dickens belongs and slides it in. *It's my birthday month, and I guess that's why I like it so much. I wonder if everyone likes their birthday month? I'm going to ask Joanie and Paul.*

Edna Louise Walters is getting ready to turn eighteen at the end of January.

———

"Eddy, wait up!" Joan runs up the stairs leading to the second floor of Thomasburg High School, huffing as she catches up to Eddy. "Have you studied for the exam in Mr. Thompson's class?"

"Not much," Eddy answers. "I figure if you pay attention in class, which I do, then I'll do fine. Well, in the classes I like. I *do not* pay attention in Government class. And my face is breaking out. Ugh. I have to use that pHisoHex more often these days."

"Your face doesn't look bad at all. It's always our own faces in the mirror that bother us, isn't it? Whoever made the rules around here just ruins our Christmas with exams being held over our heads all through the holidays. No wonder our skin is breaking out. Sadists," Joan spouts.

"Just picture Mr. Arnold and Mrs. Arendall plotting together at the beginning of time making up the schedule. Did you see Mr. Arnold standing at the lunchroom door and watching us as we ate our lunch yesterday? He looked right at me, and I wasn't doing a thing—well, that he could see."

"C'mon, Eddy, be serious."

"I *am* being serious. I was thinking about how he would be scared if he knew what we were all thinking about him. How *I* think of him. He lords it over us like a … like a …" Eddy pauses to search for the metaphor she wants. "Like a prison guard watching his prisoners."

Joan laughs. "Stop, Eddy, and hold my books a minute." The girls stop in the hall while Joan tries to get her unruly hair back into a barrette. Eddy loves her friend's wild, hard-to-control hair. Her own is tame by comparison. Even though short hair is in, she was tired of fixing it and has been growing it out. Her dark-brown strands are now just at her shoulders and rather unmanageable. When her hair falls against her cheeks, she often tucks it behind her ears to keep it out of the way. Eddy thinks she would like to have Joan's hair. It would match who she is inside.

"Okay, thanks," Joan says. "Eddy, we have to study if we're going to take the SATs. I can't believe we have only a few months left of high school and then, and then … college, I guess. *If* we can get in a college. I know it's easy for you in English, but I need help. Please."

"Okay, kiddo. If you help me with Government. I hate Government. I just don't like studying about all the people in the branches of government arguing all the time."

"That's called debating, Eddy."

"Okay, okay. Tonight, we study. My place. Dad and Mom will be at church. They're always at church." She says each word of this last sentence slowly, as if they weigh too much to say quickly.

6

After exams, life and classes return to normal. Eddy doesn't fail Government, and she's relieved.

Winter days in the Appalachians bring flurries of snow or bracing winds or sleet or all of the above. Winter coats and warm hats and gloves are de rigueur especially for some of the students in Thomasburg, Virginia, who walk to and from school rather than ride school buses. Eddy's heavy coat is stuffed into her locker, and she walks to classes on this day with forest-green knee socks and a plaid wool kilt and white sweater. After first-period English, she holds her notebook and textbooks against her chest as she contemplates the class discussion of Richard Wright's *The Man Who Was Almost a Man*. She wonders why she's not itching to be … something. And if she does decide to be or do something, will she get into deep waters of trouble like Dave in the story, who buys a gun to make himself seem more important, more manly in his world? Do the boys in her school want to prove they're men in their world? Is the war in Vietnam just such a proving ground? Mr. Thompson tried to get some discussion about this in class, but the boys didn't bite. They sat in their desks looking down. He posed the same question to the girls, but only the couple of dependable talkers spoke up. They seemed to have big plans for their lives. Mr. Thompson pointedly asked her what she would do to fit in, be adultlike, prove something. She answered that she would need to think about it for a while. He moved on to someone else who didn't want to answer either.

Eddy continues to think as she walks through the crowded halls. She's "almost" a full-grown woman. What will she do to prove that? What will the world want her to do? That word *almost* is troubling. Will she do something stupid like Dave? Maybe not with a gun, but really stupid anyway? Like losing her temper and shouting at a teacher and getting kicked out of school and her parents never forgiving her? Or running away with someone and never coming back to Thomasburg and breaking her parents' hearts? Things like that?

She meets up with Paul and Joan in the parking lot after school.

"No, I mean it, Pauley. What do you want to be when we leave here in June? Joanie and I were talking about this the other day."

"Stop calling me Pauley. We three sound like backup singers to the Crystals. Pauley, Eddy, and Joanie. Geez."

"Okay, okay," Eddy mumbles. The three of them walk in silence for a bit. "Hey, who's got money? I'm just dying for some fries from Kenny's. I need grease."

Joan looks in her pocketbook. "I have thirty-five cents."

Paul puts his hand in his pocket and pulls out some change. "Seventy-six cents."

Eddy is pulling out her wallet from her pocketbook. "I've got fifty-seven cents, no fifty-eight. We can do it!"

As they sit in the booth at Kenny's, the conversation turns to Eddy's birthday.

"Whatcha gonna do for your birthday? I bet Johnny will take you somewhere," Joan says as she dips a fry into ketchup.

Paul grins. "Yeah, like the top of the mountain."

"Shut up, Paul. As a matter of fact, we plan to go to the movies."

"Has anyone done a study of the number of boys named Johnny in this town? Or in this country, for that matter. I know about five myself, but your Johnny is maybe the handsomest! Can't compare to my Roger though."

"Johnny is handsome, for sure. But he's so doggone calm all the time, where I'm antsy all the time …. Like I need to move around or I'll come out of my skin. I don't know what I want. I can't seem to stop doing things or saying things. Sometimes Johnny looks at me strangely when I say things like … I don't know … like the universe is collapsing all around me … or … everything falls, is falling away. I don't know, he'll probably fall away from me."

"You're quite serious today," says Joan. "Is it your birthday coming up that has you down this dark path? I hope I don't feel so serious when my birthday comes in March. I want to celebrate being eighteen. Get presents. Eat cake. Kiss Roger."

Paul dips his last fry into the ketchup. "Eddy, you're not made for such dark thoughts," he says dramatically. "What's your name? Hamlet? Lighten up!"

"Paul," says Eddy, "that sounds like a quote from somewhere. Dark thoughts. Hmm …. Maybe it's the thought of that story, *The Man Who Was Almost a Man,* that makes me feel life is shit right now." Her voice drops on the word *shit* as if by using it in public, the adults will come out from somewhere at Kenny's.

Joan laughs. "You became a woman some time ago, remember?"

"You know what I mean!" She cuts her eyes over to Paul. How much girl stuff did he need to hear? She had to admit, though, that he didn't seem to care at all when they talked of girl stuff like boyfriends and fashion and changing bodies in front of him. *Maybe we should ask him when he became a man and his voice dropped!* Then she says, "And you know, of course, there's a war going on. Like I said, there's a lot of shit going on."

They all grow quiet for a few moments until Paul says, "Vietnam seems so far away. But then it seems real when it comes through our TVs on the news at night." The girls are looking down at the fries.

"Far away and in our living rooms at the same time. You're right, Paul," Eddy says.

———————

Eddy walks home with Joan, and after they say goodbye and Joan continues on, Eddy enters her house on Cavendish Road, thinking about the show she watched the night before: *Kraft Music Hall* hosted by Bobby Darin. A singer named Laura somebody performed, stirring more unrest in Eddy's insides. First a slow song about a guy who's a "runner" no woman can hold because he would take a midnight train to get away from her if she tried to hold him. After that soulful song, Laura somebody sang an antiwar song with an up-tempo tune that jumped like her hands on the piano and a voice that shouted—screamed actually—that she won't study war "no more." Laura implored the listeners to save the people, the children, the

9

country. In her mind, Eddy puts that song on her list with "Blowin' in the Wind" by Bob Dylan, "For What It's Worth" by Buffalo Springfield, and "If I Had a Hammer" by Peter, Paul and Mary.

Music stirs her soul, and as much as Eddy likes being in the school's chorus and near music, she realizes they sing no songs with an edge. Just "safe" songs, like "Climb Ev'ry Mountain" and "You'll Never Walk Alone." Safe because their parents approve. And their teacher, Mrs. Norman.

Eddy is thinking about these things when she steps into the kitchen and her mom asks about her day.

"Fine, fine."

"Edna, your dad picked up a couple of 45s for you today at lunch. They're on your bed."

Eddy runs up the stairs. On her bed is Stevie Wonder's "For Once in My Life" and Donovan's "Hurdy Gurdy Man." "Thanks, Dad," she whispers. She doesn't quite know how her father decides what to get her. Just new artists? Has he heard any of them on the radio? It's an almost unspoken bond between them as he introduces her to new music. She saves Stevie Wonder for later and hastily puts Donovan on the record player. Eddy has liked his music from the first time she heard him. She thinks he sounds like he's from another world. "Sunshine Superman" was her first single, and it made her body want to move. And lately, she's heard a strange song of his on the radio titled "Atlantis," about a place that no longer exists that is buried beneath the sea. Now she's excited to hear this single, a gift from her father. She sits down on the edge of her bed, listening as the Scotsman begins humming. Then comes a soft guitar strum. Then Donovan's wavering Scottish voice. Enter the drums and a guitar wail. Eddy is transported—to where, she's not sure. She picks up some phrases and asks herself, *Who is the Roly Poly man? Why is humanity crying?* And then Donovan's hypnotizing voice repeats the words *Hurdy Gurdy* over and over again. *Who is the Hurdy Gurdy Man who brings songs of love?* The drums, bass, guitar, and odd background instruments fill her room. When the needle finds the end and the arm rejects, Eddy jumps up and starts the 45 again. And then again.

CHAPTER 2

"Edna Walters."

"Yes, sir?"

Eddy has just left English class, and Mr. Thompson, her teacher, catches up to her as she heads to Trigonometry.

"You seemed distracted in class. Anything the matter? I think you like English."

"I do like your class. Just lots going on right now, I guess."

"Well, don't forget to work hard on the Shakespeare presentation that's coming up. It's for a test grade. You'll need a good grade."

"Yes, sir." *Yes, Your Royal Highness.*

Eddy continues on her way, knowing Mr. Thompson is watching her walk away. She wonders if her clothes look all right from behind—aware that her olive-green A-line dress, even with a slip on underneath, is a bit clingy over her bottom.

Good grief, why is everyone on my back? I'm almost through with high school, and you would think the world might end at graduation if I don't have good grades.

She hugs her notebook close to her chest as she finishes the walk to class. Arriving to her desk, she sets the notebook down with a slight bang and slides into the seat.

"What's up, buttercup?" The smartest math person in her class, Bill Norris, surveys her from his seat across the aisle. He nervously taps his pencil on his desk.

"Nothing, nada, nil. Just a lot going on."

"If you need to look over my shoulder for the homework, I give you permission."

Good grief. "Thanks, but I've got my homework. Piece of cake."

Of course it hadn't been, as she worked on the assignment last night. Trig, Algebra, Advanced Math—they all give her trouble, and she has to work hard at it, when she takes the time to work at it at all. But she likes the teacher, Mrs. Lemons, well enough. Old Mrs. Lemons sits at her desk and looks over the top of her glasses at the class. She seems to see things, *really* see right into the minds of the students sitting in front of her: She sees Bill's abilities when she has to resort to calling on him after asking everyone else for an answer to a particularly hard problem and receiving no correct answers; she sees shy Karen's red face when called upon to answer a problem in front of everyone or, worse, when she's asked to go to the board, and Mrs. Lemons is easy on her; she sees Paul, who keeps his head way down over his notebook as if he can't see well the numbers he has scratched there; and Rob, the handsome fair-haired boy who knows he could have any girl in the class as his girlfriend and is a pretty good student to boot. And the others to whom Mrs. Lemons, all-knowing, all-seeing, bestows a glance over her glasses. Her thinning hair and glasses perched on the end of her nose to look at her textbook make one think she's sickly, but she's not—just pretty old. Eddy wonders how old she really is. Hard to tell. She's probably one of those people who looked old when she was younger and never changed much when she actually aged. Mrs. Lemons seems to sense Eddy's disquieted spirit these days. She knows Eddy isn't a math whiz, and yet she encourages her, particularly being patient with her as she works the tangram shapes that Eddy just can't piece together. Eddy has trouble seeing how they fit together. But Mrs. Lemons seems like a benevolent monarch, enthroned at her desk, her large arms resting on the large black desk blotter.

Mrs. Lemons is giving Eddy extra help during lunch hour. She's sitting at her desk as usual, grading some papers while looking up at Eddy every now and then.

"Ugh! Why can't I see how to solve for these variables?"

"Edna, relax. Take a deep breath. Read the problem out loud."

Eddy holds her pencil tightly and reads out loud from the worksheet in front of her. "'A man is observing a pole of height fifty-five feet. According to his measurement, the pole casts a twenty-three-foot-long shadow. Solve for the angle of elevation of the sun from the tip of the shadow.'"

"Draw the pole. Put the sun in the sky, Eddy. Let x be the angle of elevation of the sun. Now solve."

Eddy scratches on her paper for a few minutes. She rips out the paper and balls it up and looks at Mrs. Lemons. "My drawing looked ridiculous. I'm starting over." Eddy doesn't see it, but Mrs. Lemons gives a small smile.

Eddy draws and scratches some more. Then she looks up, stands, and takes the paper up to the desk and places it in front of her teacher, looking expectantly across the desk. Mrs. Lemons looks down her nose through her glasses at Eddy's paper and isn't smiling.

She reads aloud: "Tan x equals fifty-five divided by twenty-three equals 2.391. X equals tan to negative one power, 2.391. Or x equals 67.30 degrees. Where's your work? You must show your work, Eddy."

Eddy frowns, turns, and goes back to her desk, snatching up a messy piece of paper. She returns to Mrs. Lemons and places the paper in front of her. Mrs. Lemons picks it up, looking at the frowning face of Eddy over the top of her glasses. Then she looks back down at the paper.

"You did it correctly. Good for you—although I gave you this problem because it's similar to the one we worked on in class today. Still, you got it right. But Edna, why so exasperated? I've told you over and over, you must show your work."

So that's how it is for Eddy. Exasperation, frustration, and questions. *What's wrong with me?* she constantly asks herself.

As she walks out of school that afternoon, her coat buttoned all the way up and her notebook and some textbooks hugged once again against her chest, she breathes a sigh of relief that the week is over. Her mother let her borrow the car for the day, and the teal-blue Corvair with the white upholstery is parked in the lot behind the school. When she gets to her car and leans against it to wait for Joan, she notices two guys leaning against the car next to hers. She knows them both a little. Buddy, a guy who was a year ahead of her but had somehow not graduated with his class last year and is now in Eddy's class. Jay, an intense-looking, dark-eyed guy who, though in her class year, isn't in any classes with her. She has known of him for some time but doesn't *know* him really. Jay's shock of dark hair falls over his forehead as he cuts his eyes over to Eddy. He nods at her, and she half smiles back. Buddy quickly walks over and squeezes his arm around her shoulders in a firm hug, as if they're good friends, which they're not.

"Buddy, stop that." Eddy shrugs off his arm.

"Just trying to be friendly, for God's sake. Eddy, my girl, want to see what happens when you don't pay attention in class?"

"I'm not your girl, but sure, what happens when you don't pay attention in class?"

"This." He holds up his left hand where instead of five fingers, there are only two, along with three stubs where fingers should have been. Eddy draws in a short breath through her parted lips. She stares at the hand, then she looks up at his face. Buddy is just standing there, grinning over his little performance. She looks over at Jay, who's studying her reaction with a small smile on his lips.

"Yep," says Buddy. "Shop class is filled with learning opportunities, but I was daydreaming about you that day, honey. I certainly learned one thing that day, using the saw to cut wood. Don't dream."

Eddy just leans there on her car with her lips parted dumbly. Buddy puts his arm around her shoulders one more time and squeezes. "Don't worry, honey, I'm all right now. All healed up."

Joan walks up then, and Buddy goes through the same routine. She kind of gasps too, and as Buddy has gotten the response he wanted, he walks back over to Jay and says, "Let's get out of here. We've upset these nice girls enough."

Jay walks around to the other side of Buddy's car and opens the squeaky front door. He stands for just a second, looking over the top of the car at Eddy. She meets his gaze, and later, lying on her bed listening to Peter, Paul and Mary while looking up at but not seeing the angled ceiling close above her head, she thinks about this encounter; she thinks that maybe time has gone out of whack. Was it a long gaze from Jay? Or had it lasted only a split second? Was she repulsed by the incident with Buddy? What did her face look like to Buddy as she looked upon the misshapen hand? What had she looked like to Jay, with her coat pulled tightly around her and her books armored against her body?

But she does come to know one thing: Jay's eyes are dark and long lashed, and a shock of hair falls across his forehead. Something about him has pulled her, interested her. When she thinks about his face, one she has only seen briefly in hallways over the last few years and has paid little attention to, her body now actually reacts physically. Something disturbing. But what? Disgust with his choice of friend? Thoughts of Shop class she has rarely pondered? His ... face?

She stops on the word and leaves her bed, going to the low bookcase and grabbing her yearbook from last year. She looks at last year's senior class, finding that Buddy's picture isn't in it. Then she looks for Jay in her class. Jay Nickles. There he is, staring out from the page with the same dark hair, the same dark eyes. Jay Nickles.

———

"Happy birthday to you. Happy birthday to you. Happy birthday, dear Eddy. Happy birthday to you." Joan sings loudly as she gets in the front seat of Eddy's car for school.

"Joanie, shhhhh. You'll wake the whole neighborhood! And I don't want everyone to know it's my birthday."

"You're eighteen today. A legal adult, for goodness' sake, Eddy. Live a little!"

"I'm living. Just don't spread the word at school. *Please.*"

"Well, surely I can tell Roger."

"Yes, you can tell Roger—but that's all, understand?"

"Yes, Your Royal Highness. Still, I sounded good on the birthday song, don't you think? Oh damn; I should have sung the Beatles' birthday song to you. Oh Eddy, I still love them so. Remember when we collected the Beatles cards? I think I still have mine somewhere in the attic. We had stacks of them, remember? At lunch in seventh grade we'd study them and trade them, and the boys made fun of us. I think they were all jealous because every girl was gaga over the Beatles. I loved Paul, and you did, too, but then you deserted him for John. I thought you were cuckoo; John wasn't handsome like Paul."

Eddy's two hands are on the steering wheel as she enters the back parking lot of the school. She decides to parallel park into a spot next to the PE field, reaching her arm along the seat's back as she looks over her right shoulder and maneuvers the wheel with her left hand. She speaks while backing.

"Paul McCartney *is* handsome, but John's voice is rough, and, well, it gets me. Like on 'Twist and Shout'—it's not pure, but it gets me. And he seems like a tortured soul. Sort of the same thing with Dylan, like he stays tortured by the society he lives in."

"Dylan's voice tortures me, I can tell you that, and not in a good way. Ugh. I don't get you sometimes, Edna Walters. It's almost like you want to be a tortured soul. I remember when we would lie on our backs on the bed in your room and stare at the ceiling while you played 'Heat Wave' over and over again. And we still lie on our backs in those beds pondering. Boys. Girls. Parents." Joanie looks over at Eddy as she backs and then shuts off the car. Joan sighs and then says, "I could never back a car like you can. You're a born driver, you know that? You do know that, don't you?"

Eddy smiles. It's not a tortured smile at all.

PART 2

FEBRUARY 1969

CHAPTER 3

Saturday in the little town of Thomasburg means relaxation and some time-wasting talk for Eddy and her friends. It's February 1st, and Eddy and Joan are in Eddy's basement with Saturday morning cartoons on the TV. The girls sit at a table with a plate of store-bought cinnamon rolls in front of them. The small TV sits on a portable stand against the wall. A bigger one sits in the upstairs den, but her brother Jimmy is sitting on the carpet in front of that one. The girls want to talk—alone.

"Well …" says Joan.

"Well what?"

"Well, how was the movie last night with Johnny? I know about your birthday dinner with your family on Wednesday, but how was everything else?" Joan's big brown eyes with eyebrows raised are zeroed in on her friend, and her curly ash-brown hair is uncombed this morning since there's no school. Eddy's is pulled back in a loose pony tail.

"Fine. You know Mom and Dad and Jimmy gave me an album. *Surrealistic Pillow* by Jefferson Airplane. Wait till you hear it, Joanie! It's absolutely fantastic. Grace Slick pounds out the words. Sort of sounds angry as she sings 'Somebody To Love.' I played the whole album nonstop after dinner that night of my birthday until Dad said I needed to turn it off so they could go to sleep. Typical. And the movie last night? Joanie, you know I love the movies. I go almost every time it changes, but last night's Elvis movie was silly. Really."

"You've always liked Elvis, I thought. Or maybe I liked Elvis a lot. You go with me to see his movies."

"He's okay. But when I think about Elvis in movies, I think about *Love Me Tender.* When I watched that movie on TV one Sunday afternoon, I cried at the end. Elvis was good! I really thought Elvis would go on to be a good actor. *Live a Little, Love a Little* is just okay. Can't compare with the great films we've been seeing this past year. Um ... *Dr. Zhivago,* um ... *Guess Who's Coming to Dinner.*"

Joanie rolls her eyes. "That scary one. That true one that has *blood* in the title.

"Yes! *In Cold Blood.* You're right, pretty scary stuff. Well, at least there was lots of kissing in the Elvis movie."

"And more kissing after the movie, I bet."

"Yeah. Johnny's a good kisser. Very polite, with no roving hands. Joanie, does Roger's kissing get better and better the longer you're together?"

"Roger isn't a 'polite' kisser, and his hands ..." The girls look over at each other and start giggling. "Yeah, better and better! And the place we went last night ..."

A call comes from the top of the stairs. "Edna, Paul's coming down."

"Okay, Mom."

Paul swings around the stair railing. "Good morning, ladies. What's happening?"

"Cinnamon rolls." Eddy pushes the plate toward Paul as he sits down at the round table.

"Also, Joanie was just about to tell me about the place she and Roger went parking last night."

Paul rubs his hands together in mock gleeful expectation. "Oh boy. Let's hear it."

"Well, we drove up a hill over on the other side of the railroad tracks from here. The road went straight up, I'm not lying. I wasn't sure Roger's car was going to make it. And what did we find at the top? A *big* house with no lights on. There was one of those covered places that come out over the driveway from the house so that the people who get out of the car and enter the side door won't get wet. A rich person's house. Who knew that house was there? I sure didn't. Strange to find new places in our little town we've never seen. It was spooky—like it might be haunted. Very dark—very interesting. And Roger just pulled up and killed the engine. We sat there for a while before, you know, we started doing other stuff."

"Wow," says Eddy. "What if someone had been there? You might have been arrested!"

"Yeah," echoes Paul. "Sounds like a cool place. I know, let's finish off these rolls and drive over there and investigate."

"I definitely want to see this house. Kind of dangerous but exciting. Perfect Saturday activity," says Eddy.

"All right! By the way, I have some news too. Did you hear the news about the Beatles?" Paul looks at the girls for their reactions.

"No!" both girls say together.

"Jinx!" shouts Joan. "You owe me a Coke."

Eddy smiles at this old elementary school ritual of saying things at the same time.

"Well," says Paul, taking up his story again, "seems that on Thursday, the Beatles played a concert on a rooftop in London. Set up all the equipment and started playing some songs, and people down below on the street started gathering and looking up, and then the police came and shut down the band for disturbing the peace. Unplugged them! Man, I would have liked to have been there to see it. The news last night just barely covered it. There they were: John, George, Paul, and Ringo."

"Oh man, is right," says Joan. "A rooftop. That's pretty cool."

Eddy says, "Yeah. Just think about walking down a sidewalk and hearing a famous band on the roof above. I want to go somewhere, someplace where things like that happen! I bet that concert means there's a new record coming out. Paul, when you get that magazine you like, that Rolling Stones one, I bet we can all read about what happened."

"Not Rolling Stones, Eddy. Just *Rolling Stone*."

"Confusing!" Eddy says. "There's the Rolling Stones band, there's Dylan's 'Like a Rolling Stone'—"

"There's 'A rolling stone gathers no moss.'" Joan interrupts, counting them off on her fingers.

The three friends think some more and take some bites of their rolls.

"There's that guy we read about in English rolling the stone up the hill just to have it roll right back down," adds Eddy.

"Good golly, y'all are good," says Joan holding up four fingers.

Then Paul says, "There's the stone that was rolled away from Jesus's tomb." Joan slowly adds a fifth finger.

"Paul, you've been paying attention in Sunday school, haven't you?"

"C'mon Eddy, you go as much as I do. You just don't want to admit it."

"Sunday school. As if we don't have enough school. I go to please my folks."

"Yeah, right." Paul smirks. "Joanie, you're the only one safe from the scourge of churchgoing."

"Helps if you're about the only Catholic family in town and there's no Catholic church. Of course, we go when we visit relatives in Roanoke."

"What do Catholics believe, Joanie? Really. What's the bottom line?" Paul asks pointedly.

"You're asking me? How should I know the bottom line? We don't talk religion much in our house. We don't talk about *anything* much except food. That's why I'm always over here talking to Eddy and you. My guess is you'd better respect Mother Mary. Ave Maria. Oh, and we like God and Jesus all right too. What about you two? What do Presbyterians believe?"

Eddy looks at Paul. "What does your church, Memorial Presbyterian, believe in?"

Paul laughs. "Bottom line? I have no idea. But Presbyterians at my church are always talking about doing things in good order. *And* I know Presbyterians set the model for our government. Our American system is based on Scottish Presbyterianism."

"Really?" Eddy looks over at him with surprise. "I don't think I knew that. Our youth group leader says that Jesus probably didn't know he was going to be worshipped. And Jesus called God 'Daddy' or some foreign word that means 'Daddy.'"

Joan whistles. "You two know a bunch of shit about religion."

"Last cinnamon roll—who wants it?" Eddy asks. All three look around at one another, slowly moving their hands closer to the plate, and then they grab, pinching off bits of the sugary roll and laughing as they pop them in their mouths and lick their fingers.

One day, Eddy will realize that rooftop concert on January 30, 1969, was the last public concert the Beatles ever gave.

CHAPTeR 4

Sundays for the Walterses is a routine: Harold and Mary cajoling Eddy and Jimmy out of bed and putting up with groans and protests. Breakfast is a meal slowed down to a snail's pace, and the parents start to lose patience. Then off to Sunday school by 10 a.m. Jimmy looks fairly disheveled, and so does Eddy.

Mary teaches a class for adults, while Sunday school classes for young people are held in upstairs classrooms where the teachers sit around a table with the kids and read the scripture lesson and then try—often unsuccessfully—to get the kids to react and answer some questions. Eddy figures out that if one inserts the name of Jesus somewhere in an answer, it sometimes gets the teacher to move on to the next person.

After Sunday school, the Walterses reconvene on a pew halfway back in the center section of the sanctuary. Eddy knows her mother wants her family to try to be presentable, but it seems Jimmy and Eddy look more not-together on Sundays than on any other day of the week. Sometimes Eddy thinks that she should try once in a while to please her mother on Sundays, but it doesn't happen for some reason. Eddy can't summon the effort. Today is no exception. Her hose have a run starting at the ankle, but she wears them anyway because she honestly didn't have time to look through her drawer to find a good pair. And her blouse is wrinkled.

Exactly at 11 a.m., the pastor stands up from his chair behind the pulpit on the dais and raises his arms. "Let us worship God," Dr. Stevens says rather loudly and with authority. The bulletin says this is "Call to Worship."

Jimmy is coloring in all the *o*'s on his bulletin with the little pencil he finds on the pew rack in front of him. Eddy really likes to do this as well, but today she just looks at her hands in her lap, trying to smooth the edge of a ragged fingernail until they all stand to sing hymn 303, "Be Thou My Vision." A favorite in her church. Actually, if she were pushed to remark, Eddy would have to admit that she likes it probably as well as any hymn. She likes the unusual order of the line "Naught be all else to me, save that Thou art." Sounds like an ancient language, like Shakespeare. But today Eddy sort of thinks about "the vision" as if the person writing it knows what dreams and visions are. *Why can't I have a vision for once? Do only special people have visions, like Shakespeare's characters or Martin Luther King in that famous speech, or … or …* Eddy tries to think of another dreamer. She thinks of one as she remembers a report she did in her ninth grade World Geography class about the Indian emperor who, in his grief, had the Taj Mahal built as a tomb for the woman he loved. Eddy smiles to herself, kind of pleased that she came up with another vision. How she had liked spending time in the library finding out about the Taj Mahal.

The hymn ends, and everyone makes a rustling sound as they settle into the pews. There are some coughs. Eddy looks at Mrs. Knox, sitting in the front row but on the right-hand side, probably sitting there because she wears a big hat on Sundays and doesn't want to block anyone's view. Mrs. Knox raises her chin and looks as if in rapt attention when the pastor stands to read the scripture. Eddy looks at the hymnal in her hands. She opens it and idly turns the pages. Dr. Stevens reads the scripture aloud in a boring voice. But one part grabs Eddy's attention. "For you created my inmost being; you knit me together in my mother's womb."

Eddy suddenly has a picture of an old, old God with a long white beard rocking in a rocking chair with knitting needles in his hands, knitting quite expertly and fast, and whatever he's knitting, it looks to be just a pile of red fabric in his lap. By the time she finishes with this picture in her mind, Dr. Stevens has launched into his sermon. Eddy looks at the sermon title in the bulletin. "God Reads in between the Lines."

Eddy keeps turning the hymnal pages, kind of listening, kind of not. But then Dr. Stevens gets to a part where he says that no matter what we're thinking, or no matter what we say out loud, God knows us so well that he can read our thoughts and read in between the lines of what we actually say. Eddy parts her lips slightly, and she realizes that every non-churchy image she can think of is bombarding her mind. She can't keep them out. She pictures people hitting other people; she pictures herself screaming cuss words one right after the other; she sees herself saying mean things to her parents like *Leave me alone*, or saying to a teacher *I hate you!* She pictures crude sex in orgies. Eddy looks around to see if anyone else is having this response. Jimmy is still shading each *o*, her parents are just listening, and Mrs. Knox's chin has not moved from its elevated position.

Eddy gives her head a slight shake and tries to clear out the pastor's voice. She starts reading the words on the page in the hymnal on her lap. Eddy is looking at "Jesus, Lover of My Soul" on page 216 and sees the word *Aberystwyth* on the right side of the page. *Aberystwyth?* Eddy starts to smile as she tries to sound out the word. The word is unpronounceable. A foreign language, she surmises. She turns to the back of the hymnal to look up that word under "Hymn Tunes" and sees that that tune can also be used to sing "Watchmen, Tell Us of the Night." She starts to look at other hymn tunes in the pages. "Nun Komm, der Heiden Heiland" is German, she thinks. "Besançon" is French. "Veni, Veni Emmanuel" is Latin. Eddy stops on page 18 on the hymn "We Gather Together." There are no notes, just lines of the verses to that Thanksgiving song everyone knows. It says it's a folk song from the Netherlands, which is funny to Eddy. She wonders if the people of the Netherlands know their song is in a Presbyterian hymnal.

She turns page after page, smiling at all the hymn tunes that read like a map of the world. She comes back to "Be Thou My Vision" because her hymnal opens easily to that hymn. Ancient Irish, it says. She sees that it's almost exactly in the middle of the book. The preacher's words are just a faint sound in the background now.

"Please, come with me. Pleeeaaassse," Eddy says into the phone. "It's Sunday night, and I don't have homework, and I want fries. Or ice cream."

"Seems like I'm always giving in to you, Eddy." A pause. "Okay, okay. I give up. I give in. I give with. I give under. All the prepositions. Dari Delite, here we come."

"Hot dog! Daddy says I can take his car!"

"The Mustang? You sure?"

"Joanie, you know I'm an excellent driver. Certified by my dad since I was fifteen and who taught me everything about driving."

The night is chilly, but the car is warm. Eddy's dad's 1968 Mustang is a metallic-blue two-door. Her daddy loves cars, even though he doesn't seem to know very much about them, like how fast a V8 engine could really go. Mr. Walters just likes the look of fast cars. He taught Eddy to drive first by sitting her in his lap and letting her steer. She remembers the drives in the country on Sunday afternoons—no destination, no agenda. Just driving.

When Eddy was young, she sometimes asked her mom if she could go and sit in the driveway in the car and pretend she was driving. The car was a two-toned blue Chevrolet at the time—dark blue and sky blue. When Eddy pretended to drive, she moved the gearshift up and down on the steering column. Once, when Eddy was probably around ten, her mother was at a church meeting, and Eddy was with her. Eddy became bored and asked if she could go sit in the car. Mrs. Walters said yes, not really giving Eddy her attention. But this time, the car was on an incline. When Eddy took the car out of park, the car began to drift backward, landing with a thud against a tree.

Mary Walters was so glad that Eddy hadn't been hurt that she didn't fuss at her hardly at all. But that evening, Eddy wouldn't come in from playing in the neighborhood until dark, afraid her father was going to be furious. Finally, sitting at the dinner table, her father looked up and said, "So Edna, I hear you've been doing some driving today." Eddy realized he wasn't so much angry as he was relieved that she was okay, so she didn't even mind the lecture on not getting to pretend-drive any more. He got the dent in the back fender fixed. Then when she was fourteen—and her legs were long enough—he let her drive around the flat parking lot at the nearby elementary school on weekends, going round and round. At fifteen, she legally got her driver's license. By then, the family had the two-door, teal-blue Corvair with white upholstery. Yes indeed, she and her dad loved cars. For a while he had a cream-colored T-Bird to drive to work and then traded it for the Mustang.

There aren't many cars fanned out in front of the Dari Delite on this Sunday evening. A few people are getting hot dogs or hamburgers. But over on the side of the parking lot sit a couple of cars under the streetlight. Eddy and Joan look over as they wait for someone to come out to the car to take their order. Eddy recognizes Buddy. When Buddy sees the girls, he jumps out of his car, comes running over to theirs, and opens Joanie's door. He pushes the back of her seat forward and slides in.

"Hey!" Joanie is thrown forward a bit. "What are you doing?"

"Just coming to say hello. And see this fine car. Nice to see you girls out on a Sunday night. I don't see you here very often." Buddy's crooked smile stays too long on his lips, like a clown smile that's painted on.

"We come here some, don't we Joanie?" Eddy volunteers. "We don't see you here either, by the way. And tonight, we wanted some fries."

"You wanted some fries," counters Joan. "I'm just along for the ride."

A cold-looking lady rushes out to take their order, looking like she'd rather be anywhere but out here taking orders from teenagers. Eddy rolls down her window, and the woman asks, "What can I get you?" Her pen and pad are ready in her hand.

"Just some french fries and a Coke. Joanie, are we sharing?"

As Joan nods, Buddy says, "Can you buy me some too? Pretty please?"

Eddy looked at Joan. "Do we have enough money?"

Joanie opened her pocketbook. "I have fifty-three cents."

"I've got a dollar and change. Okay, Buddy," she says reluctantly.

The waitress turns and almost runs back in with the order, and before Eddy can roll the window back up, Jay Nickles is standing at her car door looking at her. "Let me in, it's cold out here." He has his fingers already opening the door. Eddy helps open it, pulling her seat back forward so he can slide in. She then turns on the car so the heat can come on.

"Brrrrr. Cold out there. Thanks for turning on the heat. What brings you girls out on a Sunday night?"

"Fries," both girls say at the same time, smiling at each other.

"Jinx" say both girls, but Joan says it faster and then says, "You owe me a Coke. Again."

Eddy takes a deep breath.

"They've even bought some fries for me and you," Buddy says, grinning at his friend. "It's our lucky day!" Jay looks up into the rearview mirror and meets Eddy's eyes. He's smiling; Eddy is not. She's just looking.

The lights from the drive-in restaurant's overhanging roof shine into the Mustang. The fan from the car's heater whirs softly in the background. Joan is looking quizzically over at Eddy. Eddy doesn't look at her. She's looking straight ahead, then glances up into the rearview mirror again. In just another heartbeat, Buddy takes over the conversation.

"Wow, this baby is sweet! Your daddy is nice to let you drive it."

"Why wouldn't he let me? I'm a good driver." Eddy looks over her right shoulder at Buddy in the back seat. He's rubbing his hands along the upholstery and glancing all around the inside of the car.

"'Cause this baby can fly! Does he know that you might end up racing around town in this hot car?"

Eddy ponders this possibility while catching Jay's eyes in the rearview mirror. He seems to be watching her closely, and though his eyes are dark, they seem to be smiling.

"Don't think I'll be racing. But driving around? Definitely yes."

"We race, don't we, Jaybird? Man, if we had this car we would fly across the finish line." Buddy keeps talking. "Want to take this baby out on the streets after we eat?"

Eddy is shaking her head no as the food is delivered; Joan passes around the fries. Eddy turns on the radio, twists the dial a bit to lose the static, and suddenly the thumping blues sound of "Hello, I Love You" by The Doors comes into focus. Buddy starts singing while he chews his fries. Eddy is surprised. Joan's head bobs a little in rhythm, and then softly she joins Buddy. Jay starts tapping his hands on the top of the front seat—in rhythm. Eddy finally loosens her shoulders and starts swaying them a little until all in the car are singing. Then the last stanza (only Joan knows all the words) and then, loudly, all four scream the finale, "Hello, hello, hello, hello" over and over again, lifting their bodies off the seat and making the car rock. Jay pounding on the front seat. Eddy looking in the mirror. Joan's eyes closed. Buddy's too. And then it's over. The last *hello* fades, and some DJ's voice comes on in the distance.

"Well, boys, I've got to get home," Joan says as she balls up her napkin. "Guess we'll see you in the halls!"

"I'll see you in my dreams," Buddy croons.

Both girls open their doors and pull up the seat behind them. Jay, as he steps awkwardly out from the back seat, taps his hand on Eddy's right shoulder and says, "See ya."

"See ya," Eddy answers, closing the door and watching Jay put his hands in his pockets and hunch his shoulders against the cold while he walks away from her car toward Buddy's. He doesn't look back.

As they drive home, Joan says, "Those hoods. I don't know them very well, and that Buddy gives me the creeps the way he looks at me."

"What does that mean, 'hoods'? We use that word but what does it mean?"

"Well, I think it means they hang around after dark in their dark jackets and are up to no good. Knives come to mind. And they like cars. Like to look under hoods of cars. And they don't like school."

"Do you think Buddy and Jay are hoods really?" Eddy says this thinking about how Buddy's and Jay's families are not known to Joan's and Eddy's, somewhat of an anomaly in a small town like Thomasburg. "Weird to go to school with people for years and know so little about some of them. They just don't cross paths with me. They're definitely not in the Library Club. Or Chorus."

"They should try out—they sounded good on that song!"

Eddy suddenly starts singing along with the Beach Boys on the radio. "Wouldn't It Be Nice" is a song she has played over and over in her room, contemplating what it would mean to say goodnight to someone and stay together. She continues to hum. Joan looks over at her friend and then turns to look out the window at the passing lights emanating warmly from the front rooms in the homes they pass. Eddy reaches over with her right hand and touches her friend's arm, squeezing gently. Then she replaces her hand on the steering wheel. Joan turns at the touch of her friend and smiles at Eddy.

CHAPTER 5

Dinner at the Walters's house is low-key. There's an everydayness about it, for in small towns there aren't many options to go out for dinner on a regular basis, except for burger places like Dari Delite. And not enough money to make it a habit for most people. In Thomasburg, mostly the women cook, the families gather, the kids put their feet under the tables and wait for their plates. At least this is the way families end their day among Eddy's friends.

"Edna, come and set the table, please." Eddy's mother's voice rarely lifts in a command, just an expected family "pulling together" kind of feeling. The Walterses are easy, but because of that, Eddy holds in a lot, not wanting to cause ripples in their nice, plain life. They might be appalled at her thoughts, not that she would act on them. At least, she doesn't think she would act on them. She does love her parents.

Eddy comes down from her bedroom into the kitchen area where the big window looks out into a large ravine with trees that show a creek running at the bottom and then another tree-covered hill rising on the other side. The drop-leaf table in front of the window is waiting. Eddy knows what to do: old-timey handmade cloth placemats, Blue Willow china, everyday cutlery from the sideboard drawer, placed traditionally with knife and spoon on the right and the fork on the left sitting on a cloth napkin. And drinking glasses placed at the right-hand corner of the placemat. All in order.

It's a dark February night, cold and impenetrably black down in the ravine. Eddy lights the candles in the middle of the table. Thank goodness her mother likes candles as much as she does—and isn't that much of a neat freak—because there's often the risk of wax on surfaces. Eddy thinks about candles as she moves around the table placing things. She thinks that she would rather have a single candle in the dark than a room full of artificial light. She thinks of Abraham Lincoln. The story in which he studied by candlelight in that log cabin. Or maybe it was an oil lamp. *I could do that. I like doing things in half-darkness.* She smiles as she thinks of her father, who comes into any room switching on lights and fussing that Eddy can't possibly see what she's doing in the dark. While Eddy is lost in thought, her mother's voice breaks in from over in front of the stove where she's been taking the ground beef casserole out of the oven and steaming the broccoli at the last minute.

"Call your little brother. Let's eat," her mother says.

Eddy goes to the doorway of the kitchen. "Jimmy! Supper! Right now!"

"Edna. Goodness. Do you have to shout?"

"Mom, you know he purposely doesn't hear. Just wait …. We'll have to call him again in a minute." Eddy cannot see why her parents aren't exasperated by Jimmy like she is. He seems to do whatever he pleases, and he's just thirteen.

Sure enough, as Mary brings the casserole and broccoli to the hot pads on the table and begins to serve some to each plate, and Harold comes in from working at the desk in the living room, Mary tells Eddy to call Jimmy again.

"Jimmy, I mean it. Come right now. Supper's on the table!" Eddy turns and looks at her parents to see if they're going to do something, anything, about Jimmy. They're already chatting about something else. *What could it be that's more important than Jimmy's stubbornness? The cold? The bills on Daddy's desk? The casserole?*

Finally Jimmy saunters slowly through the doorway and takes his seat with the rest of the family. Eddy tries to give him an exasperated look, but he pointedly does not look at her. All the Walterses sit around the table and bow their heads as Harold says, "Bless this food to the nourishment of our bodies and us to thy service. Amen." Same blessing every night they sit around the table together. *Same damn one*, Eddy thinks, but even in her thoughts, the *damn* comes out softer than the other words in case they can read her thoughts. Or could it be that she thinks God hears her?

"Edna, what music are you practicing for the spring concert? Any we know?" her dad asks. Harold likes music and often hums and sings as he comes into the kitchen. Songs like "A White Sport Coat" and "Tennessee Waltz." Sometimes he starts waltzing with Mary and even tries with Eddy once in a while as she protests.

"We're singing 'Try to Remember' from some Broadway show, and also 'You'll Never Walk Alone' from *Carousel*."

"*The Fantasticks*. 'Try to Remember' is from *The Fantasticks*," says Harold. "Remember we sang that around the piano one night up at the Cliffords'?"

Mary nods.

"Jimmy, how's school for you?" Harold continues, looking hard at Jimmy across the table, almost demanding that he participate.

"Same old stuff, over and over. Band's good though."

"Seems you're getting a bit better on the clarinet. Does your band teacher say so?" Mary asks.

"You sure don't practice enough here at home," Harold says. "Can't improve without practice."

Jimmy just keeps on eating, looking down at his plate. Eddy smiles. She likes it that the conversation isn't directed at her now.

After dinner, Eddy is guilted into helping with the dishes, a job she's supposed to share with Jimmy, who doesn't do his share, she thinks. She finally escapes to her room where she puts the Beach Boys' *Pet Sounds* album on the little turntable that sits on a brass stand; the brass is peeling in places. She sits on the floor next to the record stand, then reaches up and sets the needle to hear the train whistle at the end of the album again—and then again.

"How's your Shakespeare assignment going?" Joan's voice comes out raspy after running in the hall to catch up with Eddy.

"Not well," answers Eddy as she steers a path through oncoming students. "*Hamlet* is getting me down. Death and dying."

"Why you decided to do a play not required by Mr. Thompson, I'll never know. Geez, Eddy, what were you thinking?"

Both girls plop down in their desks in French class, one of two classes they have together. Joan dangles one leg while tucking the other under her and sitting on it. She starts picking lint off her white bobby socks. Eddy leans toward her as other students come in.

"I saw the movie *Hamlet* one Sunday afternoon. Black and white. And Laurence Olivier was so handsome and so … oh, I don't know. Characters whisper to themselves a lot, and there's even a ghost and a skull. And there was Ophelia, floating serenely on the water. But reading the play is even more bleak than the black-and-white movie."

"There you go again with the tortured-soul stuff. What have you done with my friend Eddy who used to laugh more?"

"Sorry. But listen to these lines Hamlet delivers." She opens her big notebook and finds some paper with writing on it. "'It's a fear of something after death/that undiscovered country from whose bourn no traveller returns.' Makes me wonder, you know?"

"Good grief, Eddy. I'm worried about you. You know what you need? You need somebody to kiss you *and* have roving hands! It's almost the weekend. Let's hike over to the lookout on Saturday morning and shout down into the abyss below. And talk about people. And laugh. What do you say?"

"Deal." And Eddy shakes hands with Joan. "But first, Penny's party tonight!"

"Bonjour, mes amies," Mrs. Davis says.

"Bonjour, Mrs. Davis," the class responds.

"Joan, please pass out these worksheets. Class, spend the next fifteen minutes translating these paragraphs into English. Begin."

Eddy looks at paragraph 1, entitled "Le portrait de George":

> *George est Américain. Il est marié et a trois enfants. Il est né à New York City, mais il habite à Long Island. George travaille dans une école et est professeur de français. L'atmosphère est bonne et ses étudiants sont multiculturels. Il aime lire et aller au restaurant avec sa famille.*

Eddy sees that this first paragraph is easy. She wonders about "Le portrait d'Edna" and what it would say. She wonders if she will ever need French anywhere but in school. *Edna est un Américain; elle n'est pas marié et a non enfants. Elle est perdue dans un bois sombre.* Eddy smiles. She looks over at Joan and hears her voice in her head: Lighten up.

CHAPTER 6

"Who is having a dance party at the American Legion? Penny Jones?" Mary Walters stands at the kitchen counter playing solitaire, a common activity for Mary while she waits for something to finish cooking.

"Yes, Mom, and there will be a live band!"

"Wow, that must be costing the Joneses some money."

"Not really. I've told you some of the guys at school have started a band called Thee Purity. I told you, remember?"

"Remind me again? Who's in it?"

Eddy takes a breath. "Joey, Ben, Alan, Steve, and Mark." She counts out on her fingers.

"Ah, yes. Joey Johnson. Of course. I know his parents."

"Yes, Mom."

"Will Johnny be taking you?"

"He doesn't know Penny very well, but she may have asked him. I don't know. Joanie and I are going together."

The American Legion Hall is the downstairs room of an old two-story building in Thomasburg. The biggest room can hold the band for the party and still have room on the linoleum floor to dance. Anytime there's a live band, Eddy and Joan get excited.

The girls have talked about what to wear because they had to figure in the dancing. And they might meet new people because Penny might have friends they don't know. Eddy likes being in chorus with Penny, who sings out in class but is quiet otherwise. Will there be cheerleaders? Popular kids? Jocks? Maybe hoods? All the cliques might be represented.

There's a cold front coming through the mountains, and Eddy and Joan can see their breath as they get out of Eddy's Corvair parked along the street. When they're inside, Eddy and Joan hang up their coats on the racks just inside the doorway and then enter the hall. The air is warming from all the bodies standing around. The band is warming up too. Eddy feels as if her skin is tingling, running warm and cool at the same time. Penny's parents and some other grown-ups are behind the table, which has punch and cookies.

When Eddy and Joan enter, Penny is standing near the entrance, looking as if her parents might have said she must greet her friends as they arrive. And even though the girls are friends, a hint of formality is in the greeting.

"Hey!" she says.

"Hey Penny! Happy birthday!" from Joan.

"Yeah," says Eddy, giving Penny a slight hug.

"Y'all look cute! Nice dress, Joan!"

"Thanks," responds Joan, looking pleased.

"And yours too, Eddy," Penny hurriedly says, as if she might have neglected Eddy.

But Eddy smiles a big smile to assure her friend that all is well.

"Your dress is really cool," says Joan to Penny, touching the fabric on the sleeve.

Penny has on a fairly tight-fitting navy-blue dress with maroon trim around the neckline and the sleeves. Penny's blondish hair is in a short cut with bangs over her big blue eyes. Eddy's collarless yellow dress has a straight-across neckline, and the tight-fitting dropped waist accents the flared skirt at the hips. It's loose enough and comfy for dancing, and she likes the yellow. Joan's pink dress was chosen with just such care as well, full at the skirt, a bit blousy at the top for her more full-figured shape. The music has dictated their dress code, for both girls want to move easily.

Eddy wonders if the guys take such care, as she looks at them across the room. Their shirts have a range of pastel colors, blues, greens, some plaids mixed in, and their socks often match their shirts. But their pants are mostly khaki or dark corduroy. Seems the boys don't have much choice. Eddy thinks of Johnny and how much he dresses like these friends of Penny.

Some of the guys there are talking in the far corner, and they're not all familiar to Eddy, but she sees a couple who are in Library Club with her: Parker Helms (also in choir with her) and Andrew Stevens, who takes projectors to the classrooms when the teachers need them for films. Joan sees Roger and walks over to him, and Eddy joins some of the girls from chorus while the band finishes tuning up. The lights are somewhat dim, and Eddy feels her expectation grow. Then the band begins.

A few chords on lead guitar, and then, almost suddenly, Steve's trumpet is playing a smooth, rhythmic line, *ba ba-ba ba ba, ba ba ba, ba ba-ba ba ba, ba ba ba, ba ba-ba ba ba, baa ba ba da.* Then Ben starts the drum beat along with the trumpet, Joey on the bass guitar comes in to play the low notes, and Mark plays the melody on the rhythm guitar. It lasts less than a minute, but the crowd pays attention, if only because most don't know what they're listening to. Eddy sure doesn't.

When the music trails off, the band members seem to be smiling at the confusion on the faces of the listeners. "That, my friends, was Duke Ellington's 'Satin Doll,'" says Mark. Then he counts off "A-one, two, three, four," and the opening chords to "Knock On Wood" begin. Alan sings, and Eddy's heart lifts as she listens to this familiar tune. *Live music. The best.*

Joan is on the dance floor with Roger, and Penny and Andrew are there too. Some girls start dancing together, and Eddy senses that they feel comfortable enough to know that they don't have to wait for a male partner. *I might do that too.*

Then, looking around, she sees Parker looking her way. She smiles, willing him to come over because she wants to dance so much, when suddenly Buddy Hall is beside her saying, "C'mon. Let's boogie!" Eddy is so surprised, she follows him to the middle of the room. He's smiling that crooked smile and starts moving fairly spasmodically, and Eddy tries to figure out how to respond. Joan looks over with wide eyes from nearby, so Eddy kind of decides it'll be like dancing with Joanie. And oh, how she likes this Motown hit.

So she moves, but a bit hesitantly because she doesn't know Buddy, who erratically moves in front of her as if he can't decide which rhythm he wants. His arms sway back and forth, and instead of looking at Eddy, he glances around the dance floor, and Eddy sees him looking at Joan. Eddy notices his hand with the missing fingers as he waves his arms around. And while she's dancing with Buddy, she notices Jay Nickles standing in a doorway watching. He still has his winter jacket on.

Every time the part in the song comes when the band stops and there's the actual *knocking* by Ben on drums, everyone seems to stop with the band before starting their dancing again. The band is loud, and even some of the people not dancing are moving their heads in rhythm.

"Thank you, sweetheart," Buddy says out of breath when the song ends. "Whew! I better stop with the cigarettes." Pause. "What do you think my chances are of dancing with Joan?"

Eddy's a bit surprised. "I'd say your chances are not very good. Thanks for the dance!" And with that awkward ending, Eddy moves over toward Joan. "Well, that was interesting."

"Yeah!"

Roger says, "Buddy is Penny's cousin, I think. Don't know him very well. He's … he's different."

And just then, Thee Purity starts on another Motown hit. Eddy moves to the drink table and takes a cup from Penny's mom. "Thanks, Mrs. Jones."

"Nice to see you, Edna, and not just at a choir concert. How are your mom and dad?

"Fine, fine." And she gives a slight wave to Mrs. Jones as she sips and turns back to the room. She moves to the side of the table to watch people dance and to listen to the music, and she sees another girl has been chosen by Buddy to dance to this tune. *Poor girl.*

Eddy sees Jay move in her direction, and she can't decide whether she wants him to stop by her or not, and while she's deciding, he goes right behind her to the table and gets some punch and a couple of cookies. Then he turns and moves slowly toward her, stopping when he reaches her side.

"You didn't get a cookie," he says, offering her one of the two. "Here."

"Thanks," she says, taking the offered cookie. A pause for a bite, and then she asks, "How do you know Penny?"

"She lives kinda near me in the country. We used to ride the bus together."

"Gotcha. We're in chorus together."

"Yeah, I know," Jay says munching on the chocolate chip cookie.

Eddy doesn't exactly know how to respond to this. Then Jay says, "You always watch people."

"What? Isn't everyone watching everyone else?"

"You just seem like you're thinking hard while you watch. You judging people?"

"What a thing to say. I see you watching people."

"Just asking." Jay has finished his cookie and drink and turns his head to see what's behind him. He reaches over to take Eddy's empty cup and walks behind them and places them in a trash can. Eddy still has the partial cookie in her left hand when Jay returns, takes her other hand, and turns to face her right where they're standing on the outside of the dance floor.

The first chords of "When a Man Loves a Woman" have begun. With his left hand holding her right, he folds it in against his chest just inside his jacket edge while his right wraps around her waist. Eddy is a bit confused, her senses heightened as she feels his hand against the back of her dress. She holds on to the cookie with her left and awkwardly puts it over Jay's right shoulder. Jay moves very slowly, slower than the tempo of the Percy Sledge song Eddy knows so well. This song is one of her favorites, and for a split second she wonders if Jay knows it's one of her favorites. Or if Johnny knows it's one of her favorites.

Jay's not a good dancer, Eddy thinks, but he pulls her a bit tighter, and her temple is suddenly against his jaw, her breasts against his chest. She breathes in a sort of clean smell on the skin of his neck. The two of them are barely moving, Jay's hand warm and dry around hers. Eddy's mind is buzzing. *This is crazy. I've danced with boys before, with Johnny particularly. What's wrong with me?* She looks out over Jay's shoulder and catches Joan looking her way. Even Roger looks her way. There are questions in Joan's eyes, as if she too wonders what Eddy is doing dancing with Jay.

Eddy feels like she's in a spotlight, and she hates it. She pulls back a bit to see Jay's face and to get some distance. He glances down, his eyes dark in the half-light. His lips glisten as if he just licked them. She can't really see him well enough to read the expression on his face. She looks hard at him.

"I really like Percy Sledge's voice when he sings this song," she says because she can't think of anything else to say while they're looking at each other.

"You have bits of yellow in your brown eyes," Jay says softly with a slight smile, as if he knows, really knows, that this is going to confuse Eddy even more.

With that, the song ends and Eddy takes her hand out of Jay's, and with a nod and a "Well, see ya," she turns to look for Joan and moves away.

"First you dance with Buddy, and then Jay," says Joan. "*Verrry een-ter-esting ....*" Joan says, quoting the line from Arte Johnson on the *Laugh-In* TV show that the girls love. "What do you think Johnny would say?" Joan asks with a thinking pose.

"Joanie, I'm just dancing!"

"Better watch out, Eddy. That song will make you fall in love."

Eddy takes a deep breath and sees Jay and Buddy head out the front door.

Joan follows her look and says, "Guess that's all they can take. Back to the open road and their cars."

Thee Purity breaks into the drum roll for "Shotgun" by Jr. Walker & the All Stars. Steve's trumpet stands in for a saxophone, and as it cuts the air, Eddy and Joan look at each other and start dancing. Almost everyone is on the dance floor, and even Parker comes and dances next to Eddy. But mostly Eddy dances facing Joan, and they shout "Shotgun" every time, and every beat has their arms flying over their heads. They're not thinking of anything but the song.

CHAPTER 7

The thing about the mountains is that they're both places to see clearly and places to hide. From on top of a lookout, one can see far and wide—if the lookout is open enough. But one can also cower beneath its rocks, hiding. One can hide a treasure or a secret in the rocky outcroppings of stone after stone, and with so many hiding places to choose from, other seekers wouldn't be able to find it.

One particular place where Joan and Eddy like to go is near a warehouse on a gravel road that ends in a field stretching up to a high point where a stand of mostly pine trees edges a precipice of rock. They call it the Overlook. It's not the highest point around, but high enough to stand on some of the rocks that jut out over a sheer drop. If one stands there, she can see the train tracks below and the next rolling blue mountains stretching to the north.

All through high school, Eddy and Joan have used this place to be alone, or at least away from grown-ups. Eddy knows kids come here to smoke, drink a little, make out, and maybe more on the pine needles just under the trees—everything that seems taboo. At least that's what the place feels like to Eddy. But the two friends rarely see others at the Overlook.

"Remember when we came with Paul and Leonard up here that Sunday afternoon last fall?" Joan is leading the way from their car, up the hill, through the woods, until stopping near the edge of the precipice.

"Of course I remember," counters Eddy. "We tasted a little beer, and remember we tried a cigarette? Paul or Leonard made fun of us because we didn't like the cigarettes and only took a sip of the beer. And somebody's mom made egg salad sandwiches."

"I think Paul's mom. Little finger sandwiches she called them."

"Well, they were perfect. But remember what Leonard did, dangling from one of the rocks and scaring us to death. Why would he do that?" Eddy sits down with her legs in her old Wrangler jeans crossed in front her. Her big red-and-green plaid car coat covers the other layers of shirt and sweater; her gloves and toboggan are keeping her warm enough, although her hands are pressed tightly under her arms. "I mean, why risk falling on a whim?"

"I don't know, Eddy." Joan starts picking up loose stones near her to throw off over the ledge. She heaves the first one, and the girls lean a bit forward to hear it hit rocks and tree branches or the train tracks below. Eddy picks up a handful of loose stones to throw all at the same time, and the quiet makes them sound like distant gunshot. *Pop, pop, pop.* "You know," Joan says, looking out toward the far mountains, "Leonard isn't in any of our more advanced classes. I don't think college is in his future. So when we graduate, he may be off to Vietnam. Maybe that's why he dangled from the rock. Preparing himself for, I don't know, for war. We should ask Paul—he knows Leonard better. After all, he brought him up here that day."

The girls sit silently. They can hear a chainsaw somewhere in the distance. They hear a car engine nearby. Then, at the sound of laughing, both girls turn their heads to look toward the woods behind them. Out from the woods, Buddy and an older-looking girl come walking together, and behind them, Jay walks beside a girl Eddy recognizes named Barbara, a girl from school but not someone she knows exactly. Eddy can tell the girl has a good figure, even with her coat on. *She's pretty*, Eddy thinks as the memory of Jay's hand covering hers at the dance suddenly comes to mind. She shakes her head as if trying to shake out that memory.

"Well, well, well, we saw that car at the end of the road and wondered whose it was! Hello girls! Fancy meeting you here," Buddy says.

Joan looks at Eddy, and both seem unable to respond at first. They continue to sit where they are, the best seats for gazing out over the mountains.

Joan speaks first. "Haven't seen you out here before."

"We come much later at night than you girls do, I bet."

"Is that why I see all those cigarette butts in the woods?" asks Joan.

"And some other things, too, I bet. Condoms and bottles, you know, the usual." Buddy looks at the girl at his side, who is smiling the smile of one who knows firsthand about these activities. Jay and Barbara have just stepped up beside Buddy. Eddy looks at Jay and sees a look she can't decipher. He's looking at her, a slight smile perhaps, but cold eyes, she thinks.

"Okay, let's see who can make the loudest noise below from throwing rocks," says Buddy. He looks around and pushes loose with his shoe a bigger rock than the girls had been throwing. He walks over and stands next to where Joan is sitting, takes a step toward the drop-off, rears back on his right leg and shouts, "Look out below," and heaves the rock with his right arm. There's a sound from the ravine far below as the rock hits something. Tree? Another rock? Eddy can't tell what he hit.

"Your turn, Jaybird. Let her rip!"

Jay looks around. He takes some time finding a stone. He walks back a ways.

"Damn, Jay, hurry up. Any rock will do." Buddy is stamping his feet to keep warm, his plaid flannel coat buttoned to the top.

Jay bends down, his back to the group, and pries loose a couple of rocks. One is fairly large. He walks over to where Eddy is sitting, with the bigger rock in his right hand. He takes a step and peers over the edge of the drop. His left leg is right beside Eddy, so close she could have put her arm around it, and it crosses her mind that she might if he gets too close to the edge. Jay also steps back with his right leg and then casts the rock into the distance. They all listen for the sound of its hit. Nothing. Eddy leans a bit forward, straining to hear.

"I didn't hear nothin'!" Buddy says. "Are my ears going deaf?"

"I didn't hear anything either," Joan kind of whispers to Eddy.

Eddy is still leaning a bit forward, turning her head to look at Jay's brown corduroy pant leg, and then she looks up to his face. He's looking straight ahead. Slowly he turns to look down at Eddy. His face is in shadow, and Eddy is squinting up into the sun to see it.

"I think it got caught in a tree," Barbara offers from behind Eddy.

"Maybe Jay threw it so far it was out of our range," Buddy's girl interjects.

Buddy bursts out laughing. "Naw! He's not *that* strong." Buddy walks over to his friend and holds up Jay's arm to feel his muscle. "See, scrawny, just scrawny."

Jay pulls his arm out of Buddy's grasp, giving only a slight smile.

Everybody is laughing a bit now. Buddy says to his three companions, "C'mon, gang. Let's run along and leave these two ladies to ponder the universe. I've got some other things to ponder," he says, looking at his girl, who is never named.

Barbara and the other girl start moving off in the direction Buddy is leading farther along the tree line. Jay goes down on his haunches next to Eddy, looking out over the mountains in the distance and, while looking, places a stone with his left hand in Eddy's lap. Then he rises and walks off with his friends before Eddy can even acknowledge what he's done. She looks down in her lap and sees the stone. She then looks toward his retreating figure, but he doesn't look back. Eddy slips her right-hand glove off and picks up the rock between her thumb and forefinger. It's a smooth brownish stone with reddish streaks crossing its uneven terrain. Eddy's thumb moves over the surface, feeling its raised markings.

"What is it?" whispers Joan, looking over into Eddy's lap.

"Just a rock."

"Why did he give it to you?"

"I have no idea. Maybe this one was too small to throw."

Joan looks up into her friend's face. "Maybe. Those red streaks—looks like it has blood on it. Ewww." Joan stands up. "My legs have gone numb sitting for so long. Those guys ruined our afternoon up here. I wanted to scream out over the drop-off like we've done before, but I don't want any of them to hear us. Wonder what they will do when we've gone?"

Eddy stands up, puts the stone in her coat pocket, and puts her glove back on. "Hmmmm ... I wonder."

And both girls break into giggles, covering their mouths with their gloved hands and walking fast back through the woods to Joan's car. Eddy looks over at Buddy's car parked beside it, really looking at it as if for the first time—the peeling paint and the bald tires. *Buddy is poor*, she thinks. Her next thought centers on the stone in her pocket and the why of it. And on Jay's corduroyed pant leg that was so close to her she could have touched it. And how her stomach felt a lurch toward that leg, that boy.

On Sunday evening just before dinnertime, Eddy's family is sitting in the den, reading the Sunday newspaper (her father) and doing a crossword puzzle (her mother) and playing a game of Labyrinth on the floor (her brother). Eddy is sort of looking at the *TV Guide*, seeing what lineup is coming on and looking at shows like *The Smothers Brothers Comedy Hour*. There's a fire burning in the fireplace, and once in a while the flames crack, releasing a shower of sparks. A stack of paper, some twigs, and a few logs on the hearth sit ready to be used to build it up again if needed.

Eddy's father spends much time building a fire. He often sits cross-legged on the floor, balling up old newspapers to put under the grate. Then come the twigs. Then come the logs, which are usually too green and, therefore, take forever to catch fire. The family makes fun of him a little bit. Not too much though. He says, when picked on by the family, "You'll miss me when I'm gone."

Eddy thinks that's a morbid thought. "Dad!" Eddy says whenever he makes such statements. "Stop it." Her dad is a steady worker who goes each weekday morning to the textile mill offices without complaint. He likes coming home for lunch at noon, staying just long enough for a sandwich or a bowl of soup and a TV fix of the game show *Jeopardy!* with Art Fleming, on at noon every day. Eddy's mom and dad like the show, and when Eddy is home in summer or on school vacation, she can watch with them, trying to get some of the right answers—or questions as per the *Jeopardy!* format. But she isn't any good at the game. It frustrates her. Her mother is quite good and tries to tell her that someday she'll get better. Eddy doesn't believe her. Eddy thinks the maker of the clues on the board is conspiring to give too many hard academic facts so that young people can't play unless they're geniuses. Her mother just smiles when Eddy says such things aloud.

Her mother … another steady person. With her dark-brown hair almost always fixed in a short, curled hairdo by the weekly trip to Betty's Beauty Parlor, Mary has always seemed comfortable with her role of housewife, mother, cook, and cleaner. And churchgoer. She loves church and teaching her adult Sunday school class. And she loves bridge. She has two bridge clubs: one with women in the daytime once a month, and one with couples one evening a month. Mary Walters has good women friends and sees them often.

Eddy's whole family likes card games. All of them. The card table is folded flat behind a door in the den, waiting to be put up for family games. Playing card games is a soothing activity for Eddy. She often sits at the card table shuffling away until her dad says something like, "Edna, you're going to shuffle the numbers off those cards! Let's play." And laying out cards on her bed for many kinds of solitaire gives Eddy's hands something to do, an outlet for the excitement she feels as she listens to music.

This dark Sunday evening in February is like many others, until Eddy's father abruptly says, "Edna, have you given thought to plans for next year? What colleges you might look at? What sizes of schools? I know Mr. Ratcliffe has given you a job this summer at the Shop and Save, but beyond that? I need to plan as well."

Eddy picks up a handful of chips from the bag beside her and crunches them in her mouth as she thinks about her dad's question. Eddy and Joan and Paul have been thinking about such things lately, but Eddy is reluctant to tell her dad all that they've been wondering: whether or not their grades are good enough to get in anywhere, whether or not they want to stay close to home and attend community college, whether or not they should go somewhere together, whether they should go to a big school like Virginia Polytechnic Institute and get lost in the crowds or maybe attend a small school and feel safer instead. One such conversation left all three friends thinking that their families want them to go, so they suspect that their families must therefore have enough money to send them to college.

Eddy thinks about those conversations now. She knows her family has enough money for things, things they need and even extras. But college? Eddy doesn't even know what college costs. She thinks that she should have listened more when the high school guidance counselor talked. Why didn't she listen more, she wonders. Eddy looks at her dad who is still looking at her expectantly.

"I don't know. I'm worried about my grades. Government is killing me."

"Your grades, Edna, have always been satisfactory to your mother and me. One poor showing doesn't alter too much the overall good grades."

"You chose not to stay in college." Eddy says this softly, for she knows it's a bit sad for her father that he didn't finish college on the GI Bill after the war. He went to VPI for a year, but he and Mary decided to get married and start a life, which meant his getting a job. So to Thomasburg and the textile mills he came, managing a credit department. Eddy has wondered sometimes how he does it. How he talks on the phone or writes letters every day, trying to get people to pay what they owe. He always answers with a smile and says it isn't so bad. The people owe the money, he just has to remind them of the fact.

"Edna, both your mother and I want you to go. But I need to plan a little, maybe go down to the bank and ask John Rose about finances. Things like that. But you need to plan a little too."

"I'll get on it, Dad, I promise." Eddy knows she has kind parents. She hates to let them down, but it's hard to tell them what she's thinking. She doesn't want to scare them. They seem so, well, normal. What if she's not? What if she's an abnormal girl stuck in a normal world?

"Well …" and Harold's voice trails off, and he turns his attention back to the newspaper.

Mary, who had been following this conversation, says to the family, "Don't forget we're going to Galax for your father's birthday on the first Saturday of April after you take the SAT."

Holy crap, Eddy thinks. *The SATs. And I need a present for Dad.* In the warmth of the den fire and the glow of the TV, Eddy looks around at her family with her own warmth toward them. She gets up and plops down on the carpet beside her brother and watches him tilt the game board in all directions, trying not to let the marbles fall into the holes in the labyrinth.

"Dang, I almost had it," Jimmy mutters.

"Here, let me try," Eddy says as she reaches for the wooden box.

"You won't be able to do it. You're too impatient."

"Jimmy, let her try," Mary says, looking up from the crossword puzzle book. Even Harold lowers the newspaper and peers down.

Eddy takes the wooden box with the swiveling board on top and turns the knobs on the sides to tilt the board so that the steel marble goes through the labyrinth to reach the end without falling into one of the holes. Her tilting happens faster and faster, and the number of times her marble falls into a hole adds up until she finally sets the box back on the floor.

"Ughhh," she almost yells.

"Take it slowly, Edna," her father intones, speaking slowly himself.

"I can't. I'll never get it."

"Edna," her mother interjects. "You can do it; just take your time."

"Nope, I'm done." Eddy gets up off the floor and, noticing the slight smile on her brother's face, swipes her hand across the back side of his hair just hard enough to wipe that smile off.

"Mom," Jimmy says, "did you see that?"

Everyone in the room goes back to doing what they were doing before, except for Eddy, who goes up to her room. She puts Dionne Warwick on the record player and then lies down on her bed, taking the rock out of her jeans pocket and turning it over and over again in her fingers as the older scratchy 33 rpm record plays one ballad after another, starting with "Promises, Promises" and moving through Side 1. Eddy is barely listening, just letting the music become the backdrop for her thoughts of woods and rocks and a boy. Then she hears her mother's voice from the bottom of the stairs.

"Edna, it's EMFH for supper tonight! Every Man For Himself. And you have youth group at church tonight."

Church, Eddy thinks, continuing to turn the rock over and over in her fingers. *Always church.* "Can't go to youth group tonight, Mom!" she yells. "Big presentation in English tomorrow!" No answer from her mom. *Crap.* She gets up to go downstairs to fix her chicken noodle soup, her go-to on EMFH nights. Then she'll finish her *Hamlet* presentation.

CHAPTER 8

Joan turns down the hall and joins Eddy, who has just emerged from Mr. Thompson's English class. "Well, how did yours go? Quick, tell me; I've got my *Macbeth* next period."

"I think zeroing in on Ophelia might not have gone over so well with Mr. Thompson. I thought by looking at how she was manipulated by everyone, plus her being unable to read Hamlet's feelings for her and her father's death sending her over the edge, was a valid point. But standing up at the lectern in front of the class and looking at those blank faces made me nervous as hell."

Joan nods absent-mindedly. Eddy looks at her friend closely. "Is that a new skirt? I like it. I like the dark greens and blues of the plaid."

"Thanks. Yeah, Mom got it for me when she went to Roanoke last week. Got it from that store with the name I can hardly pronounce. Sort of sounds like Hypotenuse. What is it? Hieronymus?"

"Hieronymus? Something like that. I like Hypotenuse!" Both girls laugh. Eddy hopes the laughing will relax her friend for her presentation. "Good luck with *Macbeth*. Your reading 'Out damned spot; out, I say' will be brilliant! Really ham it up like you did when we practiced, Joanie Baloney!"

Joan gives her friend a lackluster smile and turns around to head to English class. Eddy starts walking, looking down at the floor, when she almost runs into someone.

"Eddy, for Pete's sake, you gotta look up!" Johnny puts his hand on her arm to stop her, even though all the students in the hallway are walking quickly to class before the next bell rings.

"Sorry, Johnny," Eddy is irritated, like her reverie has been interrupted and not pleasantly.

"Remember I asked you over the phone last night about this weekend's movie? You didn't really answer. We going? *Camelot* is playing. I know how you like to go to the movies every time it changes."

Eddy does love the movies. Her body seems to tingle with expectation when the lights go down in the theater, and there's that moment just before the film rolls that makes Eddy think anything is possible. She sometimes realizes that these people in the movie are similar to her. But often, they're so unlike her, having adventures or going places so unlike the movements of her own life, that she's left openmouthed with more questions than answers.

"I might be going somewhere with my parents. Let me check."

"Seems I haven't seen you much since your birthday."

"Yeah, lots going on."

A pause. "I heard you went to a dance party." His voice is slightly accusatory, like he's caught her doing something.

"Yeah. It was fun." Eddy looks up into Johnny's familiar face and suddenly sees in his blue eyes searching hers for understanding that he doesn't understand her, and she realizes she doesn't understand him. His blondish hair and tan skin along with his stocky football-playing body are handsome for sure, but Eddy realizes they don't talk much about what's inside them. She suddenly wants to ask him, *What's inside you, Johnny? I can't see what's inside you.* But she feels this would scare him. Or maybe her.

"I'll let you know about the movie," she says quickly. "You better run; Mr. Thompson will close the door on you, and you'll miss your Shakespeare presentation. Good luck!"

Johnny takes off quickly. He makes it to the door just as the bell is ringing. Eddy whispers, "Yeah, good luck doing *Romeo and Juliet*." She smiles as she wonders who Johnny thinks is the main character in that play. Then she looks around and realizes that she's late for Trig. "Geez," she whispers again while running.

That evening after supper, while Eddy is helping with the dishes, her father says from the den, "Oh, Boris Karloff died. How did I miss that?" Harold reads on. "'Boris Karloff starred in many films in the first half of the twentieth century. He earned a reputation for acting in horror movies such as *Frankenstein*.'"

"I didn't know he died. He must have been pretty old though," says Mary.

"Eighty-one."

"Pretty old then. Edna," Mary says, handing Eddy a rinsed plate to dry, "I remember when you came home scared from some horror movie. Was he in it?"

"No, I don't think so, but the movie was *Black Sunday*. I'll never forget it. How could you let me see that scary movie?" Eddy says, standing next to her mother at the sink. She's remembering something about a mask of Satan that had spikes attached to the inside so that when a person put it on you as a means of torture, the spikes went into your face. "I was only about fourteen."

"You wanted to go to the movies every time it changed. How could I know what every movie was about?"

"Well, the title might have given a hint, I guess. Anyway, I found out about scary movies, at least. But you know, I never thought *Frankenstein* was scary when I finally saw it on television. Thought it was sad. *Dracula*, however, was quite scary. No background music. Just eerie silence. But *Black Sunday*? Yikes, it was violent!"

"Well, I think you turned out pretty normal, considering."

Considering what? Considering no one knows what "normal" means? She remembers her thoughts about Johnny and whether she has looked at him correctly—and whether he has ever really seen her. Maybe he is also carrying around secrets that he doesn't want people to know. She doesn't think she'll tell her mom about these questions she's carrying around inside.

––––––––––

"Come in, Edna, and have a seat." School has ended for the day, and Mr. Thompson is sitting at his desk, so Eddy sits in the desk closest to it and puts her books down. She has her coat on.

"I want to talk with you about your Shakespeare presentation. You did fine. In fact, you earned an A minus on it."

Eddy blushes slightly, surprised by this grade. She murmurs, "Thank you, Mr. Thompson."

"But I want to ask you about Ophelia, your topic. You didn't condemn her decision to maybe end her life in your presentation. I wondered why not?"

Eddy's eyes widen a bit as she tries to understand why she has been called in after school. "Well, sir, it seemed, the possible suicide that is, a logical course for her because her life was not her own. Hamlet has killed her father, after all. She could have drowned by accident, but maybe not. Maybe she couldn't see her way forward ...."

"True enough. Do you admire her?" Mr. Thompson says this last part slowly, looking at her with a piercing look, as if to see into her head.

Eddy takes a breath. Now she understands. She quickly deflects. "Well, everyone is pulling her every which way. She's just a minor character. She certainly was drawn toward Hamlet but just couldn't read him. He has his own stuff going on. I felt sorry for her. That's all."

"So you don't admire her decision?"

"Admire her? No, sir ... except that, well, no sir."

"*Hamlet* is a violent play, Edna. And tough to understand. Hamlet is young, as is Ophelia. Yes, he debates the idea of *being* in the 'To be or not to be' soliloquy. Yes, he entertains the thought of *not being*. But do you remember how he ends the conversation with himself?"

"Uhhh ... not at the moment." Eddy does remember, but she's not sure where Mr. Thompson is headed with this conversation. Is she in trouble?

Mr. Thompson leans forward over his desk, his arms crossed on the open book in front of him. "Yes, he ponders whether he should end his life when he suffers 'the slings and arrows of outrageous fortune.' And yet, when he considers what might happen after death, he says ..." Mr. Thompson takes his arms off the book and starts to read.

> But that the dread of something after death,
> The undiscover'd country, from whose bourn
> No traveller returns, puzzles the will,
> And makes us rather bear those ills we have
> Than fly to others that we know not of?

"Taking his life, Hamlet determines, doesn't solve the riddle of what it means 'to be'. Hamlet, unlike Ophelia who perhaps doesn't have the 'wherewithal' to have such a conversation with herself, lives on until his actions determine his end. Do you see that, Edna?"

The two of them, the teacher and the student, look at each other across the desks. Eddy thinks about that word *wherewithal*. Is Ophelia found floating in the water because she can't see her life unfolding before her? Is it because she's a girl, and girls aren't listened to by the adults or by Hamlet?

"Mr. Thompson, I see you're a bit worried about me. Thank you. But I'm not Ophelia. I would never make that choice. I was just trying to write a good presentation. I thought I had a good angle, that's all. I'm not really suffering any slings and arrows." Eddy kind of laughs.

Mr. Thompson sits back in his chair and smiles. "I'm glad to hear it. You're quiet. I just wanted to check in with you to see how you're doing."

"Yes, my father says the same kind of things. He thinks I am, what's the word—'impetuous'. Or maybe he likes *frustrated* better. Or maybe *impatient*."

"Give things a little time, Edna, and everything will become clearer. Maybe not completely clear, but clear*er*. Try to qualify those words with an *e-r* at the end as I've instructed."

"Yes, sir. May I go? Joan is probably waiting by the car for me."

"Yes, yes. Thanks for coming in. See you in class."

And with that, she grabs her books and walks out, thinking that Mr. Thompson is probably watching her as she leaves. She doesn't want to know what he's thinking. She senses something between them that isn't quite clear to her. In the hall, she finds Johnny waiting outside Mr. Thompson's classroom.

"I looked everywhere for you. You in trouble?"

"Nope, just a regular old conversation with Mr. Thompson. Don't worry about me so much."

"About the movie this weekend ...?"

"Sure. Let's go. *Camelot*, eh?"

PART 3
MARCH 1969

CHAPTER 9

March in the mountains. Can be cold still. Can have snow. Can be springlike on some days. Can bring rain and low-hanging gray skies that settle into the folds of the mountains for days. But indoor sports bring warm gyms and high spirits. Football and basketball rivalries between small high schools give townspeople a reason to cheer. Wrestling bouts between those same small schools bring out supporters too, though in smaller numbers than fall football and winter basketball.

Wrestling—those one-on-one struggles that Eddy seems compelled to watch, even when wanting to turn away. Seems like raw power versus raw power, and then there's the power of the will that can only be seen in the results. Eddy has a hard time watching yet can't stop. Her body tightens, and she wonders if it would be easier to be the one wrestling than the one watching. Still she goes to the matches, drawn toward these battles of the body and the will.

It's a Thursday night, and the rain is beat-beat-beating on the roof and against the high windows of the high school gym. Paul and Eddy walk through the double doors under the basketball hoop, and they climb to the topmost bleacher behind their school's wrestlers, the better to lean their backs against the wall.

Thursdays are deep royal purple for Eddy—a color she likes. She doesn't know why; she just sees purple when she thinks of Thursday or sees the word written down. In fact, all the days of the week are color-coded for Eddy: Mondays are red, Tuesdays are orange, Wednesdays are robin's-egg blue, Fridays are pale yellow/white, Saturdays are green, and Sundays are blindingly white but turn into dark midnight blue by nightfall.

It will be years and years before she reads somewhere that there's a name for people with such sensations. Synesthetes. Words and senses can be combined. Sights can have sounds, sounds can have tastes, words and numbers can have colors. As for Eddy, she's just always assumed that everyone sees colors for the days of the week, so she's never asked others about it. Eddy's colors for the days don't change. Thursdays are definitely purple.

Eddy and Paul look fairly bedraggled from the rain and wind as they take their seats in the gym. The first match is about to begin, the lightest-weight entrants from both schools taking center stage on the huge mat in the middle of the floor. The referee stands in the center circle talking to the boys who face each other in their revealing unitards, wrestling shoes, and head gear. Eddy pulls out a box of Luden's cough drops from her raincoat pocket, offering one to Paul.

"I don't have a cough," he says.

"I don't either. I suck on them like candy. I love the cherry flavor."

"That's weird, Eddy. Why not just buy candy?"

"I like this flavor."

Paul takes the cough drop; Eddy takes one, too, and places the box back in her pocket and then takes off her coat.

Paul and Eddy stare straight down to the mat, ready to watch the wrestling. Paul's friend Leonard is a wrestler, so he likes to come to matches. Joan hates watching the wrestling matches, saying they're too intense, so she doesn't come. Eddy thinks so too, but as she's watching, she reminds herself that if these wrestlers can take this chance, this individual challenge, then she can try to make herself watch. Who will be pinned beneath another body without being able to move, arching his back until the body on top forces his shoulder blades flat for the count of three by the referee? Who will triumph, pinning those shoulders to the mat, and then stand alongside the referee, who lifts the winner's arm high in the air while still holding on to the loser's arm? Eddy wonders whether the loser finds any comfort from the referee's hand on his arm. Or perhaps the loser hates it and wants to leave the mat in a hurry. Eddy has never asked any of the wrestlers. Maybe she should, now that she thinks of it.

The two 108-pound wrestlers are circling each other, their arms ready, their hands poised to grab hold of each other. A throw down? A leg sweep? A full-body slam, one body wrapping up the other to take him to the mat? That body fighting frantically to turn over, turn the tables on the other, to stand again. Eddy is biting her middle finger's nail. She has no idea she's doing this.

Suddenly, she senses a body next to hers as someone slides in close along the bleacher. She breaks her eyes away from the mat and looks to her left. Jay is sitting there, hands in the pockets of his short rain jacket, his brown corduroy pants next to her Wrangler jeans.

"Do you like wrestling?" Jay asks, looking straight ahead down at the mat as he speaks.

"Oh, I didn't see you." Eddy knows she may be blushing. She hates surprises.

"I know. I was down a ways. You didn't look over. Hey, Paul."

"Hey, Jay. How's it going?" Eddy thinks that Paul says this as naturally as can be, as if it's the most normal thing in the world to be sitting in the bleachers with Jay.

"Okay, I guess. How's it going for you?"

Eddy thinks she's entered another universe. These two are acting as if they have shorthand at conversation. *Do boys have this way of conversing easily like I do with Joanie?*

"Fine, fine," Paul says perfunctorily as he keeps his eyes on the wrestlers. One has swept the legs from under the other, giving the home crowd a chance to cheer for a second and the referee to raise his fingers, signaling two points given for the takedown, before the other boy twists away and is suddenly on top of the one who swept his legs. The referee awards points for this reversal. The boy on the bottom is on his belly. The one on top wrestles the home team boy's left arm around to his back, hoping to lift that boy's shoulder, flip him over, and pin his shoulders to the mat. This continues for some moments, this pulling, twisting, pushing, body-against-body maneuvering. Then the buzzer sounds, ending the first timed period. Eddy is still biting that fingernail. Slowly, Jay takes her wrist and lowers her hand to her lap.

"Hey, what are you doing?" Eddy turns angrily to Jay.

"You're going to bite off the whole nail. Those little guys are working hard, but they aren't as anxious as *you* are. They do this every day in practice."

"How do you know?" Eddy asks with a slight edge to her voice.

"I know because I wrestled in ninth grade."

Jay has already released her hand into her lap and put his own back into his pocket. Eddy looks at him, noticing his hair is overlong on his forehead, thinking to herself that some teacher will soon tell him to cut it.

"Did you like it?" Eddy says as she shifts her gaze back to the mat.

Paul looks over at them briefly, then turns back to the floor. The boys are in the starting position for period two, the home team boy on all fours on the bottom, his adversary kneeling on one knee with one arm reaching around the boy's torso, his other hand on the boy's near arm.

"I did for a while. We had just moved here from Wytheville, and it was fun to be with guys after school, wrestling but also fooling around."

"So why did you stop?"

"I don't know …. I never saw any of those guys outside of the gym. None lived near me—I live out in the country—none seemed to be special friends. I don't know …. And what the coaches make you give. It just got harder. I was kind of scrawny, but I still had to be strong and weigh enough to make weight. Some of the bigger guys have to carry a cup around all day close to weigh-in, spitting into it to try to get under the weight limit. Poor guys. Anyway, my folks never came to watch, so I quit."

Eddy ponders this information, Jay wrestling. *What did I do in the ninth grade? Oh yeah, I played volleyball with about a hundred girls in the Girls Athletic Association. I was terrible.*

Paul suddenly yells as the home team guy flips the guy on top—does it so fast, as though he'd planned it in his head and then, boom, pins his adversary before the other guy has time to think. The referee pounds the mat with his open hand three times, the three stand up, and amid the home-crowd cheers, the referee raises the arm of the winner.

"Yeah!" said Paul. "That was intense!"

Eddy looks over at Jay, and they both smile at each other at the word *intense*. Eddy sees that Jay's eyes are more green than she's thought, and not so dark. There are also small light freckles over the bridge of his nose and under his eyes. Almost invisible except in this harsh gym light. She knows they're holding each other's eyes a moment too long for her comfort, and she quickly turns away. She looks down at her lap, at her jeans, and she can see the closeness of Jay's leg to her own. Again, like the time at the cliffs, she feels a desire to reach out and touch the corduroy. She doesn't. Paul is speaking.

"Leonard's up. Holy crap he must be nervous."

"He don't look nervous." Jay is looking down at the mat. "He a friend of yours?"

"Yeah."

"He'll be okay. Other guy looks scrawny. What's Leonard, about one twenty?"

"One sixteen. And he looks a little scrawny too." Paul leans his elbows on his legs, covering his mouth with one hand.

The whistle blows. The match begins. Jay and Eddy are leaning their backs on the gym wall.

Eddy glances at Jay. "What classes are you in? I rarely see you at school."

Jay's eyes are straight ahead. "The usual: some English, Math, Government. Same as you, but the kids in my classes aren't going to college. Our electives are Shop and Woodworking for guys and Typing and Home Ec for girls. You know, those kids who used to be in gym class in the ninth grade and you haven't seen them since, except in the halls and at lunch. They're all with me and Buddy in our classes—the dumb classes."

"You're not dumb!" Eddy blurts out.

Jay smiles, still not looking at Eddy. "C'mon Leonard! Move!"

Paul looks over at Jay. He gives a slight nod of the head.

Leonard has his hands full, literally. Both boys are hunched over from the waist, flailing their arms around, trying to get a good grip on the other while smacking the opponent's hands away. Then they stand up straight, and Leonard pushes the other boy outside the ring just as the buzzer sounds. The referee blows his whistle, and Leonard loses a point. The boys return to the center of the mat and begin again. The visitor gets an arm around Leonard's middle and kind of swings him around until Leonard loses his balance. Both boys fall down to the mat with the visitor on top. The referee gives the visitor two points for a takedown.

"Oh boy," whispers Paul.

Eddy places her hand on Paul's arm and squeezes. Some people in the stands yell out like Jay just did: "C'mon, Leonard!" "Get 'em, Lennie!" "Go, go!" Each coach is yelling instructions from the sideline. The visitor is trying to turn Leonard over onto his back. Leonard is striving to push the visitor off him and get out of this situation. Seconds tick off, and those two bodies, with very little movement, grapple with each other.

Eddy thinks that Leonard must feel helpless, lying there underneath another body and unable to move because the boy on top has his torso and arm in a viselike grip. Leonard has one arm he can move, so he's desperately trying to maneuver his way out. Leonard's cheeks are red from the exertion, or from rubbing against the mat. Eddy's hand rises to her mouth again. She and Paul and Jay are leaning forward now. Paul is whispering, "C'mon, Lennie. C'mon, Lennie."

The whistle blows, and the period is over. Leonard and his opponent stand and then kneel into position, Leonard on all fours underneath his adversary. The last three-minute period begins. Leonard tries hard to twist free, and suddenly he breaks his opponent's hold and stands up. The crowd cheers, and Leonard is awarded points. But just as quickly, Leonard's opponent grabs him around the waist and throws him to the mat. The crowd groans as they watch Leonard on his back, squirming to turn over with the other wrestler covering him, trying to pin his shoulders. *Is Leonard tired?* Eddy wonders. *Does he have nothing left with which to struggle and break free?*

Eddy is tense as she watches, her fingers moving to her mouth again. And while she watches the last seconds of the bout, just before the referee slaps the mat three times, Jay takes Eddy's hand once again, bringing it down between her body and his, and this time he doesn't let go. They sit there like that for seconds.

After this moment of Jay's hand taking hers, the referee slaps the mat, and Leonard has lost. The boys stand beside the referee as he lifts Leonard's opponent's arm. Leonard walks off the mat to sit with the team. Paul, looking a bit sorrowful for his friend, turns to Eddy. By then, Eddy's hands are in her lap again, but her cheeks are flushed.

"Damn," Paul whispers.

"He tried hard," whispers Eddy. She turns and looks at Jay, who's looking straight ahead. "Hope he doesn't feel too bad."

The next weight class of boys are already on the mat when Jay stands up.

"Welp, I gotta go. See you later."

"See ya, Jay," Paul says absently.

Eddy looks up at Jay. He looks at her for a second, as if he's expecting something from her. Or as if he sees her, sees into her thoughts. It scares her a little—and pleases her at the same time. Does he see that she's thinking about his corduroy pants? His touch? But she can't seem to make up her mind between these two feelings of fear and pleasure enough to form any words, and so she says nothing. Jay turns and walks back along the top bleacher before heading down to the floor and out the double doors. His hands are in his coat pockets. She watches him. She realizes she has no idea how to think about this, about him. No way to see into his thoughts like he seems to see into hers.

———————

When Eddy comes into the house after the wrestling match, she finds her dad and mom sitting on the living room couch together, her dad with a short glass of his favorite bourbon, and her mother wearing her soft muumuu dress with a glass of sherry in her hand. Mary's leg is tucked under her, and Harold has his socked feet up on the coffee table. Frank Sinatra sings from a record turning on the big record player in the corner of the room. Eddy thinks both of her parents look dreamy. *Are they drunk?* she wonders as she hangs up her coat in the closet near the door. She's never seen them have too much to drink, but there's a first time for everything. Her parents smile at her when she turns to them, and over the music, her mother asks, "Did we win?"

"We did, finally. Thanks for letting me take the car. Paul and I cheered on the team, although Leonard, Paul's good friend, lost." Her parents keep looking dreamy. "What are y'all doing? Listening?"

Harold points to the chair next to the sofa. "Sit a minute, please. You've heard us play this record before, I'm sure, but I'm not sure you know what it means to us."

"Dad ..." Eddy starts.

"Please, Edna. Sit a minute."

Eddy sighs and perches on the edge of the chair.

"I know how you like music. I like to take some credit for your love of music, of your generation's rock 'n' roll. Well, this is my music, and your mom's. We had records, but we often took sheet music to our friends' houses and someone would play the hits on the piano. Stella Randall was the best at that, wasn't she, Mary?"

"I know all this, Dad. You and Mom jitterbugged around the room."

"Yes, we did. Your mom was—is—a good dancer. Well, anyway, a couple of years ago, Frank Sinatra, one of our favorites, came out with this record. He turned fifty that year, and this record is the result of that, I think. We—your mom and I—really like it. They're songs about looking back over your life, and you know what? The singer says it was good. Even if there were times when things you hoped for didn't work out or love didn't last."

Eddy wonders if he's thinking about the Second World War and his part in it. Things he saw or friends he lost. She thinks her mother looks at her father with understanding, as if their shared history doesn't even need to be spoken. Harold stands up and goes over to the stereo. "Listen to these words."

"Dad ..."

"Just listen, please."

Harold turns up the volume and then carefully places the needle down on the right track, and instruments begin to play slowly. Frank Sinatra sings about a good year when he was seventeen.

Eddy is embarrassed. She doesn't know where to look; she just knows she doesn't want to look at her parents. She knows her mother is glancing over at her now and then while she's sipping on the sweet Harvey's Bristol Cream Sherry she likes. Eddy can feel it. She can sense that her mother is hoping Eddy will give her father a chance to tell her about their music. Harold looks down at the drink in his hand. The orchestra swells in between the verses, and even though he pronounces each year "good," the voice of Frank Sinatra sounds so sad Eddy can hardly stand it.

The song finally ends, and Harold stands up to turn down the volume. When he returns to the couch, he says, "Okay, Edna. You can go now. I just wanted you to hear a song your mother and I love, just like I can hear the songs coming from your record player that you love. Loving music doesn't end just because we get older." Eddy thinks he looks so sad, she feels she must say something supportive.

"No, Dad. It was pretty. I've always known you like his music. This is just, I don't know, a little sad sounding." No response. "Well, goodnight."

"Goodnight, darling," Mary says. Mary's eyes are loving eyes, Eddy thinks. Soft and loving.

"Goodnight, Edna," Harold says absently. As she begins to walk toward the stairs, Eddy turns to see her father reach over and tenderly take Mary's hand and bring it to his lips. Mary dips her head toward her husband and smiles slightly. Eddy is embarrassed again, but it's because she feels she's witnessing something too intimate for a child to watch.

In a few minutes, she stands in her red pajamas, the ones with a little lace fringe at the top, and peers into the mirror in the bathroom; her toothbrush is in her hand. Her face looks splotchy, and she looks at the two little lines appearing just between her eyebrows. She leans in closer. *I'm turning into my father with these serious lines.*

"Hell's bells," she mutters just as the phone rings in the hall. She rushes to answer, and as she picks it up, she hears her mother say hello.

"Hey, Mrs. Walters. I know it's late, but can I talk to Eddy?"

"Hi, Joan." But before Mary can say more, Eddy chimes in.

"I've got it, Mom." Eddy hears the click. "What's up, Joanie Baloney?"

"Paul just called a bit ago to ask a question about a homework assignment. Imagine that, Paul asking *me* about homework! Anyway, he said y'all went to the wrestling match. Poor Leonard."

"Paul called you? Interesting." A pause. "Yeah, I know what you mean about Leonard. We hated it for him, but at least our team won. Eddie Coleman won the heavyweight match. It was intense."

"Paul also said Jay sat with you for a while. What's going on with you two? Why is he showing up wherever you are?"

"Don't know. He said that he wrestled in ninth grade but gave it up. Maybe he just likes to come to the matches, I don't know." Eddy sits down on the carpet next to the phone.

"Hmm ... maybe. But Jay is, I don't know, suddenly just around—agreed?"

"Agreed. Hey, Joanie?"

"Yeah?"

"Do your parents talk to you about when they were young?"

"Sure. All parents do a little, I suppose. I think we don't like to think of them that way. Or holding hands. Or kissing, for heaven's sake. Or maybe we just can't picture a time when they weren't 'the parents,' telling us kids what to do. But mine were never rebels. Too Catholic, I guess."

"I don't think mine were rebellious either. But they had that war. I think that made all the difference. They really *wanted* normal after that. Our times seem different. I don't know what I want."

"Me neither. Except to pass Trig. 'Night, Eddy."

"'Night, Joanie Baloney. Oh, and your birthday is coming up! What do you think you'll do?"

"I think my folks want to go see my grandparents in Roanoke this Saturday. And spend the night. You know what that means …. Dinner with all the older crowd, and then we'll go to Mass on Sunday morning. What a birthday!"

"You'll do something with Roger though, right?"

"Oh yeah, we'll hang out on Friday. Maybe go to the Dari and then find a good secluded place to stop for a while. Roger told me he found a deserted alley where no cars drive through. You know what that means …."

Eddy laughs. "Watch those roving hands, Joanie! Just think, eighteen. We're practically grown-up."

A few minutes later, lying on her bed and staring at the wallpaper while she listens to Jefferson Airplane, she still doesn't know how to think about Jay. Pondering the night in the gym, she lets her mind wander. She wonders why she let Jay hold her hand. She remembers how warm and dry his hand was as it encircled hers. How long did he hold her hand really? The song "Today," number four on Side 1, comes on. How she loves the haunting guitar notes floating high above the rest of the song, even over the rush of a huge range of sounds and instruments played midway through. How she loves the constant tambourine. She looks at the album cover to see who's playing the guitar on "Today" with those haunting notes. Jerry Garcia. And through that rush of the building sounds of music, through the added harmonies and drums, through the insistent tambourine, the male lead voice pierces right through her.

She holds the pinkish-purple cover to her chest. Thursdays are definitely purple, and this one was a firework of purple. Eddy suddenly hears that first line Frank Sinatra sings. Something about being seventeen and how it was a good year for small-town girls on summer nights, and then the memory of Jay's warm hand holding hers comes to mind. *How to make sense of this*, she wonders. Maybe she doesn't need to make sense of it. Maybe she just needs to be happy feeling this way about a boy holding her hand.

CHAPTER 10

"Well, Edna, looks like you're out of luck. Paul McCartney married Linda Eastman on March 12th. He's off the market." Eddy's father is reading *The Roanoke Times* "People in the News" section.

"Oh, that's okay, Dad. It's John I like best. And I'm starting to like Frank Sinatra too." Harold looks up quickly and sees the smile on his daughter's face. He smiles too, as he shares what he thinks is Eddy's attempt to be funny.

———

Joan and Eddy are doing their homework together on the floor of Joan's bedroom and playing records on the small record player. Eddy is humming along with Gordon Lightfoot when he sings about jumping on a freight train in the early morning rain. She looks up and out the window of Joan's room at the rain. "Could you jump a freight train, Joanie?"

"I wish I could jump on one right now—Trigonometry is *killing* me! Surely together we can figure this out."

"I think Mrs. Lemons knows we can't. Oh well, we're trying. Why can't we sing songs like this one in chorus? This one fits my mood more often than 'Jesu, Joy of Man's Desiring.' Of course my mother would like that one. Anything to do with Jesus. Geez, we sing some old songs."

"Why is it *Jesu* instead of *Jesus* in that song?"

"I have no idea. Mrs. Norman may have told us, but I probably wasn't listening. Still, I like chorus class pretty well. Beats always having textbook assignments. Do you feel the same way about Typing?"

"I love it! I can flat out type like the wind. And Roger sits next to me, so we joke around a lot. He's crap at typing. I'm so glad that Mrs. Brickman recently asked me to be a helper for another typing class because I had a free period. I like helping people out. Mrs. Brickman is nice, as teachers go. Oh! I keep meaning to tell you but keep forgetting. You know who's in that class I help in? Your weird friend Jay. Wonder why he's taking Typing? He doesn't seem the kind who'd need to type. He seems like he'd just like working on cars."

"He's not exactly my friend, Joanie. I don't know what he is."

"A person of interest? I think you have a little crush on your weird friend."

"I barely know him."

Joan starts singing "To Know Him Is to Love Him" by The Teddy Bears.

"Joanie … I'll take my records and go home."

"Ha! C'mon, Eddy; lighten up. By the way, I haven't asked you about *Camelot*. Roger and I saw it too, but brother, everyone busting into songs all the time killed me. Roger and I couldn't stop laughing, and the people behind us shushed us. I suppose you liked it? Forbidden love. Songs. Tears at the end?"

"I did like it, but it was definitely sad. When Guinevere cries because she knows she won't be there to see King Arthur smile at her ever again, I teared up too. But then Johnny looked over at me when I sniffed. His nonsmiling face looked at me as if I had embarrassed him in public. It's a theater, for goodness' sake! It's dark! And poor Guinevere going to the convent. Better than dying at the stake, I guess. You're the Catholic, Joanie. Would you ever go to a convent?"

"Me? You know me, I'm made for loving a real person, not just God. I like God and all, but I like Roger a whole bunch too. What about Johnny?"

"I like Johnny …."

"Eddy," Joan says slowly, "you might need to think about not stringing Johnny along if you don't really like him that way. You're the opposite of that song 'Johnny Angel' where the girl is trying to date Johnny. I'm starting to feel sorry for your Johnny."

"Joanie, I'm not stringing him along!!"

"Okay, okay. Not my business. I'm only your best friend though. If I don't tell you shit, who will? Well, besides Paul."

"Okay. I hear you." They look down at their notebooks. Then Joan starts to sing "Johnny Angel," using her pencil as a mic, and Eddy laughs, lifts her pencil to her lips, and joins in. They can't help but sway.

"Well, well, well. Edna, you're out of luck again. John Lennon married Yoko Ono yesterday on the twentieth. You'll just have to settle for finding another fella." Harold chuckles to himself. Eddy glances over at her father from her seat on the couch. She shakes her head, but there's a little smile along with her head shake.

"Looks like the old saying 'March comes in like a lamb and goes out like a lion' is certainly true this year," says Mary Walters as she looks out the kitchen window at the wind howling through the woods out back. Eddy is helping her set the table for dinner. She wonders what her mother is thinking. The trees sway and bend, and the woods are near their house. Is her mother afraid they'll fall on the roof? Eddy, too, looking out the window, suddenly wonders what she would do if she saw a tree start to topple toward the big window she stands before. What would her mother do?

"March can just head on out as far as I'm concerned," says Eddy, not looking at Mary.

"Now Edna, don't go wishing your life away. Life is precious. Every day is precious. Why, you can learn something every day, and that will make the day worthwhile."

"Mom, I learned about trigonometry equations today, and I plan on never using that information in life, so what's the point?"

"The point is to apply yourself because you never know what you will use in life. You may get to college and decide space exploration is for you! Look at me; I took shorthand in high school and college, and although I've never been a secretary in an office, I use shorthand as the secretary for church meetings. I like it. It's like a secret only I know how to decipher. Want me to show you?"

"Sure, but not right now." Eddy looks at her mother at the kitchen counter; she's stirring the juices surrounding a pan of pork chops she's frying. She seared them first and now has added water, tomatoes, peas, and onions. It's a favorite dish of her father's, and they have it a lot in the Walters house, sometimes substituting cubed steak for the pork chops. Eddy places the silverware just so because her mother loves it just so. Eddy wonders what her mother's dreams were when she was eighteen.

"Mom, what were you doing when you were my age?"

"Hmm … let's see. That would have been 1944. Oh dear, that would have been the height of America's involvement in the war. My sophomore year at college. Remember I graduated from high school at sixteen."

"No, I didn't know that! Were you that smart?" Eddy asks with a swift turn of her head toward her mother.

"Well, I was smart enough. I liked school. But that's not why I graduated at sixteen," Mary says, laughing. "We didn't have eighth grade back then. Just freshman through senior year in high school. Don't know when they added eighth grade. I'll have to look that up somewhere."

"So tell me again," says Eddy, "what you wanted to major in. Did you dream of being a secretary, working in an office?"

"I didn't dream about much. Just took practical courses, except for lots of English classes. Always liked English." Mary looks up at Eddy.

"Does it sound silly to say that I just wanted my friends to come home safely from war? Especially one?"

"You mean Dad?"

"No, but he was your dad's cousin, Jim. You know Uncle Jim."

Eddy is curious about Jim and thinks about asking some more questions, but she decides not to. Maybe she doesn't want to know why her mother's dreams are missing. Maybe she's afraid that she has the same syndrome—the no-dreams syndrome.

After dinner, Mary and Eddy clean up the kitchen together. Mary says, "Edna, my dear, you'll figure things out. Don't fret too much."

Eddy looks at her soapy hands, then says, "Oh by the way, I have a singing part for the spring chorus concert."

"Oh Edna, that's wonderful! Hear that Harold?" Mary says a bit louder. "Edna has a singing part in the spring chorus concert!"

"That is wonderful! We'll be there in the front row!"

"No! Please not the front row! I'd just die!" Eddy exclaims.

"And what's your part?" Mary laughingly asks.

"A verse from that piece by Beethoven called 'Joyful, Joyful, We Adore Thee.' Mrs. Norman made a special arrangement." Eddy can tell her mother is so pleased. She wishes she were pleased.

Later that night, Eddy and Joan are lying in the twin beds in Eddy's room under the eaves. There's a stack of 45 records on the turntable. Joan is reading a page in a notebook.

"Eddy, your lists of songs from 1965, '66, '67, '68, and '69 tell me a lot. I know why you mope sometimes. Listen to these songs you were raised on: 'Hung On You' and 'Unchained Melody' by the Righteous Brothers, 'Tracks of My Tears' by Smokey Robinson, '96 Tears,' 'Black is Black.' Good grief."

"Can't help how I was raised. Dad's always loved music and brought home a lot of 45s. So I started keeping lists of my favorites. You know you like my records."

"I do, but gee whiz, so many are about love gone wrong."

"That's rock 'n' roll. Actually, when I think about it, that's so much of music from Broadway, and probably opera and jazz, though I don't know opera and jazz. Love gone wrong. I like the way you put that."

"Action" clicks down on the turntable, and the needle arm finds its place at the beginning. "Well," says Joan, sitting up and swinging her legs over the edge of the bed, "I like songs that make me want to dance!" She looks over at Eddy and pulls her up off her bed. The two girls stand facing each other, and when Freddy Cannon sings and beckons them to dance till their backbone slips, they dance, twisting and turning in the small space of the room while singing loudly along with Freddy.

The girls have one rule when dancing: Your arms have to go above your shoulders. The girls turn every which way, stomping and turning together all around the room. Their dances are a mash-up of the last five years: the twist, the bird, the monkey, and the jerk, with a little bit of holding hands and jitterbugging!

"Hold it down up there!" comes the angry voice of Jimmy from downstairs. "It sounds like the floor is going to cave in with all that clomping around!"

The girls don't answer.

CHAPTER 11

Lunchtime in Thomasburg High School, whichever period of the day you have it, is a game of seek-and-go-sit. Whether you bring your lunch or walk through the hot-lunch line, you must be in the game of finding a place to sit and deciding with whom. The huge cafeteria with its ten rows stretching the length of the room gives ample space, but given the rules of the game, it's sometimes hard to fit in where you want.

During Eddy's fourth-period lunch, the Black students sit as far away from the entrance as possible, taking the first table nearest the side windows and nearest the place you drop off your trays. Some of the Black guys who play sports, however, sit with members of their teams. The White kids sit with their groups. Cheerleaders and jocks sit in the first row near the shelves at the entrance where you park your books while you eat. There's a large window and radiator nearby, and some of the boys get up after eating and lean against the radiator, surveying the room.

In the second row, some nerds sit together. The hoods sit together at the ends of a couple of the middle rows, their dark jackets standing out, as do their girlfriends with the dark lipstick colors. The underclassmen who have fourth-period lunch fill in much of the middle of the cafeteria, finding their groups but having trouble maneuvering in between the tables and the large columns in the center of the room. The upperclassmen seem to have dibs on all of the tables near the windows. Sometimes there's a commotion from the middle of the room as trays drop or someone is "helped" into dropping them. Eddy is sure there's bullying going on.

Some of Eddy's friends, like Joan and Rhonda and Lynn, and sometimes Johnny if he's not with the jocks, often have to take the first empty seats they find near the ends of a table.

Lately, there's been another game afoot. The jocks have been orchestrating the building of pyramids with empty milk cartons. They flatten the tops to make cubes and begin stacking them to see how high the pyramid will reach before it tumbles. And when it does, the boys scramble and leave the mess on the table and floors. These high jinks occur only infrequently, and the administrators have had trouble pinning the mess on anyone. The boys time it pretty well, with no pattern to the day they build it and never the same table. They build the tower quickly, just as many kids are standing to head back to class, making their tower tumble close to the bell that ends the lunch period. When the scramble takes place, the administrators would have had to be monitoring things closely to see who's behind it all. They don't monitor closely, it seems, because the building happens only now and then.

So when Eddy is called to the office one day during her fifth-period class, she has no idea why. She likes the assistant principal, Mr. Dockett, even though he's the one in charge of discipline in the school. Mr. Dockett was a Biology teacher and a tennis coach before deciding to take the job of assistant principal, and Eddy had liked him in her Biology class. He was fair and didn't make things hard for Eddy. In fact, he was kind to her. Maybe it was because Eddy wasn't squeamish when it came to dissecting things. Maybe it was because she was quiet and didn't rock any boats.

After she knocks on the door, Mr. Dockett answers it and says, "Come in, come in, Edna. Take a seat." And as she sits down in the seat across from his desk, he shuts the door and sits down at the desk.

"How are things, Edna? How is your senior year going?"

"It's okay. Going fine."

"Any plans for next year?"

"Working on it."

"That's good, that's good." Mr. Dockett looks down at his desk. There's a long pause, and Eddy's curious smile that had been there when she came in begins to fade. Is she in trouble, she wonders? She begins to think about what she could have done to warrant this office visit.

Finally, Mr. Dockett speaks. "Edna you were a good student in my class, observant and trustworthy. As you know, there have been some students in the lunchroom setting up pyramids of empty milk cartons, knocking them down, and then running away, leaving a mess for the staff to clean up."

Eddy gives a slight nod.

"Now we've just got to put an end to this prank. The staff doesn't have time to clean up after these students." Mr. Dockett looks up at her. "Edna, I believe you're friends with the football player Johnny Miller ...."

Eddy's eyes widen, and her mouth opens a bit as she starts to get the drift of the conversation. Could he be asking her to give up Johnny (who she knows has sometimes been in attendance at these pranks) and the others by turning them in? Was this the reason for her summons?

Mr. Dockett looks down at his desk again. His hands are folded on the desk blotter in front of him, and when he looks up again into Eddy's eyes, he slowly pushes his chair back and stands up. Coming around the desk, he says, "You know what, Edna? Never mind. Thanks for coming in, but I think you better go back to class."

Eddy stands, not knowing what to say as Mr. Dockett opens the door to the office. She just nods to him as she leaves, and he says, "Good luck, Edna, with everything."

"Hell's bells!" Eddy says to Joan as they walk to the car after school. "He wanted me to tell on the boys who build the pyramids at lunch!"

"Good grief, Eddy, he called you to his office? And shut the door? Did you think you were in trouble?"

"No, not at first. I like Mr. Dockett, but what a terrible job he has, having to take care of every problem in the school. I had no idea why I was called in, but he started in about the boys in the lunchroom, and he mentioned that I was friends with Johnny, and then it started to occur to me that he was asking me to turn them in and give names."

Joan says, "I can't wait to graduate. Surely college won't have people watching us to catch us involved in something."

Eddy looks at her friend, thinking that Joan is coming around to her way of thinking, that school has too much adult supervision, too many rules. "Yeah, Joanie. What do you think our chances of getting into college are? If we go to college, I don't know, maybe we won't be watched so closely." There's a pause in the conversation, as if both girls are thinking of that future time that will grant more freedom, but a time when they will not be together. Then Eddy says, "You know what though? At least Mr. Dockett didn't ask me to tell. He just stopped in mid-sentence. I think he realized he was wrong. Just stopped and said *never mind*. Makes me like him still, even though he had that bad idea in the first place. Wonder why he asked *me* to tell?"

"I don't know, Eddy, but you dodged a bullet. You might have gotten a reputation as a major rat if you had caved in. Remember those kids in school who were always telling the teachers on other kids? There was one, Mickey somebody in our class in sixth grade."

"Mickey. Mickey ... oh yeah. Teacher's pet. He moved away the next year. I bet he becomes a preacher when he grows up."

Joan laughs loudly as the wind blows her hair wildly, and she tries to corral it behind her ears.

"Well, Johnny and the guys would never have forgiven you if you had given them up to Mr. Dockett."

"Yeah. And Johnny and I are already kind of on the outs."

"Really?"

"Uh-huh."

"Want to talk about it?"

"Not right now. I just want to go get some fries."

That night at dinner, Harold Walters puts his napkin in his lap and says, "You know, I've been reading about the Apollo 9 flight from earlier this month. Seems we're on the way to the moon. What do you all think about that?"

These dinnertime questions from their father to initiate conversation make Eddy and Jimmy begin to fiddle with their silverware and their napkins. They look down at their plates.

"Well, Harold, I think whatever plan John Kennedy started, we should continue and finish it." Mary has had a thing for John Kennedy for as long as Eddy can remember. When he appeared on the TV during his presidency, those were some of the few times Mary stopped what she was doing and actually sat in front of the screen for a while. She even commented on how handsome she found him. On the day of his death, Eddy came home from middle school to find her mother sitting on her knees on the floor in front of the TV in the den. She was weeping and dabbing at her eyes with the Kleenex in her hand. Eddy had rarely seen such an overflow of emotion from her mother, and it scared her so much that she retreated to her room and buried herself under the covers. Eddy felt like the world might be shifting, and a changing world was scary if it brought her mother to tears.

So it was not surprising that Mary was the first to answer Harold about the space program with Kennedy's words: "We choose to go to the moon in this decade and do other things, not because they're easy but because they're hard," which were still committed to her memory.

"Jimmy," Harold asks, "what do you think? Wanna go to the moon someday?"

"No, sir. Well, maybe if they get arcade games there. And of course bring in enough stuff to eat."

"Interesting, Jimmy, but not very serious. It's okay if you say you're just not interested. What about you, Edna?"

"I don't know. I haven't thought much about it."

"Give it a few moments of thought then, and tell me what you think?"

Eddy doesn't like being put on the spot. But she knows her dad is kind. He just wants to spur on the conversation at dinnertime. She takes a bite of the chicken dish on her plate, some Italian name she couldn't pronounce that her mother is trying out. The chicken is tasty. As she chews, she tries to find something to say. Finally: "All I can think about is that those men are disconnected from the Earth, and they might not get back. They're at the mercy of a computer, like HAL in that space movie, and they could end up just drifting, drifting, drifting away."

Harold looks at his daughter, and after a brief silence, he says, "That sounds a bit world-weary. You're only eighteen, for heaven's sake. Your world is going to be changing a lot. Best get used to it. As for me, I think the whole thing is exciting, even if I can't imagine the science involved." He lets out a tiny sigh as he looks at Mary, like he's concerned about Eddy a little, wordlessly asking her, *Do you hear what our daughter is saying?*

On March 3, 1969, when Apollo 9 was launched from Kennedy Space Center into orbit around Earth, the astronauts aboard simulated many maneuvers that would be replicated on a future lunar launch. The astronauts splashed successfully back into the Caribbean just north of Puerto Rico on March 13th, within three miles of their recovery ship. The space program is gearing up for their big launch to come: sending astronauts to the moon. But even though the Apollo 9 astronauts had returned to Earth, Eddy's thoughts are on the astronauts floating endlessly out in space.

CHAPTER 12

"Edna, may I come in?" Harold Walters says a bit loudly from the hallway. From her room, Eddy says, "Sure, Dad!"

He enters and finds Eddy lying on the bed with pillows propped behind her, a textbook in her hands. Mr. Walters turns the desk chair around to face Eddy and takes a seat. "Just checking in .... Nothing special. Just want to see how things are going." He's taken off his tie and sits in his nice pants and white shirt unbuttoned at the neck. His comb-over hides a thinning hairline streaked with gray. Eddy sits up higher against the pillows in expectation. "So how are things going?" he asks.

"Fine. Just fine. School is the same as always, good and not good depending on the class. Why?"

"You seem quieter lately, like something might be on your mind."

Eddy pauses, wondering where this is going and how much she wants to go there, wherever *there* is. "Senior year is going by fast. Every senior seems to be trying to figure things out. Me included. I'm glad you found me that job at the Shop and Save after graduation."

"Yeah, Bob Ratcliffe is a nice guy. I really appreciate his lining up your work for the summer. Anything else? I know you and Joan and Paul have stayed such good friends. How about things with Johnny? Okay?"

"Yeah. Things are fine all around." Eddy is debating in her head whether or not she should mention that she and Johnny aren't that close.

"And college? Do we need to talk some more about that? Your mother and I really want you to go, and the future takes planning. Aren't your SATs this Saturday?"

"Yes, sir."

"Nervous?"

"Maybe a little, but we've all been taking tests for years, and I'll just go in and wing it."

"Wing it … hmm. Not sure about that plan. You *are* taking it seriously, the test?"

"Sure, Dad. But you either know the stuff or you don't at this stage. Of course the math will be hard for me, but other than that I'll make it through okay, I hope. Are you worried about me or something?" Eddy loves her father, and lately she feels like she's letting him down.

"You seem out of sorts sometimes, I must admit. I don't want something creeping in on you that I don't see coming, I guess."

Eddy laughs. "Creeping in on me? You mean besides Jimmy?"

"You know what I mean, Edna Louise," Mr. Walters says with a hint of exasperation.

Not sure how far she wants to continue with this conversation, Eddy finally says as she looks up at her father, who's gazing at her steadily, "Dad, I'm pretty happy with the way things are, and I know everyone wants me to have big dreams or even little ones, but I don't. Everybody seems to want me to have a Martin Luther King speech ready or something. I'm just going along day to day with my friends."

"Dreams are good, Edna. How big you dream, or to put it another way, how you want your adult life to be is up to you. Your mother and I would like to guide you if you would let us."

"But did you have dreams?" she says a bit louder.

Mr. Walters thinks for a minute. "Edna, I was in the war, and my generation's dreams were shortsighted at the time, I think. Just survive and come home. Then, if we did—and some of my friends didn't—only then would we dare to dream other dreams, if you want to use that word.

I think for your generation, the Vietnam War is different. If the boys of your generation can go to college, they might not have to go to war. Seems like very few of the children of our friends here in Thomasburg, or Galax where I was raised, are joining the army as long as they can get into college. Do your friends talk about this?"

"Actually, no, not that I know of. But there must be boys in my class, ones who can't or aren't interested in going to college, that think about it. Do you think they want to go to Vietnam?"

Mr. Walters kind of sighs. "I don't know .... But this war is different from mine. This war isn't an 'all in' World War, and it's not going well. I read disturbing articles in the paper every day. They don't even use the word *dead* for the young men who are killed. Just the term *body count* or some such nonsense. Some of the men at the plant have children serving already, and some are worried about their children who are nearing the age to go to Vietnam. Since I'm in the office, I don't hear too much, but I'm sure the workers at the machines talk about it. Edna, every generation has its trials. I hope you know that your mother and I want to help you with yours. Hope that you don't shut us out."

"Thanks, Dad. I know how lucky I am. Joanie can't talk with her folks like I can talk with you. And Paul, well, I don't know what he talks with the Horns about. The Horns are so quiet!"

Harold laughs a little. "The Horns *are* quiet! And so is Paul, only not when he's around you and Joan! I hear you in the basement sometimes!"

Harold looks around the room as if he hasn't taken inventory in a while of what his daughter has out, what she likes. He sees all the records. On her desk he sees her school books, a framed black-and-white family photograph, and a quartz rock sitting there. Then he stands up, turning the desk chair back around. "Okay. Guess I'll head back down to the den."

Eddy looks at her book for a second and then says, "Hey, Dad. Did you ever have feelings that you just couldn't explain?"

Harold turns toward Eddy. His brow furrows a bit, showing that line between his eyebrows, and his eyes seem to squint at her. "All the time.

Oh, of course some of them were easy to explain when I was eighteen like you. I was scared a lot when I was in the war, scared I wouldn't get back to my mother and father and the girl, Betty Jean, I was dating before your mother. But I had other feelings, still do, that I simply *have* and can't explain. They seem to hit me in the stomach, and my stomach kinda lurches. I don't think we ever stop having those."

"Yeah. I get some of those. In my stomach, I mean. Thanks, Dad."

Harold comes over to the bed and leans down to kiss his daughter on her head. "We're proud of you, Edna. Can't wait to hear the solo from my favorite singer." As he heads downstairs, Eddy gets up and goes over to the turntable. She picks up a pile of 45s and starts shuffling through them. She takes one from the first stack and then picks up another stack and shuffles through them, picking a couple more. She places them on the spindle in order: "I Started a Joke," "Crimson and Clover," and her new Donovan single, "Atlantis." Eddy seems to think these last two sound psychedelic, that new word she's learned that makes her think of a world quite unlike her own. She's trying to listen with "new" ears, but she knows she's a bit behind as far as new music is concerned. She wants to catch up. But first, The Bee Gees. She hits Play. She goes back to the bed and lies down, listening to the turntable sounds: the start of the turning platform, the drop of the record onto it, the arm moving to the edge of the record, the static for a second or two, and then the soft strings of the melody and the vibrato of Robin Gibb and the Bee Gees coming through the little speakers. And she wonders, *Is the joke on me?*

PART 4
APRIL 1969

CHAPTER 13

"How was the weekend in Galax?" asks Joan as she and Eddy walk to their third-period classes.

"Good, although I was pretty tired after taking the SAT that morning. Were you?"

Joan nods.

"Well, time in Galax was the usual. Granny cooks a meal for us and some other relatives, and then we all sing to Dad when a cake comes out. Know what it is? A pineapple upside-down cake with candles! Isn't that funny? But it's my Granny's favorite, or at least one she can make. Don't know if it's a favorite of my dad's though. We sure don't have it at our house!"

"Ewwwww. Pineapple. Strange. Your trips to Galax sound like my Roanoke trips, except you don't go to church every time you visit!"

Eddy laughs at Joan. "Sometimes we go to Granny's church, but not as often as you go. Anyway, Granny showed me some china in a cabinet there in the dining room. She's done this for years, saying that these pieces, the blue-and-white child's tea set pieces, will be mine. They belonged to her cousin who died young. My dad watches, and I know he wants me to show interest in that china to make his mother happy. Mom seems to want me to like the tea set too. So I ooh and aah and hope that someday I may really want them, but for now they seem sorta sad, those old pieces of china just sitting there."

"Yeah, when I go to Roanoke and we visit family, they've got lots of old stuff in cabinets too. And crosses everywhere!" The girls laugh as they separate at the hall corner, and Joan says over her shoulder, "Good luck in chorus today with Mrs. Norman." Eddy rolls her eyes.

"I'll need it. She can be sooooo demanding."

On the top riser in the chorus room, Eddy arranges her music on the stand in front of her. Gwen Brooks is next to her, whispering to Daniella on the other side of her. Both Black girls style their hair in waves that are close to their faces. Gwen has a pompadour on top while Daniella has short waves at her temples and beside her cheeks. Gwen and Daniella have no-nonsense demeanors, and Eddy speaks to them rarely, but she can't help listening to their whispering.

"If we have to sing these old White men's songs much longer, I'm going to kill myself," Gwen spits out. "Has Mrs. Norman never heard of any songs by Black people?"

"We get one gospel song finally. But that's definitely not enough."

"You'd think that just once she might find some chorus music for *us*." Mrs. Norman, ramrod straight, walks to the music stand in front of the risers. The three risers full of students sort of come to attention. "Here we go," whispers Gwen.

Eddy is still frowning when Mrs. Norman gets ready to practice "America the Beautiful."

"Now class, we've gone over your parts for the last few days. Sopranos, sing out just a bit louder. Everyone else, listen to the parts around you and blend in. Blend in! Eddy, could you at least try to not look so dour?"

Eddy is mortified, then angry, as she's called out. Daniella is snickering, but Gwen whispers, "Don't draw attention to yourself, Edna."

Eddy doesn't know what Gwen means. She's definitely not craving attention, and she doesn't know what that word Mrs. Norman called her means either. She gives an angry glance at Gwen and says, "I don't want attention."

Gwen is staring straight ahead. Then she quickly says under her breath as Mrs. Norman's conductor wand taps her stand for attention, "Why're *you* so angry? You got nothin' to be angry about."

"And then Gwen said, 'Why're you so angry?' as if I had nothing to be angry about." Eddy is walking home after school with Joan—her mother wouldn't let her take the car today. "Really, she kinda spit it out at me. I have as much right to be mad as she does. Mrs. Norman picks on me, and even though I like singing, I can't stand her."

"Eddy, calm down. This isn't a big deal."

"Do you know how much a person who's venting hates to be told to calm down? Hates it?"

"Okay, Eddy, let's review. You know that the Black girls in our school get very few—what could I call them—well, opportunities. Not many chances to shine academically it seems, 'cause there certainly aren't many Black girls in our advanced classes. No extracurriculars except in-school Girls Athletic Association. At least Black guys can play sports after school and play against teams in other towns if they're good. They might even get to go to college on scholarship if they're really good. So Gwen and Daniella are probably pretty angry. Damn, I would be. If I had to enter the movie theater by a separate door and go upstairs to sit in the balcony because I'm Black, I would be angry all the time. I guess they think that you're White, so you don't need to be angry about anything. I get it."

Eddy is looking at Joan. "Geez, I thought you'd be on my side."

"Well, of course I'm on your side, but you get so frustrated, and I know you can see Gwen's side too. You're just mad at Mrs. Norman."

"You're right, Joanie. And that side entrance to the theater? That's just wrong. Why can't the adults change that somehow?" Eddy thinks for a second and says softly, "Maybe we should try to change it?"

Her question hangs in the air as a car pulls up beside the girls, and Buddy Hall rolls down his window and says, "Want a ride, ladies?"

Quickly, Jay gets out from the other side and walks around to open the door to the back seat saying, "Hop aboard."

Though both girls stand there a second, Eddy takes a step toward the door.

"C'mon girls, it's just a ride. You've got lots of books," Buddy says.

Joan looks at Eddy and shrugs, and both girls slide into the back seat. Jay returns to the front, and when he's in, he puts his arm on the seat back in front of the girls.

"Okay, okay!" Buddy laughs. "Now tell me which way to go." He seems to find the whole thing funny.

"Up the hill, right on Northwood and then left on Cavendish. That's Eddy. I'm farther on," says Joan.

"Hey, girls, would you like to join me and Jay here for a little street racing this Saturday night? You have to come out a little late because there need to be very few cars on the four-lane road."

"Uh … no thanks. Got plans." Joan looks at Eddy, who seems to be staring intently at Jay's bare arm on the seat back.

"Yeah, no thanks," Eddy says. She watches as Jay's fingers drum along the seat. Jay glances over his shoulder at her, and he's smiling, as if this is all predictable, Eddy thinks, like a script in a movie.

"Your loss. It's awesome out there in the night with engines revving. Right Jaybird?"

"Right. Two cars side by side. No other cars on the road. So cool. One of our gang stands in front of the cars' headlights with his arm up in the air. When he drops it, the cars shift into gear and race into the dark. Another guy stands at the finish line an eighth of a mile away with a stopwatch." Jay talks excitedly, just like so many others across the country who are street racing in 1969, usually illegally, despite the risks of traffic violations and injuries to drivers on public roads.

Eddy and Joan listen to Jay, and then Joan says again, "No thanks."

"Another time maybe," says Buddy. "Here's Cavendish. Which house, Ed?"

"It's *Eddy*, and the brick one down on the right with the brown door."

Jay takes his arm off the seat and turns to look at the house as Buddy pulls over. Eddy looks at Joan and starts to get out.

"Talk later," Joan says.

"Yeah, you'll be talking about us, I bet." Buddy laughs as he says this. Jay rolls down his window and places his arm on the door.

"Thanks for the ride," Eddy says to Jay as she stands by the car and looks down at him.

"Anytime, Eddy." Jay says this softly as he smiles up at her, his words sounding intimate and enticing to Eddy in spite of their ordinariness. She smiles in return.

"Yeah, anytime, beautiful!" Buddy yells, peeling out of the gravel in front of Eddy's house. Jay looks back in the side-view mirror to see Eddy frowning as she looks down at the gravel and smooths out the rocks a bit with her shoe.

"Well, that was just awkward once you got out of the car," Joan says on the other end of the phone. "I do *not* want to be alone with that maniac Buddy. He would not stop asking me to go out, wouldn't stop asking me questions about who I date, who you date, and then talking about the 'rich' neighborhood we live in and the big houses. They're not that big, not like the Sherwood Forest houses, and we're not rich. What a jerk."

"I agree. Wonder what they were really doing after school? Do they drive around every day? Do they cruise our neighborhood?"

"Now that's creepy to think about. But Eddy, I can't help but think that Jay was looking for you. Do you think he saw us walking home today? Don't you ever see him at school?"

"No. It's weird. I don't know where his classes are, but we sure don't pass in the halls that I know of."

"He sure does look at you intently. And Eddy, you should have seen your face. You were literally staring at his arm the whole time. His arm!"

Eddy pauses. She doesn't know why, but his arm was compelling. The hairs of his arm a soft brown. His fingers long as he drummed them close to Buddy's shoulder against the seat.

"Eddy?"

"I'm thinking, I'm thinking. Maybe that's what I was staring about. Thinking. I just had nothing to say. I was listening to find out about the races. I've heard about them, heard that guys race on the four-lane outside of town. You can even see the wheel marks on the road."

"Really? Are you interested? You and cars. And Jay. Something is definitely going on there. Eddy, be careful. Those guys are a rough bunch. I can't be with you all the time, and if you get into real trouble, your mom and dad will kill you."

"Joanie, stop worrying. We've got enough worries with our parents on us, graduation on us, and exams on us. Government with Mrs. Bumgarner on us. I need to study for the Government test tomorrow. I'm definitely glad we have that class together. Let's quiz each other in the morning on the way to school. I'll see if I can borrow the car and pick up Paul too. He's the smart one."

"Hey now ..." Joan says into the dead phone.

CHAPTER 14

The local paper, *The Thomasburg Gazette*, is delivered in the afternoons instead of in the mornings, like *The Roanoke Times*. Harold Walters often sits in the den, still in his coat and tie, while Mary works on dinner. He reads both papers with his feet propped on the ottoman. The chair and ottoman are made of a faux leather that is now cracked and worn.

He often speaks aloud of something he is reading, and Mary comments. If Eddy or Jimmy is helping in the kitchen or watching TV in the den, Harold will try to get them to respond. Today, Eddy is sitting on the couch in the den reading a magazine while Jimmy is watching TV.

"Well, well, well. The network has canceled *The Smothers Brothers*."

"Really?" Mary asks from the kitchen.

"Yeah, they must have finally gone too far with their skits. What do you think about that, Edna?"

Edna is looking at the February issue of *Seventeen* magazine that Joan has loaned her. Loaned only—Joan keeps a year's worth of magazines on the nightstand next to her bed. On the cover is *Seventeen's* favorite model, Colleen Corby. She's Eddy's favorite too. Colleen looks out from the cover with her dark hair almost moving, her lips almost in a kiss, and a fitted green leather-like jacket. Eddy wants to be Colleen, who looks so comfortable in her clothes. Eddy's not sure she would want people looking at her face on the cover of a magazine though.

"Edna?" Her dad asks again.

Eddy looks up. "Yes, sir?" Harold rattles the paper. "What do you think of *Smothers Brothers* being canceled? We watch it almost every week."

"I guess I don't care much. I mean, I can't get all the things that make you and Mom laugh."

Jimmy pipes in. "I can't get any either! And they play old-timey music."

"They must have crossed a line finally." Harold reads some more, pans rattle in the kitchen, and Eddy begins to read an article titled "I Love Him ... But Do I Like Him?"

"Mary, did you read this this morning? Nixon is going to gradually withdraw one hundred and fifty thousand troops from Vietnam going forward. Maybe it's the beginning of getting out of there."

"No, I didn't read the paper this morning. Maybe the whole thing will be over before Jimmy gets older. Thank goodness Bobby Clifford won't go while he's at VPI. So many boys in town who don't go to college have to go. Edna, do you know any at school who are facing that? I don't think Johnny Miller will have to go. He'll go to college, right?"

Eddy looks up at the mention of Johnny's name. "Oh, I'm sure he'll go to college." Her father is looking at her.

"Johnny's a nice boy. Always polite when he picks you up ...." Harold looks as if he expects Eddy to say something in answer to his statement. She doesn't. "By the way, how was your Government test today?" Mary stands in the threshold of the den, listening as Harold asks this question.

"All right, I think. Joanie and I studied with Paul this morning before school, but the best help I got was from Penny Jones. I've told you how smart she is, and I cornered her this morning and begged for some tips. She went to Girl's State last summer. She gave me some help on Democratic and Republican party platforms, so I had some ideas to write for the last essay question." Eddy stops, but her parents are still looking at her. "I just don't like politics though. Talk, talk, talk .... That's all they do."

"Not *all* they do, Edna. Politicians should also put some of the talk into action. At least Nixon is beginning to bring home the troops. Maybe some of your classmates won't have to go to Vietnam."

Eddy looks back at her magazine. Buddy and Jay come to her mind suddenly, and she realizes that she has no idea how they feel about the possibility of going to war. She even wonders, since Buddy is a year older than Jay and is eighteen, whether he might join the army after the school year ends. He sure doesn't seem like the college type. And Jay, has he turned eighteen yet like she did in January? *Jay. January. They both sound kinda the same*, she thinks.

CHAPTER 15

Eddy takes a deep breath as she sees Johnny coming down the hall toward her after the last class of the day. He sees her, but he also sees the hard line of her lips with no smile upon them, so he doesn't smile. As he reaches her, they both start walking, and Eddy says, "I wanted to talk to you."

They head outside and stand off to the side of the doors, away from emerging students heading home or to work or to the buses. Eddy takes another deep breath and takes a step closer to Johnny so that only he can hear her. "Johnny, I think with graduation coming and the fact that we'll all be scattering soon ... I just think that maybe we shouldn't see each other any more. I mean on dates," she adds rapidly.

Johnny continues to look at her. "I can't say I wasn't expecting this, but ..." His voice takes on an angrier tone. "But why? What happened? I didn't change or do anything that I can think of."

Eddy looks around to see if anyone is noticing this intense conversation. She's glad not many people are still around, although in the distance she sees Mrs. Lemons walking slowly to her car in the teacher area of the parking lot. Mrs. Lemons looks over toward her. Eddy turns slowly back to Johnny. "I've changed. I'm the one who doesn't want to go steady. Johnny, I hope you can understand."

"I can't understand at all. We had a good thing going, I thought. We were alike. We had the same plans and ... and stuff. We like each other."

This is it, Eddy thinks. She shifts her books to her other hip and decides to try to be direct and say what she feels bravely. So she tilts her face up to Johnny and says, "No, we don't want the same things. At least I don't think so. I don't know what I want. Not yet. And I don't really know what you want. But right now, this is what I want, to *not* go steady." She lets out a sigh as she finishes. She realizes she doesn't like that old-fashioned word *steady*.

Johnny's face settles into a scowl. Or maybe this is his face when he's sad. She can't tell. In any case, the revelations seem to be over, because he starts to turn away and says, "You know what I think, Edna Walters? I think you're going to regret this. Have fun at the prom—if you even go." And he walks away leaving Eddy feeling only relief.

"And what did he say?" Joan and Eddy are sitting on the beds in Eddy's room. Paul is on the floor in between the beds. They all have college applications on their laps that they're filling out. "I just told him I didn't want to date just one person anymore. That I had changed in my feelings. You know, in our school, you go out a couple of times and you're a couple. If you're a girl and date around, you're a slut. If you're a boy and date around, you're playing the field. How does that seem fair?"

"Eddy, what did he say?" Joan repeats.

"He said that he was expecting it. He kinda got mad and told me I would regret this decision, like he was the best guy I could find, and I wouldn't find another date to the prom. Like that was on my mind."

"Did you kiss him goodbye?"

Paul looks up when Joan asks this, and Eddy exasperatingly says, "Joanie!"

"C'mon, I thought maybe for old times' sake you would kiss him. I mean, Roger and I are still kissing—a lot! But our style is more like 'hello.'"

"You stole that line from somewhere. *Seventeen* magazine?" asks Paul.

"Back to the task at hand," Eddy says firmly, needing to change the direction of the conversation away from the painful topic of the breakup. "Let's get these college applications done so our parents can stop bothering us. You promised we'd do them together. Virginia Tech for Paul and me, and Loyola for you, Joanie. But remember our pact. If school doesn't work out, we'll find each other and figure something out."

"Eddy, will you please think positively for a change? Paul, tell her. Change back into the Eddy we knew before the last few months. You weren't scared of things then. Remember what my mother says: 'Nothing is certain but death and taxes.'"

Paul starts singing softly. It's Dylan's "The Times They Are A-Changin'."

At Paul's singing, Eddy throws her papers on the bed beside her, gets up, and goes over to the turntable. She picks up a stack of records, picks up another stack and goes through it, and selects one; she puts it on, turns up the volume. "Cue the organ. Cue the tolling of the bells!" She says. Organ starts, bells ring out. Tommy of Tommy James and the Shondells starts singing about friends going off to war and the young people's cry for peace and how they're not going to fight anymore. And then the chorus of "Sweet Cherry Wine" has the three friends singing along.

"Edna, turn that down. We can't hear ourselves think down here," yells her father from the bottom of the stairs.

"Yes, sir." Eddy turns the volume down.

Paul says without looking up. "Never send to know for whom the bell tolls. It tolls for thee."

"Paul," Joan cries, "you closet poet!"

Paul slowly shakes his head, knowing he is quoting John Donne's poem, "No Man is an Island."

After Paul and Joan leave, Eddy goes downstairs and says to her parents, "Do you know where my old ukulele is? I can't find it."

"In the attic?" her mom asks. "I haven't seen it in a long time."

Jimmy turns his head away from the TV for a minute and looks at Eddy. "I think it's in my closet. Up on the shelf. I was fooling around with it last year."

"Hmm … Jimmy, it's mine."

"You haven't played it since I don't know when."

Eddy frowns and heads upstairs to Jimmy's room, and there it is, lying flat on the high closet shelf. She gets Jimmy's desk chair and stands on it to reach the instrument. The dust flies off the ukulele as she brings it down. *Great*, she thinks. Back in her room she takes a tissue and dusts off the old thing.

She tries to remember how to tune a ukulele; she used to know when she played this one in the sixth grade talent show. Several of her girlfriends joined her for some folk tunes like "Blowin' in the Wind" and "Puff, the Magic Dragon." The four girls just strummed along and sang all the verses, not varying with any harmony. Eddy's memory is that the audience looked bored after a few verses, and then, when the principal came out and said, "How about an encore from these girls?" the people looked utterly dismayed. This memory always makes her smile. She starts to tune the uke. "My Dog Has Fleas"—G, C, E, A for the four strings. Eddy starts reviewing the fingering for the few chords she knows. *Man, I'm rusty.* But her fingers seem to eventually remember some of the old positions, and she strums for a while. She gets her music list notebook and a pencil from her desk and sits on her bed. She plays around with the chords for a bit, and then she starts writing down a bunch of words.

> *All the oneness now in two.*
> *If we're not to make it*
> *Who's to pay the price?*

She marks through *make it* and writes *last*. Then she strums some more, stops, and writes:

> *If we're not to last*
> *Then who's to pay the price*
> *For all the oneness now in two?*

With her pencil, she places an *F* over the first words and then a *G* over the word *last*. She strums and then stops to place an *F* over the next line until she comes to *price,* where she puts an *E-minor.* She can't remember the chords for the notes she hears in her head for the last line. But at the end of that line, she decides to place *E-minor* for *oneness*, and *F* over *now in*, and finally *D* over the word *two*. Eddy strums, sounding out the words on the paper, stopping on the last line that she doesn't know the chords for and then finishing with the last four words in *E-minor*, *F*, and *D*.

She stops. "I think I wrote a little song," she says to herself happily. She puts the ukulele on the bed and goes into Jimmy's room. He's getting into bed.

"Hey, you need to knock before coming in here."

"Oops. Sorry. I need to look in your closet again. Did you keep my old chord book?" She grabs the desk chair and looks on the top shelf again. Nothing there. "What did you do with the book?"

"I didn't do anything with it. Why do you blame me for everything?"

"I don't know .... 'Cause you're here." She hops down and puts the chair back. "'Night, little brother."

CHAPTER 16

Jay is suddenly beside Eddy at her locker. "Want to go on an adventure?"

Eddy looks up at him. Jay's forearm rests against the locker beside hers. She can't place at first the smell of him. Then she gets it. Wood. Sawdust.

"I've never seen you near my locker before!" It's not a question exactly. Just a sentence. "Where is *your* locker?" There's the question.

"Way down at the end of the Typing hall. The *N* names are far from the *W* names. Well?" There's another question.

"Where to?"

"A surprise. Trust me, it's nothing bad. Meet me at Kenny's after school."

"Alone?" Another question.

Jay laughs as he nods and turns to walk away.

———

"What? You're meeting Jay Nickles at Kenny's? Just you two? Are you sure about this? Want me to go with you?" Joan is wide-eyed.

"No, I'll be fine. Why wouldn't it be fine?"

"I have no idea. It just might not be. He might abduct you. No wait, Buddy might abduct you, and Jay just goes along with it."

"I'll be fine. I'll call you tonight after supper. I'll tell you everything. Promise."

"If he kisses you ... if he ..."

Eddy turns and heads toward the school door. She looks back over her shoulder at Joan and smiles a big smile.

———

"I have my mom's car today," Jay says when he meets Eddy at the front door of Kenny's. "Will you take a ride with me? I have something to show you. I promise to have you back home before dinner."

Eddy looks at the car in the parking lot that Jay is pointing to. "Okay." The car is a beige Plymouth Valiant, but Eddy doesn't know its name. She just knows that it looks like a normal everyday kind of car.

As they start off through town, Eddy looks out the window and finally says, "I've never seen you drive. You're always in the seat next to Buddy."

"Well, he has a car to drive every day. An old one though. I just get one when my mom can spare it for a day. Today she's staying close to home."

"Same for me." Eddy looks over at Jay as he has one hand on the steering wheel and the other on the door rest. "Where are we going? Joanie is afraid you might kidnap me or something."

"Trusts me, does she? Just taking a country drive. I know where you live, and we'll be driving by where I live. Then we'll both know."

Jay takes a turn at the base of Baxter Knob Mountain and heads out of town. Soon they're on a country road that rises slowly in the hills surrounding Baxter Knob. Eddy doesn't remember ever going this way. Most of the roads out of Thomasburg head to familiar towns or toward the New River nearby. Jay's Plymouth keeps on rolling past some fields and houses and around curves that lead to more fields and houses. He finally crests a hill, and as they start down, he pulls off into a gravel driveway. "This is where I live. Want to meet my mom?"

Eddy looks at the brown clapboard and stone house that sits overlooking the field below. Then she looks at Jay. "Is this what you wanted to show me? Your house?"

"No, but as long as we're here, thought we'd stop in. My mom will get a kick out of it. Then we'll go to the main event."

Eddy opens the car door and gets out. The wind gusts, and she pulls her lightweight coat around her. The April sun is waning, but when the wind dies down, it's warm. She and Jay move to the door next to the garage, not the front door, and go in.

"Mom? Mom, you here?"

Jay's mom turns when they enter the kitchen. She looks about Mary Walters's age, and she has the same color brown hair.

"Mom, this is Eddy Walters from school."

"Nice to meet you, Eddy." Since most adults know her as Edna, being called Eddy by an adult seems a little strange.

"Nice to meet you, Mrs. Nickles."

The house is nice—nice and normal—and Eddy keeps wondering why she keeps thinking about this *normal* word. Even during this introduction, Eddy is wondering why she would have thought that Jay lived some other kind of life.

"Jay told me he had a friend he wanted to show something to today. Are you a senior too?" Mrs. Nickles smiles at Jay warmly.

"Yes, ma'am."

"Well, I bet your parents are excited like we are that you've reached this milestone. I suppose we'll see you at graduation."

"Yes, ma'am. And my parents are excited, *I think*."

Eddy says these last two words with emphasis and laughs a small laugh.

Mrs. Nickles smiles. "Eddy, it's been nice to meet you. Enjoy your ride to the … in the country."

"Thank you. Nice meeting you too."

Out in the garage, there's an empty bay and beside it a motorcycle. The cycle is shiny and large.

"My dad's 1966 Harley Davidson. It's his baby."

"Nice. I don't know much about motorcycles, although my dad has a photo someone took of him riding a motorcycle in a Fourth of July Parade back when he was young, maybe just after the war. The photo is sitting somewhere in my house. I think my dad has always liked fast things. Yours?"

"Like I said, this is his baby. He's only let me drive it a few times. Would you like a ride sometime? We have an extra helmet."

Eddy is standing right next to the motorcycle, and she reaches out her hand to touch the seat where she would have to sit behind Jay. "Yeah, I guess."

Jay smiles, and he leads the way back out to the car. He makes a three-point turn in the gravel driveway and heads back out on the road in the direction they had been going. "Just a bit farther …." he says.

"To the *something*, as your mom said?"

"Yeah." Jay smiles at her before turning on the radio. The station comes in clearly, and the song isn't one Eddy knows. It's sort of country.

"Do you know this song?" Eddy asks him.

"What, 'Take These Chains from My Heart'? You don't know Hank Williams?"

"Not that I know of." Eddy is frowning, trying to think.

"Bet you do. I bet you know 'I'm So Lonesome I Could Cry,' and 'Your Cheatin' Heart.'"

"Wait, the B.J. Thomas song 'I'm So Lonesome I Could Cry' is a Hank Williams song?"

"Yeah."

"Shoot, I didn't know. Wonder how many other country songs were remade and I don't know the original."

Jay is smiling and then says, "Okay, we're close. We turn down this road, and then we're almost there."

Eddy is looking out the window. There aren't many homes out here. They pass an empty one sitting near the road, a ramshackle home sagging in places. They round a curve on a narrow road, and the road rises a bit over a hill. Eddy is looking out to the right when Jay pulls over into some dirt on the left-hand side of the road and stops.

"There."

Eddy looks out past Jay, and there, stretching from below this little ridge to the little house standing in some trees a good way off in the distance are daffodils, hundreds and hundreds of daffodils. Jay gets out of the car, and as Eddy gets out, still looking out over the field, she's wide eyed. And open-mouthed.

Jay laughs. "Close your mouth, Eddy!"

Eddy quickly jerks her head toward him, a frown on her lips, but then she shuts her mouth and smiles a small smile. The wind is blowing her hair so that she has to hold it back off her face with her hand. She comes around the car and stands next to Jay and looks over the field of yellow.

"What is this place?"

"Mr. and Mrs. Owens have been planting them for years. Can you believe it? Can you believe how many?"

"No. I've never seen this much yellow, this many daffodils except in pictures in books." The wind is passing over the flowers like a wave moving across a sea. After it passes over them, they stand tall again until the next wave of wind. The wind is cool, and Eddy moves closer to Jay.

"Can't believe you brought me here," she says softly. She wants to ask how many others he's brought here, but she doesn't ask.

"I should have told you to wear your yellow sweater," he laughs. He turns partway toward her and puts his arm around her waist and pulls her nearer still to face him. He tilts his head down to her and kisses her softly on her lips. For some reason, Eddy isn't surprised. Her hands move up to his shoulders. She kisses him in return, pressing her lips firmly upon his. He answers. Her hair gets caught up in the wind and blows wildly. He finally breaks the embrace and smiles at her and says, "I better get you home."

"Where have you been? Kenny's?" her dad asks when she walks in. He's barely looking up from his paper.

"Yes, I met a classmate at Kenny's, and he brought me home. Hey Dad, do you know the Nickleses?"

"Nickles? What's the first names?"

"Don't know. Jay Nickles is in my class. He brought me home." She wonders if she's turning red.

"Nickles? Something is familiar about the name. What does his daddy do?"

"No idea. Maybe something with engines?"

"I'll think. You get ready for dinner. Your mom's in there rattling around. I even made Jimmy get in there in your absence."

"Will wonders never cease."

Harold Walters looks up, but when he sees Eddy smiling at him, he smiles too.

Later that night, Eddy is sitting in the hall upstairs next to the phone table with her knees drawn up, and she works to make a hole in her old blue jeans larger. "Joanie, I don't know how to think about him. You know me, I've dated guys—a few even. What makes this feel different?"

Eddy can almost hear Joan thinking through the phone. "You know what I think? You can't believe he's been here under your nose all this time but you didn't see him. It's probably what you'll feel next year at college, new people right in front of you. And then there's the danger part. Do you think Jay is a little dangerous? And more importantly, did he kiss you?"

"Yeah. He pulled over and showed me a field of daffodils. Literally a whole field! Said this old man and woman have been planting them for years. It was … breathtaking."

"Did he 'take your breath away?'" Joan laughs at her joke. "No really, was it good?"

"Just one kiss—but good. I like him, Joanie. He seems nice but always on the edges of things. Doesn't want to be near the center."

"Sounds like someone else I know. Did your stomach do flip-flops when he kissed you?"

"He took me to his house. I met his mother."

"Damn, Eddy. What was that like? I've only met Roger's mother once or twice, and I've been seeing him for months!"

"She was nice. Pretty, like our moms. Just normal. Don't know about his dad. Jay hasn't said anything about him except that he rides a motorcycle. But Joanie, their home is just like anyone else's. Why do I think guys like Jay and Buddy and their friends, and those girls they date like the ones we met at the Overlook, are, I don't know, different or poorer or something?"

"I don't know, Eddy, but I think Buddy and Jay are strange. Does your dad know you and Johnny are no longer seeing each other?"

"I dropped it to my mom while washing the dishes one night. I'm sure she told Dad. They liked Johnny, I guess. Probably thought he was safe, and he was always polite when he picked me up for something. And they know his folks."

"You should have stayed with Johnny long enough to go to prom, Eddy!"

"Maybe. But that seems a bit, well, you know … dishonest. Wonder who Johnny is taking now? Paul says he'll go with me."

"No Jay?"

"I don't think Jay and his friends do proms. Anyway, I haven't been asked."

"I heard Johnny asked Sandra." Joan pauses to let this information sink in. "She's had a crush on him for a long time, I think. She must be thrilled. Just don't freak out if Jay shows up with someone else."

"I won't. Paul and I will have fun listening to the band together."

"Well, go dream about Mr. Jay Nickles, Eddy. See you tomorrow."

Later, lying in bed and listening to the Beatles' *Rubber Soul* album, Eddy wonders what instrument appears in the bridge in the song "In My Life." Is it one of those old-timey pianos? She can't think of what they're called. That song leads her to think about places in her life right now, like her room. Like Jay's mom's beige car. And she knows she'll remember that field of daffodils for the rest of her life. Eddy wonders whether she will dream of those daffodils long after she has forgotten Jay. Or will it be the other way around? There's the rub, wondering what dreams may come. What if no dreams come to her, besides the daffodils? Why doesn't she have strong dreams for her life, and what if she just lives day to day?

She's thinking about the daffodils, but she also wonders about Jay. What is it that she can't see about him? But oh, to drown in a sea of kisses like that one.

CHAPTER 17

Eddy is standing in front of Mrs. Rochester in the library. "But Mrs. Rochester, I really need to go to the guidance counselor to talk about something."

"There are so many books to shelve, we need to get this done first. If you have any time left over, I will give you a pass to go to guidance."

"But …" Eddy starts.

Mrs. Rochester has moved away to the checkout desk, and Eddy fumes as she stands next to the cart with all the books on it. She rolls off to the shelves in a huff. She looks down at the spine of the book on top. *I'll be here all hour.* She looks at the spines on the next books. Most are in the 800–899 section. Literature. *Maybe this won't be so bad.* Some teacher has assigned a lot of English-type stuff for a class. Eddy starts shelving the books as fast as she can. Around the edge of the shelf, Mrs. Rochester sees her and says, "Edna, don't go so fast that you place the books out of numerical order."

Eddy frowns, and as soon as Mrs. Rochester has gone, she pushes 812.52 so hard into a space on the shelf that it travels all the way through into the back and the space closes up again. *There,* The Scarlet Letter *is lost.* She smiles. She never liked it anyway. *Dim Mr. Dimmesdale lets Hester bear everything.*

Eddy and Joan are over at Joan's on Friday night, looking at her dress for the prom.

"Wow. Daring, Joanie!"

"Yeah; you can *almost* see that I have tits down there under the scoop neckline! Still, the color's nice. And I can dance and move in it. What are you wearing?"

"I was thinking of wearing last year's dress, but then Mom showed me a long skirt of hers that I kind of like. It has lots of colors and seems kind of shimmery, and I can put my dressy blouse with it. Paul won't care, to say the least."

"That's pretty radical, Eddy. A long skirt! Cool."

"What I'm really excited about is the band. Can you believe our school got The Illusions from Roanoke?"

"And guess what else? Roger is sneaking in a flask of whiskey and plans on spiking the punch."

"What? Another daring prom move!"

"Yep. What do you say, Eddy? Are we ready to be daring? I'll try if you try!"

Every year, prom night is a big deal for juniors and seniors at Thomasburg High School. It's essentially the last opportunity for the seniors to dress to the nines for a dance. It's when the school goes all out for one last revel for the seniors, and the juniors throw the party in anticipation that the following year, they will be feted. Let the revelry begin!

The juniors have picked a theme for the event and decorated accordingly. Most of the girls have been asked early enough to have time to decide on a long dress—bought in the small stores around town, unless a big trip to Roanoke is warranted to find more selection. Long gloves are a must in 1969, and shoes dyed to match are very popular. Even tiaras make appearances. The boys wear white dinner jackets and buy corsages for their dates. These rituals haven't changed much in America since the 1940s. And teachers still have to chaperone. There's a punch bowl and some small foods to nibble on at a table in the back of the cafeteria, and Thomasburg is lucky to have enough money to hire a good band for prom.

When Paul and Eddy arrive at the door of the cafeteria, Eddy really does think the everyday room has been transformed beautifully. The lights are dim, crepe paper hangs from the ceiling in cascading waves of white and blue, creating a tent effect, and the flow of girls in long dresses makes a whooshing sound. The plain columns holding up the ceiling throughout the utilitarian room now have fake ivy covering them, and the lights that are exposed have shiny tinsel hanging from them. *Somebody has really worked hard on the decorations*, thinks Eddy. Probably the class officers and cheerleaders. When she had stopped in during the decorating times, she saw junior Nancy Bowen running around everywhere, giving instructions. She must have been in charge.

Eddy knows her own dress—or skirt, as the case may be—isn't quite the norm, but it shimmers with rows of pinks and blues and purples and golds up and down the skirt. She's paired the skirt with a simple pink top, sleeveless with a high collar, and her favorite old-timey-looking necklace. Eddy feels comfortable, like she's just playing dress-up with Joanie. The necklace she's had since she was about thirteen, when she went with her family to Myrtle Beach and got to spend some money at the Gay Dolphin Gift Store on the Grand Strand. How she loved that store, wandering its different levels and trying to decide what to spend her money on. She stood over the glass counters that held jewelry of all kinds—cheap earrings and bracelets and necklaces. Some of them had shark's teeth dangling from the chains. Some had pretty shells, pierced with a hole to run the chain or leather through. Eddy still has a couple of the other things she purchased there at the magical place of joyful shopping opportunities. The necklace Eddy has chosen is a plain gold chain with many colorful glass stones hanging from it. It seems to go with her mother's skirt, so Eddy is, again, comfortable.

Eddy is greeted at the door by Mr. Dockett and Miss McDonald, chaperones and watchers, and given a small blue dance-card booklet with an open umbrella and raindrops all around it printed on the cover. The umbrella handle has a bouquet of flowers tied with a ribbon, and once again, Eddy is impressed by the junior class and all they've done to make this night special. The theme is taken from the song "The Rain, The Park and Other Things" by The Cowsills, and Eddy realizes that the ivy, the benches, and the colors all conjure up a park for lovers to enjoy. *Too bad I don't have a lover,* thinks Eddy. But she looks over at Paul in his spiffy white dinner jacket with the daisy pinned on the lapel and thinks he looks perfect as her date. The thought of Jay in a white dinner jacket crosses her mind briefly, but she tries to push it away as she turns to Paul. He's given Eddy the three daisies she wears pinned on her blouse.

Eddy thumbs through the booklet. The first page is handwritten with the words *These memories of an evening in the park were personally printed for* _____. A fill-in is necessary. The next page has all the lyrics from the song. Then come two pages of sponsors and class officers. Yep, Nancy Bowen is junior class president. On another page the handwriting says: *The music echoing through the park was performed by THE ILLUSIONS of Roanoke, Virginia.* The last page has more fill-in potential:

Remembering the park …
I shared the happiness of the park with _____.
The shower of happiness began at _____.
The color of my dress was _____.
"Flowers everywhere." Mine were _____.
We walked through the park until _____.

And then there's the last line: *We made each other happy.*

As Paul and Eddy look through these pages and then at each other, they show by their arched brows and their smiles how impressed they are with the junior class. Their own plans for last year's prom for the senior class weren't nearly as interesting. Theirs was Isle of Golden Dreams, so leis and one palm tree and crepe paper in streams were everywhere. *Why didn't we make more of an effort?* Eddy wonders.

She puts the booklet down in her little beaded purse, and she and Paul begin moving around the room, looking for friends, enjoying the general splendor. They see the band warming up, and Paul sees Leonard along the wall, sitting in folding chairs with his date. They stand up when Eddy and Paul approach, and all smile sheepishly, as if it's odd that they're here, the four of them. Leonard's date is his cousin Donna, and Paul seems to know her pretty well. As seniors at the prom, ones without steadies, who just want to attend in some form, these mismatched four are content—the girls laughing easily, admiring dresses and shoes, the boys talking about how hungry they are.

Eddy looks around the room, and her eyes fall on Johnny and Sandra. They're getting punch from the table, and when Johnny turns around, lifting the little punch glass to his lips, he sees Eddy. Eddy smiles, and with Johnny still looking, his hand still holding on to that ridiculous little handle, Sandra turns and sees Eddy too. The happiness in her smile can't be denied, with maybe a small dose of gloating in it. *She'll love filling in the blue booklet*, Eddy thinks.

The Illusions are ready, and boom, they begin the first song, "Ain't Too Proud to Beg." As she and Paul take to the dance floor, Eddy smiles as she notices Miss McDonald putting her hands over her ears. Joanie and Roger have arrived, and when they show up on the dance floor next to Eddy, the girls hug and exchange "You look beautiful" and "You look great," and then Roger moves closer to Paul and Eddy and opens his jacket to reveal a silver flask in the inside pocket.

"No Jay?" Joan asks when the band takes a break.

"Nope. I told you it wasn't his bag. Probably in those outsiders' code of conduct. 'No proms.'"

"Probably. You having a good time? Eddy, move over here with me and block the punch bowl while no teacher is around so Roger can do the spiking."

Eddy moves and stands as tall as she can with Joanie. "Yeah, I'm having fun. Paul is a great date! Slow dances are a trip with us swaying together, hands on shoulders and waist and our bodies two feet from each other! Leonard and Donna are doing the same thing. Meanwhile the lovers like you and Roger and Nancy Bowen and Blair Mitchell are in body holds like a wrestling match! I'm jealous!"

With Roger's deed done, the girls dip the ladle and scoop some of the punch into their glasses. Eddy thinks she can detect a different flavor. She feels daring. After a while, she goes out to the hall to cool off a minute, and suddenly Mr. Dockett comes walking quickly from the cafeteria followed by other adults. Students follow. "Prom crashers!" someone yells as they rush by Eddy. She follows the crowd out the door to the back parking lot, and the sound of cars and tires on gravel reaches her ears. Headlights are moving around the lot, and people are running. A few are standing in front of car lights in an otherwise dark lot.

Eddy moves around, trying to see what's going on. Mr. Dockett is talking with some students to the right of the door. Eddy walks toward the headlights and the three figures in the light. She gets close enough to recognize Buddy. Two other boys face him. Then she sees the knife in Buddy's hand. The other two boys each have something in their hands, which hang near their bodies.

Buddy yells, "This is our prom, you Millboro scum! Get outta here!"

One of the boys says, "My girl's in there. Just checking on her. Make me leave if you can." He raises his arm, and the hand with a knife is outlined by the lights. The boys just stand there, and Eddy thinks, *This isn't good. It's two to one.* Then she sees Jay standing outside the circle, just in front of a car near Buddy. He seems tense to Eddy. His arms are crossed in front of his chest. He takes a step toward Buddy and drops his arms. He has something in his hand.

122

Buddy, unable to wait any longer, lunges at the closest adversary, thrusting his knife in the direction of the boy in a dark shirt with longish almost black hair covering his forehead. Both strangers laugh at this lunge which doesn't come close enough to cause anything but this derisive laughter. One of the two boys takes a swipe at Buddy, who jumps to the side to avoid the tip of the blade. The second interloper closes in. Buddy's knife hand points first at one and then the other. Eddy is holding her breath, but not for long, for Mr. Dockett steps quickly into the circle of light and says, "All right, boys, that's enough. Party's over. Get in your cars and head out, and I won't call the sheriff."

Other teachers have reached the circle, and the boys from the other town turn around slowly and get in their cars. One yells something to Buddy as their cars pull away, but Eddy can't hear what they say. It sure sounded like a threat, though. Mr. Dockett walks over to Buddy and says, "Son, hand me that knife in your hand. You know better than to bring that onto school property."

Buddy is kind of grinning, just standing there as if he's thinking about his next move. Eddy hears Jay say, "C'mon, Buddy. Let's go." Eddy moves a little closer to where Jay stands, and he finally sees her. His arms are crossed again.

"Buddy ..." Mr. Dockett says. "Buddy, give it here or else."

"Or else what? You'll kick me out of school again? You'll get the cops to lock me up? They was trespassing. You should be thanking me for being here to set them straight."

"Buddy ... I'm not going to ask you again."

Buddy looks at Jay, and Jay is oh-so-slowly shaking his head.

"Okay, but I want that back later. That knife's been in my family a long time." Buddy is smiling as he closes the jackknife blade and places it in the assistant principal's hand

"Go home, Buddy. Take off *now*."

"Awww ... I was just coming in to dance. My senior prom and all."

"You had no intention of coming in to dance. Go. I mean it."

"Ruined my evening. Just ruined it," Buddy says sadly, shaking his head but smiling all the same. He heads toward Jay and the car parked there. Jay stands looking at him, then looks over at Eddy. Eddy moves toward him, but he shakes his head, backing up to the car and then turning and getting in the passenger side. Buddy gets in the driver's side and turns on the engine. The muffler sounds loud in the night, and then Buddy peels out by Mr. Dockett to make a grand exit. The taillights are red as they recede from the school.

"Okay everyone, show's over. Let's go back inside."

Joan and Roger come up beside Eddy. "Crisis averted, I guess," Joan says in Eddy's ear. "Who were those guys, and what would they have done if they had come inside, I wonder?"

"I heard that one of them was pissed off because Betty Anderson decided to come to prom with Mickey Millirons." This from Roger. "I bet Mickey's in the bathroom shitting himself."

"Well," said Joan, "I think Buddy was just hanging around out here hoping to get into some trouble. What do you think, Eddy?"

Eddy is thinking about the knife in Jay's hand. She's wondering about the kinds of guys who carry around knives. She's frowning. She's heard stories like this her whole life, how boys from the other side of the tracks have fights and even go to other towns nearby to stir up trouble. *Is Jay one of these boys?* Could he be one of these boys who carry knives and get into trouble? Boys she's heard about but never known personally? "I think that I want to go back in and dance every damn dance until we're told to go home," Eddy says.

When the crowd is back inside, the band, looking like they'd rather be anywhere else, launches lackadaisically into "I Heard It Through the Grapevine"—not exactly a romantic walk-in-the-park type song. More like a warning song with that ominous beat and the tambourine like a rattlesnake.

Eddy sees Mickey and Betty sitting alone against the wall. They have the punch cups in their hands. They look miserable. *They'll need what's in those cups.* Eddy and Paul are moving to the mesmerizing beat of the song, but Eddy's hands only slowly reach up above her shoulders now and then. Her mind is elsewhere. And at the next slow song, "You've Really Got a Hold on Me," every couple who's going steady grabs each other closer. Eddy is envious again; she and Paul hold each other loosely like good friends. Neither of them talks about what they've witnessed—not yet anyway. Afterward, Eddy goes back to the punch bowl.

CHAPTER 18

At lunch on Monday, Eddy chooses a seat next to Joey primarily to ask him about the band at the prom, but also to ask him about music in general. "So was the band really good by your standards?"

Joey takes a bite of his turkey and cheese sandwich. Chewing, he starts his sentence: "Heck, yeah. There's a reason they're so popular in Roanoke."

"Did they play any songs you and Thee Purity want to learn?"

"You know, we play a lot of Motown, so yeah, they had a couple of rock songs we might want to try."

"Like ...?"

"Like maybe 'Drive My Car' by the Beatles. Or 'Hush.' Or maybe 'Suzie Q.' They sounded sweet on that one."

"Good ones, Joey."

Both are quiet for some seconds until Joey says, "Man, it got tense out in the parking lot, didn't it? You were there?"

"Yeah, I ran out there like everyone else. I've never seen a knife fight before .... Have you?"

"No, never. Don't want to see one either."

"Do you know Buddy?" Eddy asks him.

"Not really. Seen him around, you know. There are a bunch of guys like that. You see them in school for years, and you still really don't know them."

"Yeah. Strange isn't it? Hey by the way, where did you get the name of your band?"

Another bite of sandwich. Then: "I think Ben was fooling around with names, and we all liked James and Bobby Purify, so Ben came up with *Thee*, not in front of *Purify* but *Purity*. Not any religious Thee though! We just liked the sound of Thee Purity, I guess, and it's a tribute to those great sounds. We're a pure blue-eyed soul group for sure."

"I like your songs. Where do you play next?"

"We got a bunch of the summer Saturday nights down at the Canteen. You can catch us there. Bring a date and as many of your friends as you can. It'll be rocking!"

"I don't know about a date, but my friends and I will be there."

"No date?"

"Well, you never know …. Something could happen. How are you and Sharon? Going strong still it seems."

"Oh yeah. She's a good one. Sorry about you and Johnny." Joey looks up at Eddy when he says this, his sandwich almost gone and his milk carton in his hand.

"That's okay. We weren't that suited for each other, I guess."

This makes Joey laugh.

Eddy stares into space for a second and then asks, "Have you read that *Rolling Stone* magazine? Paul showed it to Joanie and me."

"Heck, yeah! It's the best! I pick it up at the drugstore when I have some dough. You seem to like tunes a lot. Who are your favorites?"

"I like music more than anything! Righteous Brothers, of course the Beatles, Tommy James and the Shondells, Ronnie Spector, Donovan, Bob Dylan …"

The bell rings for the end of lunch. "Bob Dylan?" Joey stands up, balling up his lunch bag. "Bob Dylan? Are you crazy?"

"Crazy? He's the best songwriter. Ever."

Joey just shakes his head, smiling as he heads to the door.

CHAPTER 19

Jay is suddenly by Eddy's locker again. "Hey."

"Hey."

"Want to go to the movies?"

"You want me to go to the movies?"

"That's what I said."

"When?"

"I don't know. I know you really like going to the movies, so thought I would ask." Jay shrugs his shoulders as he says this, and then he leans slowly against the locker next to Eddy's as if he has all the time in the world. He has no books, so his hands just nonchalantly stay in his pockets. His head is tilted as if he is wondering what Eddy will say. But his smile makes her think he knows she'll say yes. His eyes never leave hers.

"I do like movies a lot. A movie called *Three in the Attic* is on this weekend."

"All right, then. Friday night. People might see us together. That okay with you?"

"Jay!" She exclaims too loudly. She looks around. "What a thing to say."

He smiles. "Well, I *was* involved in the prom fiasco."

Eddy whispers, "Yeah. I saw you, remember? And I saw what you were holding."

"Be prepared is my motto. Might have had to help my crazy friend."

"Scary, if you ask me."

"Eddy, it's a cruel world out there."

"What's made your life cruel?"

Jay looks into Eddy's eyes, and his brow furrows. "Okay. Meet you at the movies? Seven o'clock?"

"I'll ask my folks. You don't want to pick me up?"

"Nah, I'll just meet you there if you can get there."

"Okay."

And just like that, it's a date. *A date with Jay Nickles*, she thinks as she closes her locker. Her body seems to tingle all over, like it's smiling.

"You're meeting the Nickles boy at the movies? Why do you need my car? Why can't he come here and pick you up?" Her dad is sitting in the den after dinner. Her mother is getting ready for their couples bridge night that she's hosting. Two card tables are set up in the living room. Cards, scorecards and pencils, ashtrays, and drink holders.

Eddy has taken some time to think about what to wear and even contemplated some eye makeup. But then she looked in the mirror and washed it off, mad at herself for being so indecisive. She stared hard in the mirror as she patted her face dry and wondered how Jay saw her. Was she pretty enough? Did he like her hair? "Stop it," she said to herself. And then she finally decided to wear her Wranglers and her soft madras blouse that always made her feel like herself. They would have to do.

"Jay doesn't have a car, Dad. I guess someone will drop him off."

"And you want to drive my car?"

"Well, I thought it would be fun to park it on Main Street and give all the kids a thrill."

Eddy's dad seems to ponder this a minute, and as she stands there at the door, he finally says okay. "Keys hanging by the door."

"I know."

"Now be careful. Lots of cars out on a Friday night."

"I will, Dad. Thanks! Bye, Mom!"

"Bye, Edna! Be careful! Oh, and have fun!" Her mom adds from the kitchen.

Eddy runs to the front door, swiping the keys off the hook as she passes, and then she blasts through the door and into the night air, racing to the car like a rocket just launched into the unknown. And she's thrilled.

Fridays aren't as busy as Saturdays at the Dalton Theater in Thomasburg, but there are quite a few high school kids milling around out front when Eddy parks close to the movie house on Main Street. She's proud of her dad's car when heads turn as she gets out. She knows people are looking at the Mustang and not her, but she senses they might think she's cool to be driving such a car.

Off to the side of the theater, in between the door Black moviegoers use to get to the balcony and the doorway to the drug store, Jay leans against the wall. He's smiling as she nears, but truly, she can't tell whether he's smiling at her or at the fact that she drove the Mustang. "Hey," he says. He stays where he is, and so Eddy walks all the way over to him.

"Hey yourself."

"Let's go. Buddy dropped me off early, so I bought our tickets. Sixty cents a pop! Steep!"

Eddy can't tell if he's kidding, and suddenly she realizes how little she knows him. Eddy sees a couple of people she knows as she and Jay find seats near the back of the theater, but nobody seems to pay much attention to them. Eddy is thinking that she wishes Joanie were there. Joanie. Joanie thinks Eddy is in dangerous waters with Jay, but Eddy wonders if Joanie is basing this on Jay's friendship with Buddy.

The lights dim and the previews roll. Then the movie begins. As the sexual tension of the fairly raunchy plot ratchets up, Eddy is thinking that this is the stupidest thing she's done lately—come on a first date (or maybe second date if she counts the daffodils) to a movie about college kids that is heavy on risqué relationships. Three girls, each dating the same guy who has made each of them think he cares just for her, all decide to kidnap the three-timing guy and keep him in an attic.

About halfway through the movie, perhaps sensing how uncomfortable Eddy feels, Jay looks over at her, takes her left hand in his right, and holds it on the arm rest. Once in a while, he strokes her arm with his left hand, brushing her knuckles now and then. She's amazed that this works, that his touch distracts her from the uncomfortableness of the movie. She relaxes a bit.

"Well, that was a weird movie," Jay says as they come through the doors into the springtime night air. Others leaving the theater seem kind of reserved. Eddy looks at them closely and makes eye contact with a couple she knows. Their eyes are wide open, like they, too, think the movie was weird. "You go to movies like that often?"

Eddy laughs a little. "I go a lot, but that one was definitely out there. I mean, could that really happen at college? Could girls get away with kidnapping a boy and keeping him in the attic?"

"I wouldn't know," Jay says absentmindedly.

They're walking toward Eddy's car, and she wonders what will happen next. Jay turns and leans back against her car, and Eddy stands in front of him on the sidewalk. She's thinking that he holds his body so still, like he moves in slow motion. Choreographed almost. "I told Buddy that I'd meet him at the Dari. Can you give me a lift?"

"I guess. It's only nine."

"Good deal. I get to ride in this sweet car."

"Want to drive up there? I don't think Dad would mind since the Dari is so close." Eddy hears herself saying this, almost like it's someone else speaking. She's a little breathless with the offer.

"Really? I mean, sure!" And he opens the passenger door next to him for Eddy and then moves around the car to the driver's side and gets in as natural as can be. Eddy slides into her seat and takes the keys out of her pocketbook and hands them to him. She knows he likes cars, so she figures he'll be comfortable driving this one. He turns the key and the engine hums to life.

She rolls down the window and feels the outside air blow in as they pull out of the parking space. Jay is careful, feeling out the car's ways. He heads toward the four-lane and then stops at the red light about a mile from Main Street. Eddy has switched on the radio and is turning the dial to find the local station that a classmate DJs on weekends, and when "Brown Eyed Girl" comes through clearly, she hears "Hey" from the car next to them. Eddy looks to the right and sees Buddy in his car at the light.

"Let's see what you've got, Jaybird! It's about an eighth to the top of the hill."

"You're on!" And before Eddy can summon anything like a protest, the light turns green, Jay hits the gas, and so does Buddy. Both cars squeal off the pavement, and side by side race up the two empty lanes toward the next light, the one at the top of the low hill. Eddy sees the light turn yellow up ahead. She's frozen in those seconds. Buddy races on through the light, but Jay brakes pretty hard and stops. Eddy is thrown forward, bracing her arms against the dashboard, and then hitting the seat back fairly hard.

"What in the Sam Hill are you doing?" she screams.

"You've just had your first drag race, Eddy."

"In my father's car? What if we had wrecked or something? Are you crazy?"

Jay's right wrist hangs lazily over the steering wheel while his left arm rests on the open window edge.

"Did you feel a rush? Wasn't it fun?" Jay looks at her as if she will surely feel what he feels, a knowing grin on his face, as if they've just shared a mutual excitement.

Eddy has no response; she's staring straight ahead with her mouth slightly open.

"Close your mouth, Eddy. It's over."

They pull into the Dari Delite slowly and find a place on the edge of the parking lot where Buddy's standing next to his car. His crooked smile covers his face. Eddy looks slowly over at Jay as he puts the car in park and opens the door. Buddy is laughingly saying, "Why'd you pull up, dumbass?"

Jay looks at Eddy. "I think your dad's car had him by a split second. I think we won."

Eddy shakes her head, unable to think of a thing to say. Her breathing is shallow, and she feels half angry, half exhilarated. Jay gets out, and Eddy follows him with her eyes as he walks over to stand in front of Buddy. Jay kind of blocks Eddy's view of Buddy, and so Eddy hoists herself over to the driver's seat with the car still running, and she puts it in reverse. Jay turns around and faces her, and Buddy peeks around Jay with a great big grin that seems to say, *See? I gotcha.*

Jay just looks at her. She doesn't have time to figure out what his look means. With her right arm over the other seat back and her head looking over her right shoulder, Eddy backs out of the space, puts the car in drive, and heads slowly out of the parking lot. In the rearview mirror, she sees Jay watching her go. Eddy says to herself, her hands shaking just a bit on the steering wheel, *I will never tell a living soul about this. Not even Joanie.*

CHAPTER 20

When she pulls into the driveway of her house, she slowly walks around the car, looking at the tires to see if there are telltale signs of the race. She's relieved to see none. There are a couple of cars out front, and she remembers the bridge party. Her knees are a little weak. As she walks into the house and places the car keys on the hook near the doorway, she turns to face the bridge players, who all looked up as she entered.

"Hello there, Edna," says Mr. Clifford. The other adults all chime in with hellos.

"Hi, everyone," Eddy says sheepishly.

"How was the movie?" her mom asks. "Are you going to paste the movie stubs in your notebook?"

Eddy realizes that she forgot to ask Jay for the stubs. "Oh shoot, I forgot to ask Jay for them," she says out loud.

"By the way," her dad says, "Ken here says he thinks he knows the Nickles boy's father. He works on the machines in the factory. And he works over at Woody's Machine Shop on the weekends."

"Yeah, big motorcycle guy too," adds Ken.

"No wonder you wanted to show off my car," says her dad, and everyone laughs.

"Yeah, no wonder," Eddy says. "Goodnight, everyone." And with that she retreats up the stairs to her room, flinging herself down on the bed and staring at the wallpaper above her head. Then suddenly, she gets up and heads over to the record player. Picking up a stack of 45s, she picks out a few and places them on the turntable, hits the play button, and lies back down on the bed. Click, drop, static, and then the staccato strumming of the guitar opening of "I think We're Alone Now," followed by the lyrics about two young people holding hands and running into the night until they find a place where they can fall to the ground—alone.

Eddy is so lost in her own head that she misses "Eve of Destruction" and "The Tracks of My Tears." She's stuck on the words from the first tune about holding someone in your arms and hearing only the beating of hearts. What's her own heart telling her? She hasn't ever felt this confused before, and it makes her a little mad, that thought, followed closely by *Why do I like the way I feel when Jay touches me?* Back and forth she travels in her head.

Eddy is eating breakfast and staring out the kitchen window when her father comes through wearing Saturday clothes for working outside. He stops behind her chair. "Eddy, do you like this Nickles boy? Seems you've seen him a couple of times now."

Her father's words hang in the air. "Yes, sir, he's nice. Although I don't know him very well. He has different friends and lives in the country."

Eddy can see her father's outline reflected in the window in front of her, not fully embodied, but half there. She can tell he's not smiling.

"Well, why don't you bring him around so we can meet him next time. Not sure meeting him places is a good idea."

"Dad, I'm eighteen!"

"Your mom and I can't know everything about your life, and we know you'll be on your own next year, but let us participate while we can. And meet your dates. Marvin said that Mr. Nickles is pretty rough looking. Don't want any surprises you can't handle."

Eddy looks down at her cereal.

"Eddy ..." says her father.

"Yessir."

"Yessir you will bring him round, or yessir you've heard me?"

"All of it, Dad."

"That's my girl." And he leaves the room.

Later at Joanie's house, the girls sit outside eating ice cream on a porch glider. The gray clapboard house is situated on a slight rise with a deck that overlooks another neighborhood below. Thomasburg has a series of alleys that run behind many of the houses lining the streets, and Eddy is looking at one down below.

"Why does our town have so many of these alleys?" she asks.

"Good question. Don't know. But they sure are dark at night," Joanie says, remembering one such night with Roger as they parked in one of them. Joan smiles at Eddy, who she's sure gets the reference, and then returns to concentrating on her ice cream.

"Who could we ask to find out, I wonder? I mean, they're almost like private entrances to those houses, and they seem strange to me. When I used to go to Jackie's house—remember her from elementary school—we entered her house on Campbell Court from a back alleyway. I always thought it was cool, like she had her own private entrance that nobody could see. Our house just has the woods in the back with the creek below them."

"Jackie—whatever happened to her?" Joan ponders.

"Moved away, I guess. Thinking about it, lots of people up and move, and unless we think about them like we're doing now, they're just gone. Out of sight, like they've fallen off the planet. Like she's dead. Dead and gone, like the song says."

"There you go again, Eddy. Talking sad stuff."

"It's not *that* sad." Eddy starts singing "And When I Die" by Blood, Sweat and Tears about a child being born to carry on. "See, that's hopeful."

"Well, I must admit his voice doesn't sound too sad for someone singing about dying! Okay," Joan says as she wipes her mouth on a napkin, finished with her ice cream. "I'm ready. Tell me what happened with Jay—what you couldn't tell me over the phone."

"So ..." and Eddy slowly recounts the evening's events through the car race, and then through her having to enter her house and hear what the adults said to her about Jay and his family. Eddy had decided that she had to tell Joan.

Joan scrapes the bottom of her ice cream bowl, even though she's pretty much finished all of it, while listening. She's not even looking up at Eddy. Just listening. After Eddy finishes, Joan puts her bowl down on the table and turns to her friend with a look of concern on her face, her eyes wide and her voice a little too loud.

"What the hell is going on, Eddy? Those guys ... I don't know what to think about you and them. What were you thinking? And in your dad's car."

"I wasn't thinking much of anything. I was just wondering if I was being a little bold to let Jay drive the car two miles to the Dari. I had no idea something like that could actually happen to me. It was over in seconds. I got out of there as fast as I could, and I have no idea what Jay thought. I don't know what to do about it or what to say to Jay when and if I ever talk with him again. Help, Joanie!"

"I'm just glad you're safe." Joan is quiet. Then: "Do you like him, Eddy?"

"See, I don't know."

"When you think about him—before this, I mean—what did you think about?"

"Frankly, I think about kissing him. And more. And looking at his eyes and his freckles and ..."

"Okay, I get it. But beyond *that*, why do you like him?"

Eddy sits there a few minutes. She looks out over the porch at the dark alley below.

"I like that he's different. He speaks really slowly when he speaks at all, with a low voice that kind of makes me lean in. Not a whisper exactly, but soft, like he's touching me. I hear his voice in my head. Does that sound crazy? It's like he's the person who is me right now, except he's been that way his whole life. He's ... he's like those back alleys. Private. And then there were those daffodils."

"But what about all the wild stuff? What about Buddy? Cars? That 'almost' fight we witnessed."

"Joanie, maybe I'm the wild one, not Jay. Maybe I'm the one out of control, and I'll be the one who will hurt my dad and mom. I feel so mixed up inside, and I can't untangle myself. I can't think or see my way through. Am I the girl who sings in the chorus, goes to church, or am I some runaway train, wanting to bust out, wanting to get on the back of a motorcycle with Jay and hit the road? Wanting to wrap my arms tight around him?"

"Whoa, whoa, whoa. Eddy. You're still Eddy. Still my best friend. Still Harold and Mary's girl. Do you think that you've morphed into another being?"

"I think I may be a monster. Or at least someone new."

"I don't think so. Do I understand what's happening to you? A little, but not exactly. We live in this tiny protective town. You've met an outsider who you find out is maybe like you. I've had those strong feelings for Roger for a long time, and it does feel like falling off the edge a little!"

Eddy sighs. "Dad wants to meet Jay. I don't even know when I'll see Jay again or what the hell we'll talk about when I do. He doesn't seem like the type who'd call me on the phone. And do you think he should apologize for, you know, the racing?"

"Eddy, it's 1969. Call him up and talk to him, for gosh sakes."

"Do you call Roger?"

"Once in a while, of course. But then again, I know his folks."

"Joanie?"

"Yeah?"

"Promise me you'll never leave me or desert me?"

"That sounds like a song!"

Joan slides over closer to Eddy and puts her arms around her and says, "Never my love. Just don't go home and put on Bob Dylan and torture yourself!"

Both girls laugh and keep holding on to each other.

PART 5

MAY 1969

CHAPTER 21

The day of the choir concert, a Thursday, dawns bright and springlike. There is much on Eddy's mind now as she sits in her room and gets ready. One thing she doesn't have to think too much about is her dress, since the choir will wear their black robes. What's on her mind is the conversation she had after school with Jay. He was waiting at her locker when her last class let out, as if he wanted to talk. Eddy talked fast.

"Why didn't you just call me?" she asked. "And why couldn't you be normal and do normal things like pick me up at my house?"

Jay had trouble getting a word in. Other students were aware of the two of them in a heavy conversation and, with sideways glances, skirted around them, slamming locker doors and getting out of the alcove with the lined-up lockers. Finally Jay placed his hand on her arm. He looked straight at her. "I'm sorry. It was just a reaction. I wasn't thinking."

Jay said other things Eddy tries hard to remember now while she's getting ready. But she does remember this:

"Eddy, I want to be with you. Really be with you, and not just once in a while." Then he said something about wanting to come to the choir concert and meet her folks if she said okay. And then he stopped talking and waited for her to speak. He left the 'ask' out there.

She answered "Okay" but told him she'd hate for him to hear her sing. He smiled and said he had already heard her and reminded her of the night they sang "Hello, I Love You" at the Dari Delite. Eddy smiled at him then, like they shared a secret, and then she closed her locker, and they walked out of the alcove and down the hall together.

Also on Eddy's mind now is her small solo part in the concert. Last month, Eddy pleaded with Mrs. Norman to let her start "Joyful, Joyful, We Adore Thee" very slowly. She ventured way beyond her level of comfort to ask this, but Eddy told Mrs. Norman that singing the words loudly didn't fit her. Then Eddy held her breath, thinking that Mrs. Norman would take the solo away from her, but wonders of wonders, she didn't. And she said that beginning with a slow version might be effective, especially since the whole choir would join in eventually at a faster pace.

Then a fellow choir member, Tempest Clark, who had never been a particular friend of Eddy's, asked why Eddy got to change the music, and Gwen Brooks and Daniella Watson chimed in with "Yeah" and "I agree," and then Mrs. Norman called for quiet and said she would make the decision. Things died down after that, and Mrs. Norman, at the next class, said that her decision still stood.

So as Eddy prepares for the concert, she has all this on her mind. Her parents know nothing of her worries, know nothing of their impending introduction to Jay. Eddy looks at her reflection in the bathroom mirror and sees the unsmiling face looking back at her. *Lighten up*, she hears Joanie say, and a small smile begins to appear. She has thought of something funny. She doesn't know why she has not thought about it before, but why on earth would any parent name their girl Tempest? Could it be that the Clarks meant to name her another name like Temperance? Or were they pretty sure she was going to make them feel like they were in the middle of a storm? *It's got to be the latter*, Eddy thinks, smiling while she brushes her hair that is longer now and which, she thinks, looks a little like those mod English girls.

———

That night, the auditorium is quite full before the curtain opens. Eddy needed to be there early, and her parents drove her, choosing to mill around for a while and find good seats down front. "Please, not too close!" Eddy insisted for the third or fourth time. And Jimmy was not happy at all. "Why do we have to go early? It'll be boring." Harold and Mary ignored him. He had to go to his sister's concert.

Backstage, Eddy stays close to Penny Jones, hoping the other girls give her some space, which they do. Eddy feels they're still not happy with her. Gwen Brooks, though, has a large solo, and so do a couple of other girls and boys, so everyone is fairly excited. When the curtain opens and the students standing on the risers in their black robes look out into the auditorium, they see the nice-sized audience scattered throughout. After all, the choir is fairly large, and there are lots of family members gathered, in addition to some students.

Eddy sees her parents in the third row, and there are Joan and Paul near them in row four. As she scans, her eyes fall on Jay, sitting by his mother. His mother! They're over in the side section of the auditorium, about halfway back. Jay's elbows are on the armrests. She thinks she sees a small smile from him as he watches her discover him—and his mother. Now she's flustered. Now she starts sweating. Nothing to do but turn her eyes to Mrs. Norman, who has taken her place in front of the choir to the polite applause of the audience.

The pianist, Mrs. Coble, begins the first piece they will sing: "America the Beautiful." Eddy keeps her eyes straight ahead. Two songs later, just before it's time for Eddy's part, Penny reaches her hand over and gives Eddy's wrist a little squeeze. Eddy takes a breath and is glad for her friend's presence. Then she takes a step down from the riser and stands in front of the mic as she has practiced. Mrs. Coble gives only one note for Eddy, and in her low singing voice, Eddy begins ever so slowly, every syllable and note emphasized as if this song were sad. Her soft voice doesn't match the words she's actually singing.

> *Joy ful, joy ful, we a dore Thee,*
> *God of glo ry, Lord of love;*
> *Hearts un fold like flow'rs be fore Thee,*
> *Ope ning to the sun a bove.*

Melt the clouds of sin and sad ness,
Drive the dark of doubt a way
Giv er of im mor tal glad ness
Fill us with the light of day.

There is no accompaniment. Just Eddy's voice, and it wavers a bit at first. If she could see herself, she would see a girl who looks caught, with her eyes wide and looking hard at Mrs. Norman, who keeps a slow four-beat count with her hand low in front of her so that Eddy and not the audience can see it. Eddy's voice grows a bit surer on the last two lines, and then, holding her last note for the four beats, she steps back onto the riser next to Penny.

The choir enters on verse two with Mrs. Coble's piano coming in strong on that booming Beethoven melody. No division of parts yet. Mrs. Norman raises her hands, directing and smiling. Then come verse three and the four-part harmony for the old hymn. Finally, when the fourth verse commences, the choir sounds truly joyful as everyone sings lustily and faster.

Mortals join the happy chorus
Which the morning stars began;
Father love is reigning o'er us
Brother love joins man to man.
Ever singing march we onward,
Victors in the midst of strife.
Joyful music leads us Sunward
In the triumph song of life.

After the hymn, Penny's hand reaches over once again to touch Eddy's arm as if to say, *Good job,* and Eddy smiles. Mrs. Norman smiles at her, and she too seems to say *You did fine.* Eddy breathes and listens to the applause and dares a look at her parents. Big smiles and hands clapping hard. Eddy doesn't look at Jay. Not yet.

After "Climb Ev'ry Mountain," Gwen's solo comes up on the program. Her strong husky voice sings "He's Got the Whole World In His Hands" with the simple piano in the background, and midway through, Gwen starts swaying and clapping, and so does the choir, and then people in the audience start clapping too. Gwen's voice soars over all the clapping, and on her last note, her hands raised, she sends the crowd into loud applause.

When Eddy looks over and sees the smile on Gwen's face, she registers true feelings for Gwen's success that startle her. Eddy also wonders if Gwen is feeling glad Mrs. Norman finally chose a song Gwen likes for the concert. Eddy wonders what Gwen's dreams are. Does Gwen dream of singing, unlike Eddy who has no plans of singing in choirs again?

Eddy is thinking of all this, and of the fact that once again she's aware of her lack of dreaming, when the last song on the program begins. It's Palestrina's "Adoramus Te." Eddy feels close to tears for reasons she can't explain, and her throat tightens the way tears make it hard to breathe and speak. She's barely contributing to the chorus, and with a quizzical look, Mrs. Norman seems to notice. Eddy pulls herself to attention and tries to halt her deep feelings. Her throat relaxes, and she begins to sing, trying not to think too much. *Just sing, dammit*, she says to herself.

> *Adoramus te, Christe,*
> *et benedicimus tibi,*
> *quia per sanctam crucem tuam*
> *redemisti mundum.*
> *Qui passus es pro nobis,*
> *Domine, Domine, miserere nobis.*

There is polite applause, and once again, Eddy is thinking about why she felt tears coming. Maybe it's because of the benediction that's reversed. We "bless" Christ for what he suffered. Or maybe it's because we ask for "mercy" at the end. Maybe it's just the otherworldliness of the Latin and the tune combined. Eddy just knows that tears welled up from somewhere deep within her. Even though this piece appears last on the program, the choir knows that Mrs. Norman will lead them in one more song. The pianist begins, and the choir sings the verses of "Try to Remember," knowing that almost every family who has seniors will feel the weight of the words. This is Penny's song. It's another benediction. Eddy is dry-eyed now.

In the hall outside the auditorium, refreshments line the tables along one side. The audience members mill around, having cookies and punch in little paper cups while they wait for the choir members to come out. Backstage, it doesn't take long for the students to shed their robes and for Mrs. Norman to say a few words about how well they sang and how proud of them she is. As Eddy goes to hang up her robe on the rack that will be rolled to the choir room, she passes Mrs. Norman, who stops her and gives her shoulders a little hug. Eddy smiles and thinks that Mrs. Norman isn't the hugging type; she's pleased nevertheless, and the thought crosses her mind that Mrs. Norman might think she's not the hugging type either.

As she enters the hall with the refreshments, Eddy's eyes scan the area. She sees Jay and Mrs. Nickles standing off to the side, and then she lifts her eyes over the crowd until she sees her parents gathered with Jimmy and Joan and Paul. Her group. She walks to them, letting them gush over her for a few minutes.

"Oh Edna, you did a wonderful job!" says Mary, giving Eddy's shoulder a squeeze.

"I'll say!" Her father squeezes her shoulders from the other side. "The whole concert—everyone in it was fantastic!" Harold's eyes are livelier than usual, and Eddy can tell how pleased he is with her for singing her solo. Jimmy is standing near them, eating a cookie. But he smiles at his sister while eating.

Eddy turns and finds Jay, gives a slight smile that invites him over. As the two approach, Eddy slowly opens up her oasis to include him and his mother.

"Mom. Dad. This is Jay and Mrs. Nickles."

The Walterses both turn to look at the Nickleses, and Harold, his mouth open a bit, starts fumbling to get his cup and cookie into his left hand so he can shake Jay's hand.

"Well, hello there," he says to Jay. Mary smiles at Mrs. Nickles, who wears a floral-print dress and white sandals. Everyone seems to be sort of nodding at everyone else. Later, Eddy will think on these introductions and find them slightly comical.

Strangely, it's Jay who speaks next.

"Great job, Eddy. Your solo was good, although I thought at first you were having trouble remembering the words—you went sooo slow."

Mrs. Nickles looks at Jay askance. So do Harold and Mary. But Joan bursts out laughing. "Me too, Jay!"

All are smiling now, but Eddy wonders if her dad feels blindsided, even though he's wanted to meet Jay. Her dad speaks next to Mrs. Nickles.

"Am I right that your husband works at the mill?"

"Yes, he does. In an electrical capacity."

"Well, I hope to run into him sometime." That seems to be the end of that part of the conversation. Mary takes it from there.

"Are you excited to finish high school, Jay?" Then she seems to think that she might have said something wrong; she adds, "You are a senior, aren't you?"

"Oh yeah, I'm a senior. And I'm ready to finish for sure. Then we're out into the big world. Right, Paul?" Jay, looking handsome, Eddy thinks, in khaki pants and ironed white shirt, looks at Paul, and they seem to share a moment Eddy can't quite put words to. Do they have a secret? Eddy looks at Joan. Does she know something Eddy doesn't? Eddy feels flustered. The conversation almost stops completely until Mary says to Jay's mother, who still hasn't given her first name, "Well, we'll see you at graduation for sure then."

"For sure. Yes. Yes, I'll see you then. Nice meeting you all. Ready, Jay?" There are *goodbyes* and *nice-to-meet-yous* all around, and Jay and his mom move away.

Eddy takes a breath and says, "I need some punch."

Joanie and Paul say goodbye, and Joanie's eyes say, *Call me.*

As the Walterses make their way out, Eddy's parents make a point to stop and offer their compliments. Harold to Gwen: "Now that certainly was nice, young lady." Mary to Mrs. Norman: "We were so pleased with Edna's solo. Thank you."

On the ride home, Mary says, "Jay seems like a nice boy. His mother too." Harold looks up into the rearview mirror to try to meet Eddy's eyes. She looks up toward her father's eyes, but they're somewhat hidden in the darkness.

"Yes," Eddy says. "Yes, he is."

CHAPTER 22

May goes by quickly. This afternoon, Joan and Paul and Eddy are sitting on Joan's deck after school.

"My life stinks," Eddy says. "Government may be the end of me if I don't get a good grade on our final test next week. She hates me! Ughhhhhh!"

"She doesn't hate you, Eddy. She's hard on all of us. It's not just you." Paul is holding last month's *Rolling Stone* magazine.

"But why? Why is she so hard, Paul?" Eddy looks at Paul trying to make him answer her.

"Well, I guess that's what teachers do. Prepare us for hard times, maybe." He looks back at the magazine.

"I'm pretty sure I know life will be hard, but I'm also pretty sure a life in government isn't in the cards for me. If big-guy Randall weren't sitting in front of me to block me from Mrs. Bumgarner's eye, I'd be even worse off." Eddy looks over at Paul again, then asks, "What do you see in your future, Paul?"

Paul looks up.

"Well?"

"Oh you really want to know? I thought it might be a rhetorical question. Do any of us know what our futures will look like?"

Joan stands up quickly. "I know. Let's ask the Ouija board! We haven't done that in ages!"

"But Joanie, your mom thinks that that board is a dark, evil thing. Remember when she caught us playing when we were younger? I had never seen her mad before. We haven't played since. And where is that board?"

"I think I may have put it up in a closet somewhere. I'll look. Then we'll sneak it out and over to Paul's house."

Just then, the phone rings inside the house. Joanie takes off to answer. Paul and Eddy can hear her voice on the phone in the kitchen through the open screen door. "Paul," Eddy says, "what *do* you see for yourself? Will you be happy at Virginia Tech if you get in? Will you find people like you?"

"What do you mean, 'like me'?"

"You know what I mean. Quiet. Studious. Not much into dating. Terrible dresser. Worse dancer. Best friend to two girls, and best friend to Leonard, who probably won't be there at Tech either. Keeper of secrets for everyone. You know."

Paul looks down at the oversized magazine that is *Rolling Stone* and then back up at Eddy. "I'm not frustrated like you are, I guess. I don't have grand plans. I want to find things I like to do, and people—maybe even one person will do—who like similar things. And then I hope to stay under the radar."

"What things, Paul?"

"Oh, you know, music. And math. Traveling. The stuff I like now. Just more of it. I want to venture outside Thomasburg, I guess, but I think I could be satisfied with very little."

Eddy thinks about these last words and nods. She has no grand plans either. But why is she frustrated and Paul is not? Why is she afraid she won't be satisfied with very little?

Joan comes out and plops down on the porch chair. "Guess what, Eddy? Jay Nickles talked to Roger after school today, and he wants the four of us to go to the cliffs on Friday afternoon after Sneak Day! I'm supposed to ask you if you want to go. Wow! Jay wants to double with us? How bizarre is that? Roger says that Jay just came up to him and asked him."

Paul and Joan are looking at Eddy expectantly. Eddy just looks right back at them in silence.

"Eddy? What do you think? I'm supposed to find out and call Roger back. Although I don't know why Jay can't call you himself. Don't you two ever talk?"

"No, not much. Well, never on the phone, actually. I guess I'm fine with going. At least I'll be with you two and not with Buddy and some date of his."

"Paul, do you want to join? The more the merrier with this strange group," Joan says.

"Naw. You all go. I'll see you on Senior Sneak Day this Friday. It should be fun, right? Going to Claytor Lake. Signing yearbooks. Eating snacks. Standing around doing nothing. Really 'out there.'"

"Paul, you sound positively cynical," Joan says.

CHAPTER 23

"All right, class, quiet down." Mr. Thompson sighs as if it's a hopeless case for these seniors. "Now we have two weeks to finish your project of writing a long paragraph on a topic of your choice and reading it in front of the class. This is your chance to say something you want to say or express an opinion on a topic you are interested in like politics, or art, or a hobby. Your paragraph should follow all the best rules of writing, incorporating proper sentences and descriptive writing—and a point or two. You may even bring a prop if you desire. I certainly hope you've already started and that you won't be writing this the night before you present. The presentation schedule is posted up here on the bulletin board. If I've approved your topic, then you should be working. If you have not given me your topic, do so. Immediately."

Eddy looks up from where she's doodling in her notebook and sees that Mr. Thompson is looking at her. She lets out a little sigh of her own. On the way out of class, she stops by Mr. Thompson's desk.

"Yes, Edna. What do you want to do for your project? Time is passing."

"Yes, sir, but I just can't figure out what I should do. I've been thinking ... maybe ... if you'll let me ..." Eddy pauses.

"Yes ...." Mr. Thompson draws out the word.

"I wondered if you would let me compare Bob Dylan's 'All Along the Watchtower' with that same song redone by Jimi Hendrix?"

"Hmm ...." Mr. Thompson plays with his pen, passing it through his fingers like a baton. "That could work, I guess. Although I don't know the song. Are there questionable lyrics in any way?" Eddy shakes her head. "Is it rock and roll?" Eddy nods. "Is it controversial?" Eddy doesn't answer. "I've heard of Bob Dylan, of course, and Jimi Hendrix, I think." He continues to play with the pen. "All right. Since it's only a long paragraph, I hope you can cover the topic."

"Thanks, Mr. Thompson! May I bring in the records to play a little to show the differences after I've read my paragraph? Mrs. Rochester might let me borrow a record player, or I could bring mine from home?"

"Just a little of the two songs. We don't have time for the complete records. I'm glad, Edna, to see you excited. If you need my help, you know you can ask me, right? Why do you hesitate to ask?"

"I don't know. Just thought music might not count, I guess. Thanks again, Mr. Thompson."

"Okay. See you tomorrow."

Eddy *is* excited. More than she would have thought possible. She carries this feeling all the way into Trig and right up to the point where Mrs. Lemons asks them to take out paper for a pop quiz.

Eddy is at her locker after school when Jay and Buddy come up to her. Jay smiles, and then Buddy, standing right behind him, says, "Jaybird, you going to carry her books for her?" Eddy gets the feeling he's looking for a fight, but with whom—her or Jay? His crooked smile seems not really a smile, but more of a challenge.

"I can carry my own books, thank you," says Eddy.

"Beat it, Buddy. I need to talk to Eddy. I'll see you at the car." Jay says this to Buddy and then turns back to her.

"I'm crushed, man! I won't tell anyone what you say."

Jay half turns again to Buddy, but his mouth strains a bit to hold the smile. Eddy was never smiling to begin with. Her expression is watchful, wary, like a cat preparing to run. Jay, with a soft elbow to Buddy's ribs, again says, "Go on, now!"

Eddy can't quite figure out what's going on. Is Buddy angry that Jay is paying attention to her, even seeing her some outside of school? She doesn't think Buddy likes her. She waits. Buddy smacks a locker near hers with his fist and walks out to the hall.

"Hmm …." Eddy murmurs, looking after the retreating Buddy.

"Yeah, well, that's Buddy," Jay says quickly. "Hey listen. I know we'll see each other tomorrow night with Roger and Joan, but I was wondering if maybe after school one day I might ask my dad if I could give you a ride on his motorcycle?"

Eddy thinks a minute. "He'll let you? Really?"

"I'll ask him. We could just ride up to the daffodils and back. A short ride. I've got the extra helmet. Would you have to ask your folks?"

"Don't know about that. If we just take that short ride, maybe they wouldn't have to know?"

"Up to you. I could meet you at Kenny's, and if you have your car that day, we could go to my house and pick up the cycle. I don't know, just a thought I had."

"Let me see if I can get the car. You could call me sometime, and I could tell you which day I'll have the car. It's Senior Sneak Day tomorrow, and I know we're going to the Overlook afterwards. Are you actually going to come to Sneak Day now?"

"Eddy, I've been sneaking around forever. Skipping school isn't a big thrill for me—or Buddy or any of my friends. Nah, I won't come around until the end when we take off with Joan and Roger. And I won't be buying a yearbook for you to sign either."

"Who says I'd sign your yearbook? Are you even in it?"

"Yeah, I got my picture taken for my mom. But unless someone snapped a picture of me slipping out a window in Shop, I won't be anywhere else."

"Jay, why don't you call me at home tonight, and I'll tell you if I can get the car. My folks would probably like it if you called me at least once!" She doesn't say *And I would like this too.*

Jay pauses. "Naw, that ain't me, you know. I can't play the Eddie Haskell part."

"Eddie Haskell?"

"You know, the friend of Wally on *Leave It to Beaver*. He was always *too* polite to adults, kind of sneaky and not sincere. Besides, I met your folks at the concert. That'll have to do."

"Jay ... why do you, I don't know ... do what you do?" She's been finished with her locker for a while, but she closes it now, and they start walking along the hall, which is now fairly empty.

"Do what? Hang with the wrong crowd? Or like cars? Or tell the truth? Come on, things ain't so bad, Eddy .... You've been talking to me lately, so I can't be all wrong." That makes Eddy smile. The two stop before reaching a door to the outside that she rarely uses, and then Jay touches her cheek with the backs of his fingers and leaves her standing there as he heads to the door. He bumps hard the metal bar that opens it, then lets it clang shut behind him. Eddy watches him get smaller and smaller through the small pane of glass at the center of the door. She thinks to herself how strange that he never looks back as he walks away from her, even though he must know she's watching him. *Maybe he just likes a dramatic exit*. She smiles.

CHAPTER 24

A letter addressed to Edna Walters sits on the kitchen counter when Eddy comes in from school. Her mother is watching her as Eddy asks, "What's this?" The return address says Virginia Polytechnic Institute. It seems a long time ago that she and Paul and Joan sent off their applications. Once in a while Eddy has thought about getting into VPI and what that would mean for the fall, but she usually cuts off that thinking because she just can't see that far ahead.

Eddy glances up quickly at her mother. "Uh oh. I don't want to look." The envelope feels as though it has more than one piece of paper in it.

Mary smiles. "Want to wait for your father to come home?"

"I think I might."

"Chicken," Jimmy yells from the den.

"Shut up, Jimmy."

Mary looks sternly at Eddy. "Edna, he's just teasing. Don't say shut up to anybody. It's rude. I know you're nervous. Just decide. Now or later."

"I'll wait for Dad." Eddy leaves the letter on the counter and heads upstairs.

———

Eddy is *in* at Virginia Polytechnic Institute. The whole "opening of the envelope" event brings such smiles to her parents' faces. The letter turns out to be a congratulations letter, and the rest of the papers are for her to mail back and pay the money to hold her place. Her dad says that he will go down to the bank and start the ball rolling. He can't stop grinning at her.

That night, when Eddy is lying on her bed looking at the contents of the letter, she thinks it odd that she doesn't even know what *polytechnic* means. She decides to look it up later. Then she hears the phone ring and jumps up to answer the upstairs phone. It's Paul.

"Did you get a letter this week?" he asks.

"I did. I'm in. And you?"

"Yep. We made it, Eddy. Even my parents are pretty happy."

"Yeah, mine are too. Paul, I'm so glad we'll be going together. Think we'll see each other on campus? It's a big place compared to Thomasburg."

"Sure, Eddy. Remember our pact."

"Not to change. Not to lose each other. Yes. I wonder about Joanie. I'd hate to call and say, 'I got in, what about you?' She'll call us, I guess. What's Leonard going to do after graduation?"

"Going to try community college."

"Hey, Paul, what does *polytechnic* mean?"

"A college that offers lots of technical courses, I guess."

"So I'm going to a school specializing in technical stuff, and I'm the least technical person I know. Please tell me they won't make me take more Trig."

"No sense in worrying now, Eddy. We don't know anything yet about where we're going and what we'll be learning. We're both sailing into the unknown."

CHAPTER 25

Friday, Sneak Day, comes along, and in spite of herself, Eddy is looking forward to it. All the seniors ride in school buses to the lake. The yearbooks are in the backs of the teachers' cars—the seniors get theirs at Sneak Day, while back at school, the rest of the students get theirs in homeroom at the end of the day—that is, if they've purchased one. The day is one of those nice spring days with only a few clouds in the sky and the temperatures around eighty. The girls and boys are all in shorts, and the school has reserved a picnic area near the public access to the lake.

But there will be no swimming today. Several years ago there was an accident—a senior boy who couldn't swim very well waded out too far and almost drowned before his friends found him and helped him back to the shore. That was the end of Sneak Day swimming for all the senior classes that followed. Now there were just some games planned and yearbooks to sign, and time to hang out with your friends. Paul was right. Nothing far out.

"I'm determined to get a little sun on these legs," Joan says as she stretches them out on the picnic table.

"I'm with you, Joanie. The sun feels great," Eddy says, sitting atop the table and stretching out her legs as she looks over at Joanie. Her friend's hair looks wild. Her shorts are bright orange, and she has on a sleeveless white blouse with pleats. Eddy thinks she looks positively wonderful. Eddy looks down at her own madras blouse and sky-blue shorts. She knows she'll see Jay later, so she likes what she has on and hopes he likes the way she looks.

Eddy looks around at her classmates while Joan closes her eyes and turns her face up to the sun. Some of the guys and girls are already starting a softball game in the grassy area near the tables. Eddy looks over at them and sees that many of the popular kids, the jocks and the cheerleaders, are leading the charge to organize the game. Their voices rise slightly louder as they try to make even teams. Then someone finally decides it will be girls against boys, and even though everyone probably knows how the game will end, the girls involved don't seem to mind—at least Eddy hears no protests amid the laughter.

Joan opens her eyes and sees the unfolding scene before them. "Want to play, Eddy? We can stand in the outfield and talk until a ball comes our way."

"No thanks. Didn't bring a glove. Well, I don't *have* a glove, but I guess I could have borrowed Jimmy's if I had thought of it."

"We don't need gloves. We wouldn't actually have to catch a ball. Just run after it and throw it back in! Then go back to talking and watching."

"Just my luck I'd be talking to you and get hit in the head. No thanks. Go ahead. Or go over to the horseshoe pit where Paul and Leonard are. I'm going to sit here and watch. And wait for the teachers to pass out the yearbooks."

Joan jumps off the table and heads toward the softball group. Her friend Jennifer is in the outfield, so she joins her, and the two stand talking and not really watching the pitcher and batter. After a few plays, there is suddenly a crack of the bat, and sure enough, the ball flies fast toward Joan and Jennifer with Jimbo Goodson starting to run to first base. Everyone is yelling.

"Jennifer!"

"Joan!"

"Watch out!"

"Run, Jimbo!"

"Get the ball!"

"Throw the ball!"

Jennifer and Joan turn at all the yelling and then watch as the ball rolls right by them at an accelerated speed and heads to the trees behind them. They just look at it going by.

"Get it! For gosh sakes, get the ball!" yells Diane, the cheerleader with the loudest voice, who has perfected that loudness after a few years of leading the cheers. *She's impressive*, Eddy thinks. *Wonder if I could give orders like that?*

Jennifer and Joan half run toward the trees where the ball entered, and Jennifer walks in and finds it on some pine needles, blows it off, and throws it back into the grass. It doesn't go far. Joan walk-runs back into the field to where the ball rolled and picks it up and tries to throw it back toward the field of play. It gets sort of close to second base. Jimbo has long since headed for home on his home-run hit, so mostly there is exasperation from the girls and taunts from the boys.

Joan shrugs her shoulders at the girls in the infield and turns and jogs back to join Jennifer. They start talking again. Eddy can't help but smile. *Nothing seems to phase Joanie much.* She wonders what they're talking about out there in the middle of the field. She looks over at the different clusters of girls and boys. The Black kids are hanging out nearby at a couple of picnic tables. Over on a large blanket spread on the ground, some White girls Eddy hardly knows sit together talking. Eddy only remembers being in classes with them early in high school when everyone took the same classes to start, things like PE and Home Ec, and general math and science. All general. Everyone starts together. But by junior year, the students start separating into "higher-level" courses like Geometry and Trigonometry, World History and Chemistry. Who places them there? The guidance department, after all the standardized tests have come in from the ninth and tenth grades? Eddy realizes she doesn't know how it all came about. She has just followed along, almost blindly, only half seeing the path she's been walking. And what should she call the other classes?

"Lower"? *Ugh. Don't go there,* her mind tells her. *But what is it? What pushes people to do what they do? By the time you consider these forces, you're caught. And if you try to change course ...?*

Eddy ponders this as she turns her head from group to group. Her classmates hang together based on likenesses, she thinks. The color of their skin. The church they attend with their parents. The people in their neighborhood. Their love of cars and engines. The factories where their parents work and therefore where their friends and their friends' children come to know one another. The jocks. The cheerleaders. The ones on the edge of these groups like Joan and Paul and Eddy. She looks around, and in the sun's glare, she feels as though all these people on the edges are walking in shadow. *Is that what I do? Stay in the shadows where it's safe? Is that what Jay does?* Joan arrives at the table with two bagged lunches, and Jennifer follows with hers.

"Let's eat. I'm starving after all that physical activity," Joan says.

"I saw it all." Eddy laughs. "I saw you two thrill everyone with your baseball know-how. Great throwing!"

"Your sarcasm is *not* amusing, Eddy. Jennifer and I had lots to discuss. Roger and her boyfriend, Tommy, being first and foremost. Speaking of which, there's Roger." Joan waves him over. He had been watching the horseshoe games.

"Roger, you missed it! Your girl is a stellar baseball player!" Eddy is relishing this whole scenario. All four friends open their bags and take out ham and cheese or turkey and cheese sandwiches and chips; everyone is to pick up a soft drink from a table nearby. There's a moment of switching around the sandwiches, Roger and Joan carrying over drinks for their table.

Roger speaks with his mouth full. "So Joan, what did you do out there that was so stellar?"

"Nothing. That's Eddy's point. Jennifer and I didn't do much. But we did touch the ball one time each. We watched, we retrieved, we threw. All words part of baseball lingo. I'm quite proud of us, Jennifer."

Music drifts over from the building that houses a concession stand on weekends, the bathrooms, and the jukebox. Someone must have put in a quarter. Gwen and Daniella, along with some other Black kids, begin to dance to Sam & Dave's "Hold On, I'm Comin'." Gwen has on tight shorts and a tight V-neck T-shirt. Eddy watches her move, watches how fluid her motions are as her feet traverse the cement floor, how unfrenetic and, well, just plain graceful she is as she dances and twirls under the arm of Doug Mayes, a tall guy Eddy doesn't know well but who she thinks was in a history class with her a few years ago. What she thinks now is that he, too, can really dance.

Eddy would like to join them, or get closer to hear the music, but she won't act on this desire, sensing that Gwen or Daniella might think it weird. She thinks about this for a minute; at the few school dances Eddy went to through the years, the Black kids dance together near one another, and the White kids do the same. *How strange*, she thinks. *The music is for everyone.* Now she has half a mind to get up and go over there to dance. *Half a mind. What does that even mean?* It's just a phrase her family uses. Now that she does think about it, it seems to fit her perfectly. She's split down the middle. *Maybe I will. Maybe I won't. Half of my brain says do it. Half of my brain says don't.*

Roger interrupts her thoughts. "Hey, Eddy, Jay says he'll be waiting at Kenny's around three for us to pick him up when we're ready to head to the Overlook. We're still on, right?"

"Far as I know, Roger. You'd know more than I do. You've got a car?"

"Yep."

"This should be *verrrry een-teresting* ...." Joan adds. And everyone laughs except Jennifer.

"I have no idea what y'all are talking about." She looks around at them. "Who's Jay?"

"You know, Jay Nickles. He's in our class? Hangs around with Buddy Hall?"

"Oh. Yeah, I think I know him." Eddy doesn't think Jennifer does, but then, which of them could have said they "knew" Jay Nickles six months ago?

Just then, the teachers start coming around with the yearbooks, marking off names from a piece of paper that says they've paid. Paul has come over to join Eddy's table, and Leonard is with him. Everyone at their table has paid, and they begin the grand opening. The outside cover is black with "THS" and "1969" written in gold. In the right-hand corner, two gold profiles, one with a smile and one with a frown, are connected. The picnic table is quiet for a few minutes as the friends take in the yearbook.

"Ooohhh … I like the cover. Cool." That from Jennifer.

"Me too," says Eddy.

"I don't get the jagged lines." This from Roger.

"Roger, they stand for comedy and tragedy. The top line outlines an upturned smiling profile and the connected bottom line is a sad profile. See? Comedy and tragedy. You know, the story of our relationship." Joan laughs. Roger looks perplexed.

"Joanie, that's really funny! Way to go!" Paul laughs.

"Paul, for your information, I'm often funny. Just not always around you."

They all continue turning the pages of their yearbooks and offering comments: "Look at this" and "Oh my God" and "Why is that picture in there?" And so they search. Search for themselves. Search for others whom they know after all these years. Search for revelations and surprises perhaps, like a candid photo they appear in that they didn't expect. Search for lasting images of this time in their lives.

They already know which classmates have won the Senior Superlatives of Most Likely to Succeed, Friendliest, Funniest, Most Popular, etc. because these categories were published in the school newspaper after the senior class voted. Only one of their group has earned a title: Paul is "Quietest." He and shy Betty Anderson—of the prom night almost-fight fame.

Eddy, who's in the choir picture and the Library Club picture, knows to look there for her own image. She stares at the clothing choices she had made the day the pictures were taken. She looks at her hair. She sort of smiles in the pictures. Half-smiles at best. And of course there are the class pictures. All the seniors had to sit for Mr. Randolph as he took their picture. Eddy quickly looks for Jay under *N*—and there he is, looking quite handsome in the white jacket and bow tie the photographer gave all the boys to wear over their white button-down shirts for their pictures. Jay looks a bit serious. A little like he's worried. Eddy wonders if his mom liked the proofs they sent out some months ago, and whether she bought one like Eddy's own parents did. One eight by ten.

The girls all wear a white drape across their shoulders in their class pictures. Months ago, each girl undressed behind a screen, placing the drape over her bra, and the lady assistant pinned it in back. Then each girl stepped out and sat on a little stool in front of the giant white screen with large lights all around it while Mr. Randolph, the local photographer for just about everything, clicked away behind his big boxy camera.

But there's a surprise in each senior's yearbook too. Back in the winter months, the seniors filled out a sheet for the yearbook staff with their interests, their activities outside of class, and their hobbies. This information was given to the two literary editors on the yearbook staff who wrote the senior captions. Just a couple of phrases placed beside the picture that try to capture the person. As Eddy and her friends begin reading the captions, their reactions are all over the place, from nods of approval to shouts of surprise.

> Paul's: The quiet of falling snow,
> The contentment of solitude.
> Joan's: Finding joy in everyday people,
> Friendships deep and true.
> Jennifer's: The practice that rewards,
> Her hands on the piano keys.
> Roger's: The sound of train whistles,

The call of faraway places.
Leonard's: If at first you don't succeed …
The thrill of hard-won victory.
Eddy's: The call of words and music
That bring meaning and wonder.

The group of friends all talk over one another, laughing and exclaiming over whether the captions hit the mark. No one but Joan knows that Roger and his father have a model train set started in the basement. When she explains, the group nods in understanding. And only Joan knows that Jennifer plays the piano.

"Jennifer, why is Joanie the only one who knows?" Eddy asks.

Joan responds, "I was in sixth grade talent show with her at Campbell Court, and she played in it. You don't remember, Eddy? Surely you remember my dance number in the show?"

Eddy shakes her head. She doesn't remember.

"Can't believe you remember that, Joan," Jennifer says.

Paul turns to Leonard. "Leonard, yours can't be because of your wrestling, can it?"

"Well, I finally won a match or two, so I guess so."

Everyone laughs at that.

Then Eddy says, "Joanie, I love yours. So you."

"Eddy, yours fits! But I didn't know it was music calling you. I thought it was just Jay Nickles!"

At that, everyone laughs again.

"I think Karen wrote this one for the yearbook. She sits beside me in English, and maybe she liked my Shakespeare presentation," Eddy remarks, tucking her hair behind her ear only to have it fall back down across her cheek.

The group goes on turning the pages of their yearbooks. Eddy looks up Jay's picture again. The caption beside it reads: "An observant character; a muffled roar." She figures *muffled* relates to cars, but somehow she likes that it could mean something else, like how his voice is soft and muffled a little so that she has to lean in to hear.

She searches for Buddy in their class pictures, but he's not there. Then she begins searching all the other sections of the yearbook. She sees no pictures of Jay or Buddy anywhere. Not even in Vocational Shop. She finds a candid one of Joan, Paul, and herself standing in the hall, looking at a poster on the wall. The photographer must have been standing to the side; all three of the friends are in profile, with Paul the tallest and then Eddy and then Joan bending slightly toward the poster. Eddy is looking slightly to her left at Joan, her face illuminated on one side and the other in shadow. She looks closely at the photograph, trying to discern what the poster says that they're so interested in. She simply can't remember. Neither can Joan nor Paul. *Typical*, she thinks.

The rest of Sneak Day is spent signing yearbooks and just wandering around. Eddy is glad someone keeps feeding the jukebox quarters until it's time to leave. She doesn't sign Paul's or Joan's yearbook—she'll need more time for that. Two events, though, Eddy finds interesting. Government's Mrs. Bumgarner comes over to her group, and since everyone else asks, Eddy, too, gets Mrs. Bumgarner to sign her book. Afterward, Eddy looks at the teacher's remarks. "Edna Walters, good luck in the future! Mrs. Frances Bumgarner." So formal, full names and all. *Just like her*, thinks Eddy.

And because Mrs. Lemons remains seated at a table close to the parking lot the whole day, Eddy makes up her mind to ask her to sign her book. She thinks Mrs. Lemons looks pleased as she smiles up at Eddy over the top of her glasses before looking down and signing under her picture in the math department section. Eddy reads it as she walks slowly back to her friends. "Edna, you are a fine example. I have enjoyed you so much. Best wishes in all your endeavors. I think you will do interesting things in your life. Your teacher, Mrs. Lemons." Eddy holds the book against her chest as she walks. "A fine example," she whispers to herself. *A fine example of what?* she wonders.

169

CHAPTER 26

Back at school around two thirty that afternoon, all the seniors scatter. Joan, Roger, and Eddy leave to meet Jay at Kenny's so they can head to the Overlook. The day is still fine, a light breeze blowing. There's Jay, leaning against the glass window of Kenny's. He straightens when he sees them pull in, and he opens the back door of Roger's car and slides in next to Eddy.

"How was Sneak Day?" he asks.

Different answers come from the group. "Fine." "It was okay." "Kinda fun."

"We got our yearbooks, so after lunch that's all we did—look at yearbooks and sign yearbooks," says Joan.

Eddy picks hers up off the seat next to her. "Want to see?" She turns to the senior class and finds Jay's picture and holds it in front of him. "There you are."

Jay leans down to look at the words written under his picture. He has a smile on his face when he says, "Wonder who wrote that? Seems strange for a person I don't know to write something like that about me. What does yours say?" He takes the book from Eddy and finds Edna Walters. "Hmm ... do you like what they wrote about you?"

"It's all right, I guess. I like Joanie's! And Roger's too."

Jay looks up their pictures. He looks up into the rearview mirror at Roger's eyes. "Train whistles, eh?"

"Yeah. I must have put my model train hobby on the sheet we filled out."

"Interesting." Jay looks next to him at Eddy and gives back her yearbook. They share a smile.

"Hey, Roger," Jay says. "Hear that clicking noise your car is making?"

Roger and the girls listen. "Yeah, it's been making that noise this week. Is it bad? Do you know what it is, Jay?"

"Sounds like one of your valves might not be getting enough oil. You could bring it into Woody's tomorrow, and I'll check it out. I'll try to do it for free."

"Thanks, maybe I will. Or my dad will. I'll mention it to him."

The radio is on, but the local station has one of those afternoon programs where people advertise things they want to sell and give their telephone numbers so people listening can call if they want to buy. Soft voices and phones ringing drift from the radio.

"Oooohhh, listen," Joan says. "Someone's selling a ham radio set. Why don't we get it, Roger? Then we can call Australia."

"Yeah, after we put an antenna in the yard. Your mom would like that, wouldn't she?"

Roger drives on toward the Overlook, which isn't too far of a drive, and as they draw closer, Jay says, "Hey guys, want to see what's under the Overlook?"

"What's under it? What do you mean?" asks Joan.

"Yeah, there's just rock, isn't there?" Eddy is looking at Jay. So is Joan from the front seat.

"Look, instead of turning at the usual road up ahead, go to the next light at the four-lane, turn left, go down the hill a ways, and then take the first left. I'll show you. I promise it's worth it."

"Okay with everybody?" Roger asks.

They agree. And Jay is smiling. He seems to enjoy knowing something they don't.

When they take the second left, the road follows the train tracks and then ends at a barrier put up to stop any further driving. A field of weeds has grown up on the other side.

"Okay, we park here and walk," says Jay.

"You sure about this?" Joan seems less than enthused. She's looking out the window at the tall grass and weeds. "Hope there's no snakes in there."

"Nah, we walk along the train tracks. You'll see."

They get out of the car, and Jay takes Eddy's hand, and they walk around the barrier. Roger and Joan follow. Jay leads, his khaki pants parting the tall weeds, which the girls appreciate since they have on shorts. They haven't gone far when the railroad tracks come up alongside them, and then they walk beside the rails on the gravel.

"Oh, I see," Eddy says, looking up. "There's the Overlook." She points to the sky and the ridge up ahead where the rocky outcropping appears beneath the trees. Roger and Joan are holding hands now, and all four walk carefully beside the tracks, not wanting to step into the weeds to their right. When they're even with the outcropping, Jay turns and faces the rocks and says, "There." He stretches out his hand as if he is presenting something, and they all stare straight ahead into the openings in the rock. Caves. There are three good-sized ones, large enough for a person or two.

"Wow," Joan says. "I never knew these were here."

"Neither did I," Eddy whispers.

"Close your mouth, Eddy." Jay laughs. They stand there a moment, and then Jay crosses the train tracks and the few steps to the first cave entrance. "C'mon, y'all."

The three friends look at one another for a moment, then Roger shrugs and takes Joan's hand again to cross the tracks and follow Jay. Eddy brings up the rear, but she can see Jay smiling when he looks back at them. When she reaches him, he takes her hand. Standing in front of the openings, they all take turns peering into the first cave, the biggest one, and Jay shows them by demonstrating that if they stoop a bit to enter, they can stand inside. They take turns going in. Then Roger goes to the second largest cave. He has to take a large step up to get to it, and he pulls Joan up too. They kneel at the entrance, looking in while Jay and Eddy stand waiting for their turn. Suddenly, Roger pulls something out from inside the cave. "Look, a bone!"

"Ewwww!" Joan yells, but it's just a stick, and everyone laughs a bit nervously. The four of them walk back and forth looking at the caves. Jay then pulls Eddy back toward the largest one, and they lean over and enter again, this time together. He holds her to him for a moment, and then he sits down with his back against one side of the cave and brushes the earth with his hand to move some pebbles. He pats the ground next to him in a motion for her to sit. Roger and Joan come to the entrance, and Jay says, "Find your own cave!" And they disappear from the light at the entrance.

Eddy pulls her knees up and wraps her arms around her legs. The dim cave is cool and dry, and as Eddy looks around and then at Jay, he takes her legs and places them over his, and he lifts her up to sit on his lap, wrapping his arms around her. Their legs form a 90 degree angle, and Eddy twists her torso toward Jay and rests her arms loosely around his neck, looking down at his face. He tightens his embrace, and she leans down and kisses him. Their kisses are hard and insistent, then Jay pulls Eddy against him, tilting sideways toward the ground, and it only takes a moment till they're stretched out on the cave floor.

They stop their kisses for a moment and look at each other and smile, and then the kiss starts again, their bodies now pressed against each other so tightly that Eddy feels she can hardly breathe. Jay's left hand moves under her arm, finding her breast. Eddy feels a bit lightheaded, a bit out of control, like there's a sense of urgency. Their bodies make a scuffling noise in the dust. And then some pebbles begin to move on their own. Eddy and Jay feel a strange rumbling just before they hear in the not-so-very-far-away distance the long call of the train's whistle.

"Eddy! Jay!" Joan calls. Eddy and Jay sit up, and Joan and Roger are at the entrance.

"Train's coming!" shouts Roger.

Eddy and Jay rise awkwardly and then step outside, dusting off their clothes to stand next to Roger and Joan.

"Look! It's coming around the curve!" Roger shouts. The four of them wait, transfixed, as the engine comes into view, too close for comfort. They're all only about ten feet from the tracks. Roger shouts again. "Should we run back across?"

"Too late, I think. And what if we stumble?" Jay yells. "Let's step back to the caves and watch it go by."

"I want to get back across," shouts Eddy.

"Me too," Joan yells.

"No time," Jay shouts, and he and Roger look at each other. "Stand back, and we'll be fine."

"Turn toward the cave and cover your eyes in case any rocks fly toward us," Roger offers. "Jay and I will block you with our bodies!"

The four of them face the wall of rock, lining up, with a girl in front of each boy. Eddy reaches out her left hand and flattens it against the rock to brace herself as the engine passes by first. She feels Jay's body pressing up against hers, his two arms encircling her against the rock. Roger is doing the same for Joan. The train engine is so close Eddy can feel its heat, like a massive black beast that runs right past her. Its power seems overwhelming, and yet there's a force between that power and her, protecting her. Jay.

After the engine passes, Eddy ventures a look up the tracks and sees the engineer's arm resting on the open window. Did he see them? Will he report them? The boxcars begin their steady rumble, iron on iron in a drone of clicking and clacking that seems like it might never end. The beast's long tail. Jay's right arm reaches around and encircles Eddy's shoulders, and as the rumble continues, her body begins to relax. In the distance, as the train nears the town, the whistle blows again. Roger looks back over his shoulder at Jay while he's holding on to Joan. His eyes are wide. He looks positively elated. Yes, thinks Eddy. And the yes means this is what joy looks like when you're eighteen and you love train whistles and you're holding the girl you love. She can't see Jay's face behind her, but as she leans back against his body, she's no longer so afraid, and sensing this perhaps, he tightens his embrace.

CHAPTER 27

"Roger says that since we survived, I should look back on it now as a great adventure. I'm not so sure." Joan is lying on her back on the twin bed in Eddy's room. It's Sunday afternoon, and the spring rain is steady and gray.

"I know." Eddy is lying on her own bed, staring at the ceiling. "I bet if anyone had caught us there, they would have seen some terrified faces, even the boys'. I guess we have to believe Jay that he had no idea a train would be coming? He said afterwards on the way home that he'd never been at the caves on a Friday afternoon. What do you think?"

"Who knows what Jay knows?"

"I still can't believe we did it. Actually went there. Actually made out in the caves. Actually stood by the tracks as a train went by."

"Yeah, I think it made Roger's day ... year ... *life* up to this point!"

Both girls look over at each other and laugh.

"Roger and I didn't have much time for making out in our little cave— that whistle came pretty quick. How was your cave experience?"

"Good. All good. I really do like him, Joanie. I like the way he moves. He seems so sure of himself when he's around me. Makes me think he's been around—with girls, I mean."

"Well, you've been around a bit yourself. You're eighteen, for gosh sakes. But he likes you for sure. He looks at you like he does. And when you look at him? It's a ... a ... a heat wave." The girls look over at each other again, and then, as if on cue, they sing the Martha and the Vandellas' song about burning with desire. Then there's a pause.

"Wonder if the guys talk about us like this?" Eddy says. "Wonder what Jay sees in me?"

Joan sighs. "Besides the fact that you are so darn pretty, you mean?"

"Joanie, I'm not pretty. I'm all right, I guess, but my boobs have stopped growing, and my bottom has not. I mean, why did Jay choose to be with *me*?"

"I don't know, but who can explain mutual attraction? Look at Roger and me. We were doing an experiment in science one day, and our fingers kinda touched, and we laughed and made a mess of the experiment, and we've been together ever since. It's all a mystery."

"Or science. Take your pick. And Joanie? Friday was one of the best days ever. And you were there."

"Ditto, Eddy. Now I've got to run. We both have that English assignment to finish. When do you present yours? Oh, and I almost forgot! I got in to Loyola! Letter came yesterday! My parents are very happy. Very, very happy, like they wondered if I could do it."

"I knew you'd get in, Joanie! I'm happy for you too. Very, very happy. In fact, I'm happy for Paul, you, and me. It's the beginning of an adventure."

"And the end of this one." Joan pauses, then adds, "And you and I won't be together." Joan isn't smiling, her wild hair spread out on the pillow under her head. She turns her head to look at Eddy.

Eddy turns toward her friend when she hears the plaintive note in Joan's voice. She nods at Joan. They share a look. Then Eddy turns back toward the ceiling.

———

Sunday supper is once again a catch-as-catch-can, and the Walters family has decided not to go to church in the evening because of the rain that hasn't let up much since the morning. They're eating eggs and bacon and toast—breakfast for dinner—and they're sitting in the den using TV trays while watching television. There's a bit of a haggle over which shows to watch. *Lassie* is on; so is *The Wonderful World of Disney*. Then comes *The Ed Sullivan Show*, *The F.B.I.*, and, of course, *Bonanza*. The problem is that the whole family is there, and Harold says they all must decide on one show to watch at seven o'clock and another at eight o'clock. Eddy tells them she has homework to do later, so they should let her choose the 7 p.m. show.

"No way," Jimmy says. "That's no fair. Then I'm left to watch what Mom and Dad want to watch. I'll have to watch the Glen Campbell one!"

"Now Jimmy. Calm down. I'm sure we can decide on something together. Don't you have homework?" asks Mary, ever the peacemaker.

"No. I have the weekend off from homework. I should get to decide for a change."

"For a change?" Eddy splutters. "You sit in front of the TV every night!"

"Okay, enough. I'm the father, and tonight, before I have to face a whole week at work, I think I deserve to choose. Let's see ..." Harold picks up the *TV Guide* and turns to May 12th. "I choose *Wild Kingdom* so we can learn something, and then we'll watch *The F.B.I.* so we can learn something else. Like how not to get in trouble with the law."

The family members turn their attention back to their TV trays as Harold flips to NBC.

It's nine o'clock, and Eddy is looking at her notebook and the scribblings and the cross-outs and general messiness of the rough draft of her English project. She's had a hard time concentrating since the phone call earlier that evening. She looks at the top of the page in her notebook and sees Jay's name. She had written it several times after the phone call that came in right before *The F.B.I.* began. Mary had gone into the kitchen to answer the phone, and then she came back and said, "It's for you, Edna." She was smiling when she sat back down on the couch.

Edna went to the phone in the kitchen and said hello and heard "Eddy, it's me, Jay."

"Jay." Eddy was surprised. "Hang on a minute."

"Mom, I'm going to go upstairs to talk. Will you hang up this phone when I pick up?"

She took off up the stairs and sat down on the floor in the hall and picked up the receiver. "Okay." Nothing. "Okay, hang up; I've got it." No click. "Hang on, Jay." And Eddy placed her hand over the receiver. "Mom, make Jimmy hang up the phone!" she yells. She heard her mother downstairs say something, and then she heard the click in her ear.

"I'm back. And I can't believe you called me!"

"Yeah, listen." Jay paused a second. "Just wanted to see if you're all right after our cave experience."

"I'm fine. Although Joanie and I did talk about how scared we were. So much happened so fast. It was exciting, but only when we thought about it later. At least nothing bad happened but a few rocks in the air."

"Good. Good. Um, I won't be at school for a couple of days."

"Really? Why not?"

"Family stuff. Nothing to worry about. Just wanted to let you know."

"Jay, your voice sounds a little funny. You okay?" Eddy thought it sounded like he was hoarse. "You have a cold or something?"

"Nah, well, maybe a little. Anyway, I gotta roll. See you later on in the week. And Eddy? I was a little scared too on Friday. But those caves and all ... being with you—and Roger and Joan—it was great. Really."

"Jay. You called. Thanks."

"You bet. Bye, Eddy. See ya."

"'Night, Jay." She heard the phone disconnect on his end.

CHAPTER 28

Now in her room, she once again is left pondering her conversations with Jay. Once again she feels as if they never say quite enough. Like one or both of them is holding back. She sighs and puts on Dylan's album and plays "All Along the Watchtower," but she can't focus.

She takes Dylan off the turntable and lifts her record player off the stand to put it on the floor where she sits in front of it. She places the adapter on for 45s and places Hendrix's "All Along the Watchtower" on the turntable instead. She turns on the player, and with her notebook in her lap, she lifts the arm, placing it on the record's edge.

Static.

Then comes the guitar and drums. She begins taking down the lyrics, stopping the record by lifting the arm and replacing it over and over again as she writes the words that Hendrix sings.

Then after each line or two of the song, she scribbles down notes like "Who is the thief in the song?" "What does the thief try to steal?" And she wonders about the line about life being a joke; who (besides herself) feels this way? Dylan? Hendrix? Is the song hopeful? Or full of dread? Is the song about the Vietnam War? What's the watchtower? Who are the princes? Who are the women? Why a wildcat? And who are the two riders seen from the watchtower?

Eddy stops and looks at what she's written. She plays the records again to hear the lines she can't discern. She switches out the Hendrix for the Dylan and tries again. She hears a few lines more clearly. *After all*, she thinks, *he wrote the damn thing.* But as to what it all means, she remains unsure. She sighs and skips to Dylan's "I'll Be Your Baby Tonight" on Side 2 of the album. It's her favorite after "Watchtower," and as he uses that kind of country lilt to his voice, she thinks of Jay's love of country music.

Her legs are stiff from sitting so long. She decides to go downstairs to get a snack. Her parents are still in the den, and so is Jimmy. *Bonanza* is on.

"Edna, did you have a nice conversation with Jay? That was Jay, wasn't it?"

"Yes, Mom. It was fine. Short but fine. I don't think he likes to talk on the phone." Eddy thinks that maybe this will please her folks; so many girls talk to boys for hours on the phone. "Hey, Mom and Dad, what was a watchtower exactly, in the old days of kings and princes?" She says this from the kitchen as she puts some Oreos on a plate. She pours a glass of milk too.

Her dad thinks a minute and says, "Most forts had watchtowers for protection. The guards paced up and down the ramparts, and there were towers along the walls. Why do you want to know?"

Jimmy looks up. "I know why …. She's been upstairs playing that song about a watchtower for an hour."

"It's 'All Along the Watchtower.' Mr. Thompson is letting me do a short presentation on that song in English class. I'm comparing Bob Dylan's version to Jimi Hendrix's version." If she had been looking at her parents when she said this, she would have seen Mary looking at Harold as if her daughter is speaking a language she does't understand. Her father just smiles.

"Now that's interesting," her mom says.

"But what could it mean that Dylan is writing about a watchtower now in my day. That's what I need to figure out. I guess I could look up watchtower in the Encyclopedia Britannica." Eddy is standing in the doorway to the den, eating an Oreo.

Mary is looking at *Bonanza*, but she says, "I know watchmen and watchtowers are all through the Bible." Eddy stops eating and looks at her mom.

"Really?"

"Really. There are some good things in there, you know," she says, smiling at Eddy. It's the closest to a joke Mary can come. "Maybe Bob Dylan grew up reading the Bible a lot."

"Or Shakespeare," Eddy adds. "There were men standing guard in *Hamlet*, and they see the ghost of Hamlet's father."

"Go look in the concordance of my Bible. See what you find."

Eddy looks at her mom. "The what?"

"The concordance. It's a big help when you want to find a verse that has a certain word in it. Look under *watchman* or *watchtower* in the back of the Bible." Mary turns back to the TV. Harold is smiling at this exchange, a smile that seems to mean he's pleased that Eddy and Mary are discussing a topic Mary knows about, and he doesn't need to chime in at all. Eddy heads up to her parents' bedroom and takes the King James Bible off her mother's nightstand.

Back on the floor in her room, Eddy turns to the back of the Bible. She looks up *watch* and finds references in Psalms, Proverbs, Matthew, Luke, Hebrews, and 2 Corinthians. After looking up those references, she sees nothing that relates to her project. Next word in the concordance is *Watchman – men*. Psalms again, and Isaiah, Ezekiel, Hosea. She reads in these books. *Now these are better*, she thinks. *Watchmen are being set on walls. Way to go, Mom.*

In the cafeteria the next day, Eddy looks all around until she spies Joey at a table. She rushes over to him, still clutching her books and her lunch bag.

A little out of breath, she sits down at the only place near him and says, "Joey, I need your help with something."

"Hey, Eddy. Sure. Music again?"

"Yes. For my presentation in Mr. Thompson's class. He's letting me compare Dylan's 'All Along the Watchtower' with Jimi Hendrix's version."

"Really? Cool. But I don't know Dylan's. I've heard Hendrix though. Whatcha need?" Joey looks over at Mark sitting next to him. "Mark, you know Dylan's?"

"No, man. Just Hendrix."

Eddy opens her notebook. "That's okay. I can wing it, describing Dylan's folk strum and harmonica on that version. What I need help with is Hendrix's electric guitar and the sounds of his band. I don't know what I'm hearing exactly. Like, what do you call it when he plays his guitar in between the words?"

"That's a riff usually. Sort of a repeated few notes, although sometimes a guitarist is just picking and jamming in a free kind of way while the other band members strum and bang the drums." Eddy is writing in her notebook, her lunch bag lying unopened next to it.

"A 'riff,' got it. I think he opens with one. And there's some weird sounds in the background, but I don't know what they are. Like maracas or something. Anyway, what if he makes a sound with his electric guitar that sounds like a wail, or a *wah*. I don't know what to call these things."

Joey looks at Mark, and Mark nods. "She's got it—the wah-wah pedal," says Joey.

"Yes," agrees Mark.

"Really? That's the name of the pedal? Okay. Anything else I should know about electric guitar playing?"

"It can get loud—real loud. Turn the volume up, Eddy, and rock on! Wish I were in English class with you guys. Mark, you'll have to tell me how it goes!" Joey stands up.

"Joey, what's your presentation about?"

"Music and our band Thee Purity. What else? See you!"

Eddy opens her lunch bag as the bell rings for the end of lunch period. "Damn!" says Eddy.

Mark laughs. "Ain't it worth missing lunch to talk about music? Wish I had thought of something like that to do for English. I'm writing about the John Deere tractors on my dad's farm." Eddy laughs too.

That night, Eddy sequesters herself in her room to finish her assignment for English. The other homework from Trig and Government will be deferred. She knows she shouldn't, but she works on the English assignment first because it excites her. She hopes she has time to finish the others later.

First she types out all the lyrics to Dylan's song on her little portable typewriter. Then she returns to her notebook to work on the rough draft of the paragraph she'll need to present before she ends by playing a little of each record.

How should she start? She looks at the album cover of Dylan's *John Wesley Harding*. The cover shows Dylan with two Indian musicians and an older man. Nope, nothing comes to mind looking at them in relation to the song she's chosen. She reads the sleeve cover about three kings. Nope. She can't make heads or tails of the story Dylan writes there. She writes for a while, crossing through lines, writing some more, crossing out more lines.

Finally, she draws a line down the middle of the page. Left side is Dylan's version; right side is Hendrix. Back and forth she moves, wording the likenesses and differences, only she finds more differences between the two than likenesses. Hendrix bases his song on Dylan's words and melody, and he sings some lines with the same emphasis as Dylan.

Differences are pretty easy: Dylan strums an acoustic guitar, bringing in some not-so-loud drums and a harmonica before starting to sing. Dylan's voice is his usual kind-of-insistent, nasal voice that puts emphasis in odd places whenever he phrases a line. Hendrix plays an electric guitar, makes the drums louder, and rattles some percussion instrument in the background; in between words, his guitar plays riffs, and he hits a wah-wah pedal to make the guitar wail. When Hendrix sings, his voice is louder and, Eddy thinks, more urgent. It makes the listener sense danger.

Dylan's story builds to the end, with the listener trying to figure out who the Joker is, who the Thief is. He seems like one of those storytellers of the olden days, a bard, who traveled from town to town. But Hendrix rages from the beginning, warlike. His voice growls like the wildcat he mentions at the end of the song; he howls like the wind he sings of at the end of the song, an ancient howl that anyone who has ever lived would understand. That Eddy understands too.

Eddy stops and looks at all this and then thinks, *What can I say about what the song means?* She picks up her mother's Bible and starts reading in Isaiah, finally reaching Chapter 21. She reads for a bit and then starts again at 21. The note says that the prophet seeth in a vision the fall of Babylon. She reads on.

Verse 6: For thus has the Lord said unto me, Go, set a watchman,

Let him declare what he seeth.

Verse 7: And he saw a chariot with a couple of horsemen, a chariot of asses,

and a chariot of camels; and he hearkened diligently with much heed:

Verse 8: And he cried, A lion:

My lord, I stand continually upon the watchtower in the daytime,

And I am set in my ward whole nights:

Verse 9: And, behold, here cometh a chariot of men, with a couple of horsemen.

And he answered and said, "Babylon is fallen, is fallen;

And all the graven images of her gods he hath broken unto the ground.

Eddy takes a breath, looking up from the page. She can hardly believe it—it seems like Dylan has used this? It's almost the same as his song! Why would he use these Bible verses? Eddy suddenly realizes that she doesn't know anything about Babylon and why it has fallen. So downstairs she runs to get the Encyclopedia Britannica from the bookshelf in the den. Back upstairs with the fat one-volume encyclopedia, she sits on the floor and opens to Babylon. She reads until her eyes burn.

Babylon, that ancient city of the world, did fall. It fell during the time Isaiah was writing about. Now what city does Dylan want to fall? Any city that uses power to wage war against others? And what time is at hand that is making Jimi Hendrix rage? Is it our time? Yes, she decides. It's time for justice. It's always time for justice to win.

Eddy plays the songs one after the other, and she writes her long paragraph, scribbling through lines, getting frustrated, writing more lines, and forgetting about Trig and Government. Her parents say goodnight as they come up to their room, and her dad says not to burn the midnight oil. Eddy barely hears them.

Jimmy has long since closed his door. It's quiet as she peck-peck-pecks on her little blue portable typewriter, the sounds overly loud in the stillness, the margin *ding* enough to wake someone from sleep, she thinks. She messes up a few times and has to start typing all over again with a new piece of paper; whenever that happens, she lets out a few more cuss words as she noisily rips out the paper from the machine.

Eddy finally types up a draft that she thinks will do. She doesn't even wash her face or brush her teeth. She falls into bed, realizing she will pay the price in Trig and Government tomorrow, but in her head, she sees watchmen on towers and horsemen in the distance urging their horses on with the good news she feels they're delivering. Injustice is falling. But wildcats still growl, and the wind still howls. She knows this world is dangerous—and yet a crescent moon lights the way in her mind. It gives a little light for the riders and the watchmen on the tower.

CHAPTER 29

Tuesday is over, and as Eddy walks home, she thinks that this Tuesday has been warm and bright, like the color orange she sees in her mind. Joan isn't with her, having been picked up by her mother for a dentist appointment after school, so Eddy is walking slowly and just thinking. She wonders why days are such a mix of good and bad. The good? English went very well, and Mr. Thompson and her whole class seemed to like her presentation. Mr. Thompson seemed impressed, she thought. He watched her intently and joined the clapping at the end when she took her seat. And as Mark and Eddy walked out of class together, Mark said he thought she'd captured the sounds of the song and of Dylan and Hendrix really well. Then he asked how she knew about the Bible verses. She gave her mother all the credit. It hasn't escaped Eddy's notice lately that a lot of writers seem to find inspiration in the Bible, for it certainly has enough stories in it to use as metaphors and examples. *Shakespeare had to know enough to use those stories too,* she thinks as she walks along. Eddy had expressly thanked her mother after breakfast.

And the bad that comes to mind now? The Trig answers that she had scribbled down in the car as her mother drove her to school were wrong, and Mrs. Lemons looked disappointed when she called on Eddy in class. And she didn't even want to think about Government, when she had to confess that she didn't have her homework and had to grovel to Mrs. Bumgarner for extra time to complete the assignment. It was granted, but grudgingly so. *Oh well*, Eddy thinks. *Mrs. Bumgarner won't have to put up with me much longer!*

The Good, the Bad and the Ugly. She smiles as she thinks of that movie title. And what really is the ugly? Is it that she doesn't know how Jay is doing and why he isn't in school? Something seems just out of reach that she can't see. Getting to know him is hard enough without all these other questions. When she gets home, she gets a plate of Oreos and sits in the den for a while. Her brain hurts from thinking. Her mom lets her be.

———————

Jay isn't at school on Wednesday either. Eddy and Joan discuss it on the walk home.

"I just don't know how to think about it," Eddy says. "I mean, what could have been so pressing that he has to miss three days of school?"

"Maybe someone is sick? Maybe he's sick?"

"Should I actually try to call him, Joanie?"

"Wait a couple more days. Then let's do it. I'll sit by you when you call. By the way, Roger still can't stop talking about that day at the caves. As for me, I think I can still feel the wind from that train blowing by!"

"Me too. Caves and trains and rocks and ... and ... those kisses. Geez, it was exciting."

Thursday morning before the first bell rings, Eddy decides to go down the hall past the typing classes to see if Jay is at the lockers there. And sure enough, as she walks the few steps to that hall, she sees him in the distance, standing at his open locker and fumbling with something. She hurries to where he stands, and she sees he has a sling holding his right arm.

"Jay." Eddy is next to him, and he turns at the sound of his name.

"Hey."

Eddy sees a purple patch of bruised skin above his right eye.

"What happened?"

Jay turns back toward his locker. "Fell off my dad's cycle. I'm all right. My arm didn't break."

"Holy cow. Looks like you hit your head."

"Yeah. It's healing."

Jay seems pale. This time it's Eddy who leans her shoulder against the locker next to him, trying to look into his eyes. "Jay, you missed three days of school. I'm sure you could have come back, even with this arm and that bruise."

"Just felt like staying home." He seems to keep his face turned from her on purpose as he looks in his locker.

Eddy doesn't know what else to say, and the bell rings for first period. Jay slams his locker, and the two of them walk slowly toward the stairs to the main hall.

"Want to meet at Kenny's after school?" Eddy is a bit breathless as she tries to hold the conversation steady when it doesn't feel steady. Something seems off. Or over.

Jay is looking over her head and down the hall. Then he tilts his head toward her, looking into her eyes intensely, and Eddy is sure he is going to say something that she doesn't want to hear. And then with a half-smile, and some tenderness she thinks, he says, "Sure."

The school day is long for Eddy as she stays preoccupied with Jay and what he might say to her. She wrestles with how she will respond if he says in some way—or says by his silence—that he doesn't want to see her anymore. She acknowledges once again that she doesn't know him well. She also thinks that she misses the fairly uncomplicated life she was living just six months ago.

At lunch, Joan says, "I saw Jay in Typing. A motorcycle accident? Could have been much worse, I guess."

"Yeah. We're meeting at Kenny's after school. But something seems off. Do you think he took the motorcycle without his father's permission?" Eddy is staring at her peanut butter and jelly sandwich and then slowly lifts it off the wax paper and takes a bite.

"I saw him talking to Buddy in the hall after Typing. I bet Buddy knows the whole story, but I don't want to ask him."

"Strange that I don't see either one of them in the halls between my classes. They must have most of their classes on the hall heading out to Shop class. Or maybe they just don't go to class. Like I said, it's strange."

"Want me to come to Kenny's with you?"

"Nah, he might not talk much if you're there. Thanks, Joanie. I'll call you tonight."

"Righto. Roger and I are thinking of going over to Blacksburg and VPI this weekend, just to look around. I can get Roger to ask Jay, if that's all right with you."

"Okay. That sounds good to me. Thanks, Joanie."

Kenny's isn't super crowded when Eddy gets there, and Jay is already in a booth, so Eddy slides in across from him. She puts her books on the seat next to her and can't resist saying, "Where are your books, Jay?"

"No homework for me. My teachers have pretty much given up on homework for these last two weeks of school. We wouldn't do it anyway." Jay seems to be daring her to say something.

Just then the waitress comes over. She's chewing gum while asking what they'd like. Her apron over her blue gingham dress is soiled. Eddy says she would like some fries and a Coke.

"Me too," Jay echoes. After the waitress walks away with their order on her little lined green pad and her pencil behind her ear, Jay says, "Man, she can't make much money in this job. Hope she isn't supporting a family."

"She's pretty young." Eddy follows her with her eyes as the waitress walks behind the counter. The image of Patty, a girl in their class she hardly knew, who got pregnant and left school, comes into her mind. Eddy suddenly wonders what happened to Patty. Did the father of the baby marry her? She shakes off that thought and comes up with another scenario. "Maybe she still lives at home and just helps out her parents with her money."

"Or maybe she's married and is stuck."

Eddy looks at Jay and crosses her arms on the table in front of her.

Then Jay extends his hand, reaching over and taking her right hand in his left. He grasps her hand tightly, rubbing the tops of her fingers with his thumb. His slinged arm rests on the table too. "I missed you these last few days."

"Ditto," she says.

"So are you ready to graduate?"

"I guess. I got my letter from VPI. I don't think I told you. I got in. So did Paul. And Joanie is off to Loyola. Seems like the earth is spinning faster." Eddy looks at Jay's hand, seeing some scratches on his knuckles. She looks up at him. "What about you?"

"Graduation? I'm ready; never was too good at school stuff, as you probably know."

"What'll you do after graduation?"

"I honestly don't know. I guess I can get a permanent job at the repair shop. Would sort of like to go somewhere. Anywhere. But you know ... takes money. "

"Is something wrong, Jay? You make me think something has happened."

"Nothing has happened; just the same old shit."

Eddy feels like he's holding back. Like a dam could bust any minute and she would be overwhelmed. His bruise seems a deeper purple suddenly.

Quietly, Jay says, "Eddy, you live in this bubble. Your world is, well, nice. Most people don't live in bubbles."

"I do not live in a bubble. Not any more than you do. I've seen your nice home, met your mom. You think I'm naive, oblivious. But I'm not. I know how things are. Stop judging me," she says more loudly than she intended. Eddy doesn't know why, but she feels tears coming. Jay gives her hand a squeeze and releases it, and then the waitress is there, setting down their fries and drinks.

It's not more than a couple of minutes of silence later when Buddy comes in the door like a whirlwind, shouting at Jay, "There you are!" He approaches the booth and slides in next to him. Eddy and Jay look up at the shout. Neither smiles when he slides in.

"Hey there, Ed. What's happening?"

"Hey, Buddy. Just fries and a Coke." Eddy looks at Jay, hoping he'll take the lead in responding to Buddy. Buddy starts dipping one of Jay's fries into the ketchup on the wax paper.

"Buddy, get your own!" Jay says, sliding his pile farther from Buddy.

"Best friends share, don't they, darling?" Buddy looks to Eddy but gets no help. "What are we talking about today? Jay's little accident? Are you making him feel all better, Eddy?" Buddy reaches over Jay to get a fry. Jay blocks him with his left arm and looks at him sternly, his lips pursed much like a parent who is about to discipline a child.

"Okay, I can take a hint. You two lovebirds want to be alone. Ole Buddy sees how it is." Buddy slides out and stands by the table for a few seconds, looking at Jay. Jay keeps on eating his fry and says, "See ya." Anyone could look at Buddy and see that he's waiting for something. Some sign. Eddy holds her breath, wondering what secret code this is. It's as if there's a fog, and she can't quite see well enough. She knows there are things happening just beyond the fog, but she can't quite name them, not yet anyway. Finally, Buddy walks to the door and leaves.

"Jay, is it my fault Buddy's mad at you? Haven't you had lots of dates and girlfriends? I saw you two with those girls at the Overlook one time."

Jay slowly dips a fry in ketchup and then looks up at Eddy. "Buddy's got a lot on his mind, but he wouldn't want anyone to know it. The war is calling; maybe signing up would be a chance to sort out what to do with his life. He and his parents are having fights about it, I think. They probably want to keep him from going, but they don't know how. Maybe he wants to run away from all that. I don't know exactly. Buddy doesn't say much about things that matter."

"What about you? Is the army calling you too? Are you going to have to ... to go?"

"I don't turn eighteen until August, so I have some time to sort things out. But I won't have college to help me put off decisions."

"Couldn't you go to a community college? Wouldn't that work?"

Jay looked at Eddy for a couple of minutes. "And the money for that? Even that kind of college takes some dough."

"I just thought maybe … maybe your folks would …"

"Not in the cards, not right now. My mom's father left her our house when he died, but my folks can hardly keep it up. My dad … well, he thinks I should go into the army to grow up. Or work in that auto shop in Thomasburg my whole life."

"And what does Jay want to do?" Eddy whispers.

"The impossible … go to Charlotte and work on engines for NASCAR."

"Why is that impossible? If that's your dream …"

"Who knows … maybe. It's just that … Vietnam might ruin things for me. I don't know."

The two sit there in silence for a bit. Finally Eddy says, "Does your arm hurt?"

"It's just a sprain. Kind of a wrench in my arm. It'll be fine."

"Jay, the accident, as Buddy said …"

"It'll be fine. Let's talk about something else. Let's talk about Blacksburg this weekend. Roger asked me. Let's go and pretend we're college students, drink a couple of beers, smoke some dope. You know."

"Smoke some dope? Would you? Have you? I mean, I would like to try some, but I'm not even good with cigarettes! When I tried one at the Overlook with Paul and Leonard, I couldn't stop coughing."

Jay just looks at her and smiles. He takes her right hand in his left again, and moves his thumb over her knuckles. Eddy's stomach flutters; she wants to get out of there, to go somewhere, anywhere, with Jay. But there's nowhere to go. Not today anyway.

———

Before dinner that night in the Walters home, the family is sitting in the den with Harold watching the five o'clock news and Eddy looking at a magazine and Jimmy on the floor trying to perfect his Pick-up Sticks method. Eddy glances over once in a while. "Hey, I saw one move, mister."

"You did not," Jimmy answers. "You're lying."

"Okay, you two. Stop bickering. I'm listening to the news."

Eddy thinks about that word. *Bickering*. So old-fashioned. So parent-like. Then something on the news makes her look at the TV. It's the words *young people*. The newscaster is explaining that one person was shot at People's Park near UC Berkeley in California. Ronald Reagan sent in twenty-seven hundred National Guard troops as the protests continued.

"Another protest gone bad," Harold says, shaking his head. "What's this world coming to when college kids keep trying to insert themselves into the bigger picture?"

"Shouldn't they protest if it's the war and they'll do the fighting?" Eddy says softly to her father. "Was it a protest against the Vietnam War?" Eddy asks.

"Seems it was about something else," her dad answers, his attention on the TV. The commentators are discussing this May 15th protest. Bloody Thursday it will come to be called.

"The young people think they have the right to gather at that park because they fixed it up and made it nicer than it was. Now there's chaos in the park with every side staking a claim as to whose it is. Scary," says Harold. "Whenever there's chaos, people always get hurt."

"California seems so far away," Eddy says. "I used to think of surfing and the Beach Boys and Gidget when I thought of California." She doesn't speak of how lately she has been thinking of justice—or maybe injustice—in her time. The kind that inspires Dylan to write and makes Hendrix rage.

"You'll be heading off to college soon, Edna, and there may be protests happening around you. You'll have to decide whether to join or watch. I worry about your safety."

"She's too chicken to protest," Jimmy says, not looking up. "She'll just watch, like she watches me."

"You need watching, Jimmy."

Harold is about to say something when Mary calls, "Supper's ready."

CHAPTER 30

Paul, Joan, and Eddy are sitting on Joan's back deck after school on Friday. The three are looking through their yearbooks. Eddy and Joan talk about riding to Blacksburg the next day to walk around with Roger and Jay. "What are you doing this weekend, Paul?" Eddy looks up at him while chewing her cookie. Joan's mother has always made the best chocolate chip cookies, and Eddy has wondered lately why her own mother doesn't do the homemade ones, just buys them in packages from the store. But she doesn't want to hurt her mother's feelings, so she hasn't asked her.

"Leonard and I are going to the lake this weekend. His folks rent a campsite there for the whole summer, and it's pretty neat. Campfires and swimming and sometimes a boat ride and skiing with their family friends. And now his parents trust us to stay there alone sometimes."

"So they trust you not to get into trouble?" Joan asks.

"We make sure that nobody suspects what we do. Keep a low profile is our motto. Then we can do what we want. We just make sure there are no signs left around. You know, no cigarette butts or liquor bottles."

"Can you water-ski, Paul?" Eddy asks. "Remember when we went to that church camp by the lake for a few summers? But we didn't ski."

"I've gone a couple of times with Leonard. I stink at skiing though. What about you, Eddy?"

"I learned back in middle school when I got to be good friends with Carol Lannister," Eddy chews on her cookie. "Her folks had a boat, and they taught me. Carol was good, and I got up on the skis a few times, but

I was smaller back then. I'd be crap at it now. And Carol and I haven't been close for years. She went to the other side—cheerleading side, the 'in' side—and became the most popular girl in school. We still speak sometimes and all, but we're not close anymore."

"Now you have *us*! Big step up, I'd say. Here's to our side, whatever that is." Joan raises her cookie. "To our forever friends!"

Eddy and Paul smile at each other and raise their cookies. "Forever friends," they say together. Then the three of them laugh as they finish their cookies. They seem to know they sound like elementary school kids.

Saturday, a bright yellow day, and the four young people are off to Blacksburg. Roger is driving and Joan is in charge of the radio, turning the dial to find the clearest station. She stops when she hears "Do Wah Diddy Diddy." She looks over her shoulder at Eddy and announces to the boys, "Eddy and I love this song." Joan sings along as they drive toward the college.

VPI in 1969 still seems as if someone had just decided to build the college in the middle of a field. The campus is surrounded by acres of open farmland, and all the main buildings are built of limestone, creating a pleasing symmetry. The town of Blacksburg adjoining the college is small and, therefore, teems with students walking around. In 1969, this is a school for studying agriculture and English, vocational skills and science. It's a public college for students of all walks of life who can piece together the money for tuition and room and board.

"What should we do first?" Joan asks the twosome in the back seat, where Jay is holding Eddy's hand in the little space between them. Both the quiet ones in the back seat seem content to just ride along, enjoying these moments of just being together.

"Remember that other time I drove us over to Blacksburg, Joanie? We felt so adventurous going to the college town, but we didn't know what to do exactly. We found a parking spot near Main Street and just started walking. We found some interesting places though."

"Like food places, I hope." Roger looks in the rearview mirror at Jay. "I'm already hungry!"

"Likewise," Jay says and grins back at Roger.

"Okay, sounds almost like a plan." Joan, who has been looking back at Jay and Eddy, now turns back around. The opening horns of Aretha Franklin's "Respect" come on the radio, and Joan turns it up. Aretha calls out, and the background singers respond "Ooh" after each opening line. Then after the saxophone solo, Joan and Eddy begin singing along with Aretha Franklin, finally shouting "Sock it to me" eight times along with the backup singers. Roger and Jay seem to find the girls' singing quite entertaining, if the smiles on their faces are an indication. The car rocks with good vibrations—the freedom of being young and on the road.

"The plan" starts as the four young people walk the streets of Blacksburg, looking in windows and pointing out things and people that interest them. The couples walk two by two, holding hands and turning their heads toward each other now and then. Jay and Eddy talk in quiet voices until they want to tell Joan and Roger about what they're seeing. Soon they stop in to eat at the counter at a drugstore that reminds them of one in Thomasburg. Roger and Jay insist on paying for the hot dogs (Roger's and Jay's fully loaded, Eddy's with mustard and coleslaw, Joan's with chili and coleslaw) and Cokes. Afterward they meander down the side streets of the VPI campus; they stop in front of a little sign outside a store that reads: Books, Strings and Things. Eddy looks at Joan; Joan looks at Eddy. They go in.

After looking around for a few minutes at the tall bookshelves, lots of them, and at some displays of VPI merchandise to buy, and choices for beverages like coffee and sodas and tea being served by a serious girl behind a counter, the four arrive in the adjoining room that holds the bins of albums categorized by genre and alphabetized. A song is playing over a sound system, but Eddy doesn't recognize it. She stops at one of the bins to start checking out the albums.

Jay stands just over her right shoulder, looking down at the records she peruses one by one. He slips his arms around her from behind, and his touch startles her, makes her jerk her head up, and she accidentally hits Jay in the head. Jay pretends she has really hurt him, and her face registers an anxious moment, her mouth slightly open. But when she sees he's just fooling around, she laughs and turns back to the albums, taking her left hand and bringing Jay's arm back around her like before. He rests his chin on her shoulder, watching her thumb through more albums.

The ride home is uneventful. Jay's arm is wrapped around her shoulders in the back seat, and the four of them talk easily about the music playing on the radio and graduation and nothing of importance really. Joan sits close to Roger, so close that she can lean her head against his shoulder as he drives. Eddy and Jay hold hands again, his thumb, as usual, rubbing her knuckles gently. When Roger pulls up in front of her house to let her out, Jay releases her hand, guides her head toward his, and kisses her twice. First he kisses her softly, and then pulling away, he looks into her eyes with such a longing expression that Eddy parts her lips a little before he takes her face in both of his hands and kisses her hard. These kisses make Eddy lean in and want more, but not here. Not in front of her house.

"I'll call you," he says. Then he releases her. Eddy gazes for a moment into his eyes. Did he really say he would call her? She smiles goodbye, an over-the-rainbow smile if there ever was one.

"It was interesting, wasn't it, Joanie?" Eddy and Joan are on the phone later that night.

"Yeah. I can't believe we're double-dating our senior year! I think Roger and Jay get on pretty well, considering they barely know each other."

"Caves and trains will do that to you." The girls laugh. "Joanie, can you see me there at VPI next year?"

"I think so. I can definitely see you at Books, Strings and Things. You'll be poring over all the latest albums, standing there for hours, possibly flunking out because you spend all your time there."

"I definitely like that store. I even think Jay liked it." A pause. "Wonder what he thinks about college and stuff after walking around Blacksburg today? I mean, I haven't really asked him except generally. Last time I sort of asked what his plans are, he dodged it and told me I lived in a bubble. Then Buddy came in and interrupted us. It was all awkward. Maybe Jay will go to community college like Roger."

"Eddy, Jay does seem kinda sad, don't you think? When you were looking at albums, I saw him standing behind you looking over your shoulder, and then he put his chin on your shoulder and his arms around your waist. It was such a sweet moment. Maybe he and Roger are just quiet. Maybe they can't get words in since we're talking so much! I mean, Jay doesn't seem like the college type, or at least the studying type. But he studies you, and then he bought you that album today. Cool!"

"I know; that was so nice, but he didn't need to spend that four dollars on me. I don't even like country music!"

"Well, he did say on the ride home that he was trying to educate you, that that guy was one of the greatest singers of all time."

"And I'm trying to educate him. Did you hear the song playing in the store when we were walking around? I asked the girl behind the counter, and she said it was Pink Floyd. 'Set Controls' or something like that. Eerie. I may save up to buy Pink Floyd. Maybe I should have asked Jay to buy me that album instead of Hank Williams."

"He bought you what he wanted to. Maybe there's a hidden message in there somewhere."

"Oooooh, maybe. I'll try to listen to that twangy voice and find it. Now that I think about it, one of our first conversations was about the song 'I'm So Lonesome I Could Cry,' which Jay said was written by Hank Williams. I only knew the B.J. Thomas version. But it's one of the saddest songs I know. Is that the message? Hang on, let me get the album

Jay bought me." A pause while Eddy finds the album. "I'm back. Well, every other song is about the blues, so I guess Jay doesn't mind being sad. 'Long Gone Lonesome Blues,' 'Lovesick Blues,' 'Moanin' the Blues' …"

Joan laughs. "I think he might be tormented just like you, Eddy!"

"Maybe. I can't tell what he's thinking. What if the war gets him? What if he doesn't have a way out like the college boys seem to? Wouldn't it make him sad to see all those college kids walking around today being, I don't know, free?"

"What if, what if … I don't know, Eddy. Ask him, dammit! It's like you both are moving around each other in slow motion. Even when you touch or hold hands, it seems kind of slow. C'mon, Eddy, grab him if you want to! Just be careful of that arm he hurt."

"Ah, Joanie, you're the best." Eddy hears her father at the bottom of the stairs. "Supper, Edna."

"Comin', Dad. Gotta go, Joanie. See you."

"See ya!"

Later, Eddy is in her room, listening to that album, determined to listen all the way through, even though she's not crazy about Hank Williams's voice. Too country. *But*, she thinks, *Dylan's voice ain't the purest either. Maybe I can learn to like Hank Williams's.*

Jimmy stands at the doorway to Eddy's room. "What in the world are you listening to?"

"It's Hank Williams. Jay gave me this album."

"Yodeling is funny. Do you really like this stuff?"

"I like the words. Don't know about the instruments. What is it when you play a guitar by laying it on your lap?"

"It's wrong, just wrong." Jimmy turns to go to his room saying, "Yo-de-lay-hee-hoo!"

Eddy wonders about all the songs with *Blues* in the title and thinks about Jay. *Do his parents like country music?* Eddy pictures Jay's mom listening to this music. *Does she have the blues? Does she think about the times when she was young in the very same house she lives in now? Does home feel different now?* Eddy decides to go out in the hall to the phone table. She looks up the Nickleses' phone number in the phone book on the table, pulls the phone into her room, and closes the door. The cord just barely makes it. She wants to talk to Jay, enough to call his house. She dials his number. It's nine o'clock on a Saturday night.

"Hello," says a man's voice.

Eddy almost hangs up, but after a second hello from the man's voice, she manages "Is Jay there? This is Edna Walters."

"No, he's not here." Eddy hears a muffled voice in the background. "We'll tell him you called so he can call you back."

"Oh. Okay, thank you." And she hangs up, putting the receiver back in the cradle. She takes a deep breath, as if she's managed to escape from something. Eddy listens again to the record on the turntable, hears that strange country voice sing about the blues always coming around. Eddy says his name out loud, "Jay." The day at VPI was so nice, like a taste of days to come. Now she thinks about her favorite song on this album, but she hears in her head B.J. Thomas's voice singing about being so lonesome he could cry.

Eddy realizes that she's not lonesome. She's home with her family, warm and happy after her day, and even though she wonders where Jay has gone, she only feels a yearning for his kisses, his hands on her skin, his green eyes looking at her as if … *As if what?* she wonders. She turns her attention to some song about "Honky Tonk Blues" on the album, and her mom says from outside her door, "Edna?"

"Yes, Mom?"

"May I come in?"

"Sure."

Mary slowly opens the door, looking down at the phone on the floor and Eddy sitting next to it. "Seems like you had a nice day today," she says. "I enjoyed hearing about it at dinner." Eddy looks up at her mother standing there in the doorway, her hand still on the doorknob. Eddy stands up and sits on her bed. Mary continues. "Did you get excited thinking about being there next year?"

Eddy looks at her hands and then at her mother. "I did sorta. I guess Joanie and I can picture ourselves there with college kids a little bit, but Roger and Jay … well, they probably can't picture themselves there. They just went because we wanted to."

"Where will they go?" Mary's smile has gone, and she furrows her brow a little as she asks this question.

"I don't know. Maybe community college? At least that's what Roger says. Jay says nothing about next year."

Mary comes and sits next to Eddy on the bed's edge. "We know Jay hardly at all. What's he like, Edna? You like him, don't you?"

"Sure. He's nice. Quiet. And he likes music. And he likes cars—like Dad. He works at the auto shop on weekends."

"Hmm," Mary murmurs. "One more week of high school for you all …. And then graduation. Are you happy?"

"I guess. I don't know." Eddy looks down, rubbing one hand over her knuckles. "Mom, what's a honky-tonk?"

Mary laughs, surprised. "What?"

"A honky-tonk. Jay bought me this album by Hank Williams. He likes country music, and this guy sings about honky-tonks."

"Well, let me think. It's a place out in the country where music is played. People who don't have a city nearby go to these kind of run-down shacks to dance and hear music—and … and other things, I think."

"Like drinking moonshine? Is that the other thing you're talking about?" Eddy is smiling at her mom.

"Yes, Edna." Mary looks at her daughter. "You know about moon-shine?" Mary pauses. "Have you been around it?"

"Moonshine? Not that I know of. High school boys seem to like beer."

Mary seems hesitant to ask, but then does. "Have you tried it?"

"Beer? Yes. Tastes yucky. I don't know why the boys like it."

Mary continues, "I guess I'm not surprised you've tried it. Glad you don't like it. Your father and I can't be with you when you make these decisions, and next year, well, you'll be making them a lot. Just promise you'll be careful."

"Don't worry," Eddy says, patting her mother's arm next to her. "I'm only an hour away, for gosh sakes!"

Mary stands up then. She looks around the room. There are a couple of stuffed animals sitting in a chair in the corner. She looks down at the bed, remembering going to Roanoke and helping Eddy pick out the pretty yellow bedspreads and dust ruffles for the twin beds. The desk is cluttered with papers and books and also has a small black-and-white family picture in a frame. It's a few years old. It shows the four Walterses in their Sunday clothes, standing in the yard of Mary's parents' home in Fredericksburg, Virginia, a home that was sold after her parents died. Every one of the Walterses is smiling as they pose for the camera, but Eddy's eyes are looking off to the right in the photo. Mary continues to look around; the closet door is open, and the black graduation gown hangs on a hook just inside.

Eddy watches her mother looking around. Then she too stands up, as if she's going to escort her mother out of the room. Her mother looks at her and smiles and gives her daughter a hug. "Shall I take the phone back to the hall?" she asks.

"Sure. I'm done for the night."

Mary picks up the phone. "Goodnight, Edna. Sleep tight."

"You, too, Mom! Tell Dad goodnight."

"And Jimmy too?"

Eddy laughs. "Okay, if you insist." And Eddy closes the door behind her mother. She goes over to her record player and picks up stacks of records, shuffling through them. She finds the one she wants, takes the Hank Williams album off the turntable, and puts the small adapter for 45s around the post. She places the needle at the beginning of "More Love" and hears the familiar static as she plops down on her bed.

Then she hears the piano and drums and the silky voice of Smokey Robinson singing. For some reason, Smokey Robinson's voice is how she imagines Jay's might sound if he were singing to her. Soft, slow, like that slow dance at Penny's party. Like that first kiss today. Smokey is singing about a love that will last forever and will never be worn down. The song goes on, but Eddy is aware that her response isn't soft and slow anymore. She wants to grab Jay and pull him to her. The yearning in her has a fierceness that scares her a little. But just a little.

After the song, she goes to the record stacks and looks for another one. She takes off "More Love" and places the next record. She thinks of Joanie and how she would approve. When Martha and the Vandellas reach the end of "Heatwave," screaming "Yeah, yeah" over and over, Eddy feels like screaming too.

And then she hears the phone ringing out in the hall.

CHAPTER 31

It's Sunday. Eddy stirs and opens her eyes. She's in bed, and yet, there's Joan sitting on the other bed, holding the stuffed tiger and the stuffed red dog. Mary is sitting in Eddy's desk chair on the other side of her bed. They're talking to each other quietly.

And then Eddy remembers.

She closes her eyes, squeezing them shut.

The phone call. Her father's voice in the hall, low and muffled. Her parents speaking low to each other. Eddy opening her door ....

———

"Who was that?" she asks.

Her parents look at each other, and then her father says, "Come in here, Edna. Sit down." Edna obeys and walks into the bedroom and sits on the edge of their bed.

"What?" Eddy's mind goes immediately to her grandmother. After all, grandmothers are older and something could happen.

"Edna ... that was my friend Ted Chinault, who is a volunteer fireman here in town. He said there was an accident this evening and that the two boys in the accident were in your class at school. He wondered if you knew them, so he thought he should call me and let me know. Some kids were drag racing just outside of town, and when the police came, the kids all took off in their cars in different directions. A boy named Buddy was driving one of the cars, and as they were being chased by the police, he tried to make the turn up on Ridgewood Street onto Maryland Avenue, but he must have lost control, and the car ran into that big wall there. Buddy is in the hospital." Harold pauses, looking at Mary and then back at Eddy.

Did Eddy's mouth drop open, she now wonders. Did her eyes open wider than usual, looking first at her father, then at her mother as they stood in front of her? She's not sure. But she remembers her dad kneeling down in front of her and putting his hands around her clasped hands.

"Edna, the other boy was Jay Nickles. He took the brunt of the crash into that wall and … and … Oh honey. He died."

Now it's Sunday. Now Eddy keeps her eyes closed. Her dad uttered those words last night, and now she tries to remember what happened next, but it's like she's standing in her parents' room watching a play being enacted. The problem is that she's looking through a mist at all the characters in the play.

Maybe she stood up. Maybe she took in a big breath of air. Maybe she let it out. She can't quite see all the details. She seems to remember saying, "But I was just with him. But, but, are you sure it's him?" But, but, but.

She remembers that her parents must have called Joan to come over with her mom and dad to comfort Eddy ….

Waiting for the Richardses to come, Harold goes downstairs, and Mary sits next to Eddy on the bed. Jimmy stands near the bedroom door, watching. And when Joan comes up the stairs and sits on the other side of Eddy on the bed, when Mr. and Mrs. Richards stand in front of her with sad eyes and solicitous comments, the Eddy now watching the play wants to scream, *Stop staring at me!*

But they don't stop. They keep looking at her, looking at her, looking at her. All of them. Eddy doesn't scream out loud though. She lets Joan hug her and lead her to her room, and Mary gives Eddy something to drink "to help her sleep," and like an automaton that's been turned off, Eddy sits on her own bed under the covers still in her clothes, her back against her pillows and Joan sitting at the foot of the bed with her. They stare at each other.

"I can't believe it," Joan whispers.

Eddy just stares.

"I just can't believe this has happened." Joan looks at Eddy for a response, but Eddy, as if she doesn't trust that any words will come out, or fears that a dam might burst inside her, finally just shakes her head.

"Try to rest now, and we'll try to figure some of this out tomorrow." And with that, the two friends sit there, just sit there with the faraway voices of adults penetrating through the stillness of the night. Somehow, Eddy slips into sleep ....

That's what Eddy is picturing in her head as she lies there with her eyes closed. She tries to picture what happened to Jay and Buddy last night right up to the moment Jay's body in the passenger seat is thrown out against a cement wall. She can picture the "beforehand," when Buddy convinces Jay to come out with him, to be the old friend who goes places with him, gets into trouble with him, rides with him everywhere. Jay would have said yes, for old times' sake, she thinks, because Jay and Buddy have sorta had a break in their friendship—they've had Eddy break in. So Jay must've gone.

She thinks they might have had a few swigs from a bottle, might have been joyriding around town when they decided to race some other cars out on the four-lane, which drew attention from the police, and then comes the chase. Maybe, maybe. What she can't quite picture is Jay in the passenger seat. What was he doing? What did he say to Buddy? What did he think just as Buddy was trying to make that turn? Did Jay brace himself? Did he shout, *Look out, Buddy!*

Did he think of her?

Eddy replays these thoughts in her mind. It's Sunday. Sundays are white. Bright white. Eddy opens her eyes again and sits up in bed, turning her head from one person to the other. "Joanie …?"

Both Joan and Mary stand up quickly.

"I'm here. Just slept here in my old bed in your room like always."

"I don't even remember your folks leaving last night," she begins. "Mom, what do we do now?" Eddy sees her father in the doorway and turns from one face to another.

"Edna, there's nothing to be done except grieve for your friend. How are you feeling? What can we do to help you … as you …" Her father falters.

Eddy thinks for a minute. "So Buddy is alive? And he's in the hospital?"

Mary nods. "He has a broken leg and a broken arm, his jaw is wired shut, and he has cuts and bruises."

Eddy says nothing. She gets up and makes her way to the bathroom and closes the door. If she could see the three faces she's left inside her room, she would see that grief is contagious, that Joan's face mirrors her own grief, that her parents' faces are pinched with worry because they want to comfort her when there is nothing to be done but to stand there, that all three of them don't want Eddy out of their sight, even to go to the bathroom.

When she flushes the toilet and comes back out, she sees nothing but pain, whereas when she had looked at herself in the bathroom mirror, she saw nothing but a blank, numb face staring back at her. Nothing but blankness. She crawls back into bed. She's sitting there hugging her knees under the covers. Joan sits down once again at the foot of her bed with the stuffed animals.

Eddy says to Joan, "He said he'd call. Did you hear him? He said he'd call." And then Eddy's face falls into a face of tragedy like the one on the yearbook cover: a downturned mouth, a forehead of lines. A riverlet of tears is opened, and Eddy gasps for breath. Joan moves quickly forward on the bed and enfolds her friend in her arms. The stuffed animals are squeezed between them, as both girls cry and cry and cry. Eddy's parents decide wordlessly to go downstairs to do something, anything. Jimmy walks by on his way downstairs and turns his head and looks quickly at the girls and then goes quickly down the stairs.

It's Sunday afternoon. Eddy still sits cross-legged on her bed, her back against the wall now. Paul sits on one side and Joan is on the other, and in front of Eddy rests a plate of Joan's mom's cookies. Nobody says much. Some crumbs fall on the yellow bedspread, and Joan licks her finger and reaches over and dabs at them.

"Leonard says to tell you he's so sorry. He said he liked Jay." Paul looks at Eddy, who keeps on chewing.

Joan is still sniffling and holds a tissue in one hand. "Roger says the same thing, Eddy. Word is spreading, and our class can't believe it. I wonder about Penny—" Joan stops. "Eddy, should I put on some music?"

"No!" It comes out loudly. "I mean, no, please don't." Eddy looks straight ahead and then asks, "Someone please tell me what happens next? What am I supposed to do? I feel like everyone will look at me to see my response, to gawk at me. I don't want to go out for a long, long time. I'll hate that. Hate, hate, hate. Poor Mom and Dad. The phone keeps ringing."

Paul and Joan look at each other. "Eddy, your folks are okay except for watching their girl be sad," Joan says, then looks at Paul. He nods.

"My folks looked at me a little differently today," Paul says, "to see how I am. Jay was my friend too. Everyone feels helpless. I heard that the teachers at school are torn up as well. And here it is just before graduation."

The three hear the phone ring in the hall. In a few minutes, Mary knocks on the door. "Come in, Mom," Eddy says.

"Eddy," Mary starts, her hand still on the doorknob. "Eddy, Reverend Stevens would like to stop over in a while to see you."

"Oh Mom, no. Please ..."

Mary purses her lips and tries again. "Honey, he only wants to comfort you somehow. It's what reverends do at times like this. Maybe he will—"

"Mom, not now," Eddy interrupts. "Maybe not ever. I don't know …. Please tell everyone to leave me alone." Each word she utters seems heavy, like she's lifting a heavy weight.

Mary slowly backs up and closes the door. Silence returns. Finally Eddy says, "I can't breathe. Why can't I breathe? What if this is the way I will feel for the rest of my life—like an invalid. Where can I go without people looking at me?"

Each friend reaches out a hand to touch Eddy. Then Paul takes Joan's other hand. And outside the sun is shining, and the breeze rustles through the trees, and Eddy wonders why.

———————

Eddy doesn't go to school on Monday. Her parents let her stay home, and she wanders around, not knowing what to do with herself. Harold comes home at lunchtime, and her parents stay quiet around Eddy, and very polite, as if she were a stranger. Harold brings a turkey sandwich and chips up to her room and knocks. He doesn't wait for a *come in* but just walks through the doorway into her room where she sits on the bed looking at a magazine. He places the plate on her desk and pulls up the desk chair next to her bed.

Eddy looks up at her dad. He notices the darker-than-usual skin under her eyes. She let him give her a little something last night to help her sleep again.

"What, Dad?" The strangely ambiguous question makes him pause.

"First of all, we're concerned about you of course. What a blow you've had—we've all had, even though we hardly knew him … Jay. But you, you were getting to know him better and better, weren't you?"

Eddy looks out the window. "A little better, I guess. But I still didn't know him, not really."

"But you wanted to. That's the important thing. You saw something in him you liked. I'm so sorry. Sorry for his mother and father. Sorry for that poor boy up in the hospital with his leg in traction. Sorry for you and your school friends."

Eddy keeps looking out the window.

"Edna, what can we help you with?"

"Nothing."

"Please talk to us. It's a blow, as I said."

"Dad. I don't know what to say. I don't know how to feel. I don't know where he is. I don't know anything."

"Dr. Stevens would say we know Jay is in heaven. I think that's what he would have said if he had talked with you. Your mother would say that too."

"I don't want to go to school anymore." Eddy says this in a low voice.

Harold thinks a while before he answers. "Edna. The longer you wait to return, the harder it will be. Seems the best course is to go back, take the hard parts of people seeing you, and let the good parts of people come through. Joan will help you. And Paul. Everybody who knew him is hurting."

"I'm not sure how many friends he had. I didn't know his friends, I guess, except for Buddy and Penny."

"Edna, we want you to try to go to school tomorrow. It's almost graduation. I didn't know Jay, but he would want you to walk across that stage. His mother would too, I'm sure. She seemed kind. And now she won't ..."

Eddy looks quickly at her dad. Her eyes are filled with tears. Then she looks back out the window. The sun shines on the leaves of the tree outside her room in a blur of light through the water of her tears.

"We'll all stay close today, and then tomorrow, well, tomorrow will come." Harold stands up and leans over Eddy's bed and kisses his daughter on the forehead.

Joan comes over after school, running up the stairs to Eddy's room and opening the door a bit slowly. "Hey, kiddo. Got something for you."

Eddy looks up from her magazine as she sits on the bed, watches Joanie walk over to the record player.

"No, Joanie. No."

"Please let me. I looked all through all the records at Roses and picked out this one. It's from me. I picked it out because her name, the singer, is Joni. Joni Mitchell. I listened at home before coming over."

Joanie looks at the record that's on the turntable, and sensing that this is the last record Eddy listened to before she heard the news, Joan quickly takes it off, moves it to the side, and slips off the 45 adapter. She slips the new album out of the sleeve, turns on the player, and puts on the LP, placing the arm on the last track of Side 2. She hops up onto the bed across from Eddy as strumming becomes audible. Then a voice.

"Wait," says Eddy. "I know this song already."

"You know that other singer singing it. This singer wrote it. AND her name is Joni."

The two girls sit facing each other but looking down. Joni Mitchell sings "Both Sides Now." When that pure, clear voice sings about the two sides of loving, two sides of living—how even though something is gained from living, some things are lost while living—Joan looks up hopefully at Eddy.

"Well, didn't I tell you? It's good, isn't it?"

"It's you, Joanie."

"No, silly. It's you. And when you come to school tomorrow, just think about this if you think they're looking at you. You've seen things from both sides now. Me too. And maybe a lot of people have. Who knows what goes on inside people's heads. Or hearts. They may be dragging their hearts around behind them. We'll get through this together."

"When did you get so smart?"

"Hey, I've always been smart. You just now noticing?" There's a tiny movement at the corners of Eddy's mouth.

CHAPTER 32

Eddy hardly remembers the Tuesday, the tomorrow that came, the earth's turning that continued whether she wanted it to or not. Tuesdays have always been orange and usually warm, but today she feels all the colors melt into a haze. Somehow Joan and Paul try to find her to walk with her between classes. A few of her friends who know her pretty well and know she was seeing Jay recently murmur things like "So sorry," and some place their hands on her arm as they pass or on her shoulder if she's sitting at her desk. But most people just pass by her, going along with their day as usual.

As for Eddy, she only looks straight ahead or down. She has the sense that besides the awful news spreading these last few days and articles being in the papers (which she knows about but hasn't read), the word has also spread to people who didn't know that she was seeing Jay recently. Eddy feels a sense of *There she is* as she moves through the day. It's the worst kind of feeling to be talked of that way, in whispered conversations out of her hearing but known about nevertheless. She's angry that her parents seemed almost angry with her for not wanting to go to school. She just didn't have the strength to fight them this morning.

Jimmy had been lying low since the news of Jay. But the night before, after sitting in the bathroom for a while, Eddy came out and found the ukulele chord book on her desk. She wondered where he had found it. She picked it up and went to stand at his doorway. "Hey, Jimmy. Thanks."

"Sure thing. Found it in a stack of things in the bottom of my closet. Figured you'd want it."

Eddy nodded.

"Hey, Eddy. I'm sorry about everything."

She nodded again. It was about the most they'd said to each other in days. She thought to herself that it was the kindness of people that was the hardest to bear when you wanted to crawl under a rock. Also, her dad mentioned last night at dinner that Jay's funeral was on Wednesday afternoon at a church out in the country near the Nickleses' house. Tuesday night was the visitation at Stafford Funeral Home. "Eddy, would you rather go to the visitation or the church service to pay your respects to Jay's family?"

Eddy looked at him, mouth open. "You're kidding. Right?"

"Edna Louise," he said in a soft voice, "it's the right thing to do. It will be hard, we know."

Mary nodded and said, "We'll go with you, dear."

"Oh no no no."

"It's the right thing to do to honor your friend and to acknowledge the pain of his family, even if it's the hardest thing to do. I know you know that, Edna?" her dad said hopefully.

So now, on this terrible Tuesday, she bears all the spotlight she hates. Mr. Thompson stops her on the way out of English. The other students move hurriedly around her to get out the door, and when she's all alone with Mr. Thompson, he asks, "Are you coping all right? I know you, and others of course, lost a friend, lost a friend tragically."

Eddy clutches her books to her chest and barely looks up. Her throat is tight. She can't seem to speak.

"Please know that we all grieve such a thing happening, among the young particularly. I know this is hard to bear, but you understand tragedy, I think. It isn't the first, and it certainly won't be the last tragedy for any of us, right? I know you understand this. Shakespeare certainly wrote about it in *Hamlet*, didn't he? And that was a long time ago. But this tragedy is so close to us, to you. Just hang on until breathing comes easier."

Eddy wonders how he can tell she can't breathe.

"If you need to talk …"

Eddy nods again and whispers, "Thanks" and leaves the classroom.

In Trig, Eddy thinks Mrs. Lemons looks at her so tellingly as Eddy takes her seat. Since Mrs. Lemons is a senior class adviser, she's in charge of telling the seniors about the logistics for graduation night.

"Before I go over some instructions, I just want to say to all of you how sorry I am that you've lost a classmate. Even if you didn't know the young man personally, I'm sure you feel the weight of knowing that something terrible has happened." She pauses, looking slowly around the room, making sure her gaze encompasses them all. She pauses a bit longer on the downturned head of Eddy and then continues, "It's okay to talk about this loss. Talk with one another. Even talk to a teacher if you're having feelings you don't know how to process. We care about you."

Even looking down at her hands in her lap, Eddy can feel the unease in the room, as if everyone would like to be somewhere else. As if they would like not to be reminded of this shadow in their lives that hovers, that won't go away. Eddy knows that she'd like these serious words from Mrs. Lemons to end.

Her teacher looks around once more and then looks down at a page in front of her. She begins to tell the seniors where and when they will gather, how they will march in, how they will walk to the stage, and what will happen on stage. The students settle a bit, and some even take notes. Eddy gets through it, and as she leaves class, she glances at Mrs. Lemons and gives the hint of a smile, a smile that says, *I heard you.* And Mrs. Lemons smiles back.

Eddy's chorus class practices strenuously because they have to sing at baccalaureate and graduation. Mrs. Norman barely looks at Eddy, for which Eddy is grateful, and Gwen and Daniella and even Tempest seem to give her space. Or is she imagining it? Penny seems just as sad as Eddy, and there passes between them a look so full of knowing that it brings Eddy some comfort.

Mrs. Norman is definitely not happy with the way they're singing. "Do it well, or we won't do it all!" Mrs. Norman says, raising her voice.

Mrs. Coble nods her head from the piano bench. Of course, everyone knows that they'll have to sing, whether it sounds good or not. The programs are already being printed, and their selections have been put in long before this. Still, the choir senses that they better step up, and it seems to Eddy that when they sing "The Lord's Prayer" and "The King of Love My Shepherd Is," they sing a little more together.

Eddy keeps her head down until Mrs. Norman announces, "Class, Penny has written a song for graduation. It's to the tune of 'Try To Remember,' and so you'll know it quite well and can lead the senior class in singing it. Gordon, will you pass these sheets out to the choir?"

Choir members begin turning to Penny and congratulating her. Penny smiles, a sad sort of smile, Eddy thinks, but she smiles anyway. Eddy looks at Penny. Penny's friend has died, and her cousin is in the hospital, and she's carrying all that inside. Eddy stares down at the sheet and sings along with her class. The song captures moments throughout their high school years. The last two verses are as follows:

> *Try to remember our senior year*
> *Mrs. Lemons's math, to us so dear.*
> *Try to remember our English class*
> *And all those of us who hope to pass.*
> *Try to remember Homecomings and May Days*
> *The proms and the formals now lost in a gray haze.*
> *Chorus:*
> *Try to remember a gay, carefree Sneak Day*
> *We laughed, we ran, we danced, we played.*
> *Try to remember a class that was clever,*
> *The tassel moved, then gone forever.*
> *Try to remember this class worth remembering*
> *As seen through our own eyes.*
> *We now reach for blue skies.*

Chorus:

Eddy waits to walk out with Penny. Penny seemed to sense her waiting, and after accepting more *wows* and *good jobs* from the choir, she joins Eddy.

"Penny, you did it. You made us remember. You made us feel good about our class."

"Thanks."

"How *are* you?" Penny knows what Eddy is referring to.

"You know, we're all so sad we can't even speak of it. How about you?"

"I don't even know how to think about this. It's not real. I didn't see Jay much. He didn't come to my house or … or anything. He didn't call me on the phone. We just …"

"I know. Your situation isn't the same as ours. Jay and I were neighbors, and we saw each other that way. Not often, but sometimes. Jay and I, well, Jay was always just *there*. Buddy… Buddy is family. Our family, my cousins and aunts and uncles, have taken turns going to the hospital."

Eddy nods.

"My parents and I went up there to see him briefly. He's just stuck in that room hour after hour. Do you think anyone else we know has been to see him?"

Eddy looks at Penny. If Eddy has thought of Buddy at all, and they have been fleeting thoughts at best, Eddy has pushed them away. And here is Penny, nice Penny, sad Penny, thinking about Buddy. Eddy says, "I have no idea."

When Eddy gets to the library, Mrs. Rochester tells her, along with another helper, that there are many, many books to shelve since it's the last week of school. *Good*, Eddy thinks. Something to do, something to pass the time. Some work to do to get through the day. Eddy sees Mrs. Rochester looking at her with something like pity. Or does she imagine it?

Lunch somehow passes with no one coming near Eddy as she sits there next to Joan. Joan talks in a normal voice about all the instructions they keep getting for graduation. Eddy thinks Joan is working on staying normal with her, talking about nothing so as not to hint about anything. Eddy appreciates the effort her friend is making.

Then Joey Johnson walks by her table and stops and says, "Eddy, I'm sorry about Jay. And so are the other members of Thee Purity. And Sharon, of course. Thee Purity is planning to dedicate a song to Jay at the first Canteen this summer. Hope you'll be there."

"Thanks, Joey." If he was waiting for more, he doesn't get it. He moves on past her.

In French class, they're to practice conversational French in small groups, and voices go on around her, and no one seems to mind that she just sits there. Joan looks at her and helps divert the conversations in their group. And after French, Eddy makes a decision. Instead of going to Government, she tells Joan that she's going to the bathroom, and then Eddy heads to the bathroom farthest from that classroom and sits on the floor in front of the radiator. She decides to skip her first class—ever. *Maybe I should try to go out the window.* She thinks Jay would smile at this.

CHAPTER 33

Joan is incredulous that her friend skipped Government class. She finds Eddy at her locker when the last bell rings for the day. "Geez! I sat there wondering about you the whole class! Don't scare me like that!"

Eddy apologizes. She's sure Joan understands. Joan seems to try to understand everything. Tonight is the duty-bound, frightening visit to Jay's parents at the funeral home.

At seven o'clock, Eddy and her parents leave for the funeral home. They let Jimmy stay home. She hears her parents in the front seat wondering which people they might see there. Someone from church? People from Harold's work? The low voices of her parents are soothing in a way, but they don't stop the feeling in Eddy's stomach that might make her throw up. When Eddy and her parents pull in to the parking lot of Stafford Funeral Home, they get out of the car and see a short line of people at the entrance. The three of them move to the sidewalk and take their place.

"Edna, you just want to say something to Mr. and Mrs. Nickles. Anything will do. Just being here will hopefully be remembered. They're too sad, I'm sure, to take in much."

"I never met Mr. Nickles," Eddy ventures.

The line moves, and they're inside the vestibule. "Want me to sign the book for the three of us?" Mary asks, then proceeds to sign.

The room down the hall in front of them is where everyone is headed. There's also a room off to the right. As they get closer to the threshold of the door to that far room, Eddy can see the receiving line walking by a casket. The casket is open. Eddy opens her mouth with a sharp intake of breath.

"Dad, I can't do this. I can't." Eddy is breathing shallowly.

"Hang on, hang on, Edna." Harold looks at Mary, and they steer Eddy to the room on the right to sit down. One of the funeral directors sees what's happening and brings a cup of water. A couple of other people are sitting in chairs in this room. Harold says, "Mary, why don't you go back in line and greet the family, and I'll stay here with Edna until you come back. Then we'll see …."

Mary goes back to the line. Harold holds Edna's hand for a few minutes, and then they just sit there waiting. After a while, they see Mary coming back.

"Edna, Mrs. Nickles is coming in here in a minute to see you. She understands you might not want to go in there."

And right as Mary finishes this sentence, Eddy sees Mrs. Nickles coming through the doorway. Harold stands and reaches out to try to help Eddy to her feet. Eddy still holds the water cup.

"Mrs. Nickles, we are so, so sorry," Harold says, placing his hand on her arm.

"Thank you for coming. I … we … thought you might come, Eddy, and I … we … brought this along for you. Jay planned to give it to you at graduation."

Mrs. Nickles reaches out to place a gift wrapped in tissue paper in Eddy's hands, and Eddy reaches for it, spilling the cup of water over their hands and on the tissue paper in the process. An "Oh!" comes from Eddy. Harold and Mary reach out to help, and Mrs. Nickles says, "It's all right. It's only water."

Eddy looks up from her hands into Mrs. Nickles's eyes. They're red-rimmed in her face so drawn with grief that she doesn't look like the woman Eddy met that day in the kitchen or at the concert. "Mrs. Nickles," Eddy begins. "Mrs. Nickles, I can't believe this has happened. I can't believe it."

Jay's mother moves to draw Eddy into a hug of sorts, loose and awkward, but long enough for Eddy to say "I'm sorry" in a gulping sob into her ear and for Emma Nickles to say "I had hoped ..." She stops and starts over. "I'm glad you two became friends."

And then she turns and heads back to the other room. As the three Walterses leave and turn to head back out the front door, Eddy looks to her right into the far room, and she sees Mr. Nickles standing at the end of the casket. He sees that she sees him.

When the family is finally in the car, Harold turns to Mary and says, "Mrs. Nickles ... so brave."

Eddy looks down at the gift in her lap. She pulls back the damp tissue paper to reveal a metal flower. It has yellow petals fanning out around a small yellow dome in the center, and there's a small curved green stem delicately hanging below the petals. On the back stretches a pin for attaching. She knows Jay meant for it to resemble a daffodil. Her mouth and chin tremble a bit as she places the tissue back over the flower and looks up to see her father's eyes seeking hers in the rearview mirror. Her eyes fill with tears, and she knows her father will assume they're for Jay and the gift and everything else, but they're really for herself. They're angry tears. Anger rises up from deep within her because she hadn't yet thought to get Jay a gift.

CHAPTER 34

The week *does* pass. After the initial shock of Jay's death, life returns to last-week-of-school activities for most Thomasburg students. Turning in textbooks, signing yearbooks, practicing for graduation for the seniors. Eddy, Joan, and Paul are standing in the hall after school on Thursday and picking up their copies of *The Tiger Rag*, their school newspaper.

"Why do they call it that?" Joan asks. "I've been here all these years and haven't had the curiosity to ask?"

Paul replies, "Rag is slang for a newspaper. Or a musical piece."

The girls share a look of appreciation for their friend and then keep looking at the paper. There is a whole short story entitled "Renascence" by George Pepper, the senior who won first place in the school's short story competition. Eddy thinks that she should say congratulations to him when she sees him. She also needs to read it to find out what the title means. She wonders if it has something to do with the word *renaissance*, but she's not sure.

There are sports articles about the track team, baseball team, tennis team, and golf team. Under the heading "Puttering Putters," there's a picture of Leonard with the golfers. And along the back page are advertisements for upcoming movies: *Doctor Doolittle*, *The Wrecking Crew*, *Angel in My Pocket*, and starting June 18th, *Romeo and Juliet*. The three friends walk through the parking lot reading as they head to Mary Walters's car. Eddy knows she's hovering, but it's okay. She's noticing how Joan and Paul and Roger and her family almost tiptoe around her, as if they don't want to trouble her sorrow. But each day after school, Eddy goes to her room and curls up on her bed, sometimes pulling the covers over her head, sometimes just staring out the window. Her parents watch her, gentle yet watchful, like they might be trying to get to know a new person. As for Eddy, she sees herself as waiting—only she can't figure out what she's waiting for. *Why does the world keep on turning day after day as if nothing of importance has happened, no tragedy has occurred? What if something else terrible happens? What then?* She feels scared of the world.

On Saturday morning, Eddy is sitting at the kitchen table. It's not early. Mary has pleaded and cajoled to get Eddy to come and eat breakfast. So she has complied. Now Eddy sits staring out the window, and as she watches, the woods fill up with light, striking a tree trunk here, illuminating a green bush there, and then the light moves to warm another part of the woods. Her thoughts remind her of something, but she can't quite remember it. And then Joan and Roger show up at the Walters's front door and ring the doorbell. Harold, who is reading the paper in the den as Jimmy watches something on TV, answers the door and ushers the friends into the kitchen.

"Hello, you two! What a nice surprise! Look Edna," Mary says to Eddy.

Eddy looks their way. "What are you all doing here?"

"Eddy." Joan starts in. "Eddy, Roger has something he wants you to see. It's kind of a surprise."

"Oh no. No surprises." Eddy looks stricken at the thought.

Roger says, "It's not any great shakes as a surprise. Don't worry. You don't even have to say or do anything. Just come with us. In fact, the surprise is really for me. I just thought … Joanie and I thought you might want to ride with us."

Eddy looks at the faces looking at her. Each one holds a hopefulness that she will say yes. Each holds sympathy for her, she knows, but she can't seem to see clearly or express how she's feeling inside. Her thoughts are moving in slow motion as in a dream, and even though she registers what those around her are saying, their voices seem to come from far away.

Then Joan says, "Eddy, we're still hurting too. Let's just go do this for Roger. You don't have to do anything but tag along."

Eddy stands up. She goes upstairs, with Joan following her, and changes out of her pajamas into pants and a blouse. Joan looks around the room while Eddy goes to the bathroom. Things in the room appear just a bit off from Eddy's usual room. The records are stacked too neatly, and the record player's top is down. The closet's clothes are hanging oddly, shoved back on hangers and sticking out every which way. Shoes have just been thrown in the closet on the floor. The desk is cluttered, the bed sheets are wadded up in a tangle. Joanie sees some scraps of tissue paper on the desk. She sees some boxes stacked on the chest of drawers. And when Eddy comes back in the room, Joanie walks to Eddy and straightens her hair a bit. Eddy lets her.

"I see you've gotten some graduation presents," Joanie says, pointing to the boxes.

"Oh yeah. Pajamas. More pajamas. People seem to think I need them for the future. And Grandma Walters gave me an alarm clock."

"When did you pick up the little Lane Sweetheart Chest from Porter's Furniture? I picked mine up yesterday." Joan goes over to the small cedar chest on the bedside table. The store gives one to every girl in the senior class when she graduates. Joan lifts the lid and sees the key taped to the bottom. The cedar-lined box smells fresh and outdoorsy.

"Mom picked mine up this week for me," Eddy says, glancing over at the chest as if she's surprised it's there.

"I think I'm going to put some of Mom's recipes in mine to take to college. Not that I would need to lock them up!" She hoped this would make Eddy smile. "What are you going to put in yours?" Joan asks.

Eddy shrugs. Then she goes over to her desk and turns around with the tissue paper in her hands. "Look, Joanie. I haven't shown you this.

Mrs. Nickles gave it to me and said that Jay had bought it to give to me for graduation."

The girls stand facing each other, looking into Eddy's hands as she pulls back the paper.

"Oh Eddy," Joan says, placing her open hand over her heart, like it hurts her.

"I know. I think he meant it to be a remembrance of the daffodils."

"Of course that's what it is. And the Lane box will be a perfect place to keep it—when you're not wearing it, of course."

Eddy looks thoughtful. Or maybe just absent. "We'll see."

Joan looks like she might say something else about the yellow flower pin, but she doesn't.

———

Roger drives out of Eddy's neighborhood and heads through town. It's Saturday in Thomasburg, and there's a slight hustle and bustle to the morning as people come in from the surrounding communities and from out in the country to shop on weekends. Eddy looks at her town as if for the first time. It dawns on her that she might see Jay's family, and the thought scares her. She turns her head to stare straight ahead while Roger and Joan talk about which street they'll turn on.

"I think it's at the top of Cedar Street. My mom called Dr. Meyer yesterday and asked if we could come. He's expecting us." Roger seems to be saying this for Eddy's benefit, but she's hardly listening.

Roger drives across the four-lane, takes a right on Pine Lane, and then turns left on Cedar and accelerates up a hillside. When they crest the top of the hill, there ahead of them waits a fairly large home with a columned front entrance. The cedars and giant spruce trees almost hide the old home. They park at the front door, and Roger and Joan open their doors to get out.

"I don't think I want to go in," Eddy says, but her friends seem not to hear.

"Here we go," Joan says to Eddy. "This is for Roger. We're just along for the ride."

"Joanie, I remember you said that. I'm not deaf." Eddy's voice has a little edge to it.

Eddy gets out slowly and follows behind as they climb the few steps to the front door. Before Roger can ring the doorbell, the door is opened wide. "Come in, come in! Welcome!"

Roger shyly shakes Dr. Meyer's hand as the local dentist guides him across the threshold; Joan looks at Eddy, and together they walk in.

"Well, well, well. So you have an interest in trains, young man?"

"Yes, sir, I do."

"Right this way, then. June, this young man has a hankering to see my train set." Dr. Meyer's wife June has come in from another room, wiping her hands on a tea towel while smiling at the three friends standing there awkwardly.

"Glad to have you. Billy, come in and say hello to our visitors," June says over her shoulder, and Billy comes into the vestibule from a room in the back. Billy is about Jimmy's age, with a shock of blond hair covering his forehead.

"Hey," he says.

"So who are your friends, Roger?" Dr. Meyer asks.

"Oh, this is Joan Richards, and this is Eddy Walters."

"Nice to see you, Joan, that is, besides in the dental chair!" Dr. Meyer says. His eyes crinkle at the edges because he's smiling. Joan laughs because she has just recently been in to see him. Eddy wonders why her family goes to Dr. Brenner instead of Dr. Meyer. "And young lady, are Harold and Mary Walters your folks?" he says to Eddy. Eddy nods, and Dr. Meyer says, "Billy, you're in school with Jimmy, right?"

"Yes, sir."

Eddy looks at Billy closely but says nothing. She thinks she's seen Billy before but can't remember when. Dr. Meyer looks at Roger and says, "Billy here used to like model trains. Used to help me with mine, and I bought him one of his own, didn't I, son?"

"Yessir. But you took mine out to build that bomb shelter in the basement."

"Well, thank goodness after that missile crisis we didn't need that bomb shelter," Dr. Meyer says. He smiles fondly at his son and then turns to Roger. "So you and your dad are starting a model train of your own?"

"Yessir, we've just started with a small round track and an engine."

"Let's go down and see my setup, shall we?" He leads the way through the hall to the basement door, opens it, and starts down. "I turned everything on for you this morning. Watch your step," he says over his shoulder.

All three friends follow the doctor down the stairs, and Billy comes last. They turn right at the bottom of the stairs, and a huge room opens before them. For a moment, the group just stops and stares. Roger speaks first.

"Holy cow! I mean, golly! What a setup!"

"I'll take that as a compliment, son. Now come on over here, and I'll give you the ten-cent tour." Dr. Meyer has his arm around Roger's shoulder, leading him forward under the overhead fluorescent lights. The girls follow. Before them stands a large low white table about seventy-five feet long and twenty-five feet wide. And what it holds is truly mesmerizing—it's a complete model of the town of Thomasburg, and the railroad features prominently. Dr. Meyer has built the tracks and everything else and displayed his train by recreating the town for it to pass through. He has all the buildings of Main Street lined up perfectly, and the Thomasburg Depot and businesses appear just as they are in real life. The water tower, the churches, the theater—they're all there. Eddy's mouth is open as she looks. Joan keeps glancing at her as they stand next to the gigantic table. She whispers, "Have you ever seen anything like it?" Eddy slowly shakes her head.

Then, to the delight of all, Dr. Meyer flips a switch, and a train engine starts up, and soon thereafter a train whistle fills the air, along with the clack-clack of the train on the tracks. The three friends look up at one another in surprise. It's a good surprise.

"Holy cow," Roger says again.

Then Dr. Meyer moves to the side of the table, and Roger follows him while the girls step closer to the tiny town. Billy is leaning against a far wall.

"Now Roger, my buddy Billy Ride—my son there is named after him—helped me get started on this here project. You know, Thomasburg was once known as a railroad town. People rode the train through here for years, staying at the old Maple Tree Hotel that's now torn down, and even taking in the theater. Did you know the theater once had live shows that featured horses? The boxcars used to bring in everything from livestock to cars to whatever the town needed. Now look, we used a scale of a quarter inch to the foot, which means that everything you see is forty-eight times smaller than the real thing. See these tracks? I had to hand lay these two Brass Code 173s down on fiber and individual wood ties. Used roofing shingles for the rock ballast. Looks real doesn't it? Go ahead, you can touch the tracks; just don't let the train run you over!" With these words, Dr. Meyer tenderly touches the track in front of him. Roger follows, doing the same. Even Joan reaches out to touch the track.

"Eddy, touch it. It's so real," Joan says. Eddy reaches out her fingers just as Joan asks.

The train just keeps circling the huge table, traveling through a tunnel in a homemade mountain painted green with miniature houses and trees painted along its sides; then the engine pulling the boxcars emerges on the other side, chugging by the stores and the businesses and by the depot. Then it begins its trek all over again.

Dr. Meyer is explaining to Roger: "Now the DC power comes from Lionel's Type B transformers from the 1930s, and I use four-inch selenium rectifiers. The cloth wiring is ..."

The girls are leaning over the table as far as they can to see the little buildings of their town, the replicas of the stores they've been visiting for years. "Look," Joan says, "Cato's looks just the same! And The Jewel Box, and the bank, and, and ..."

Eddy adds, "I can't believe he's made every store on the street. There's Mrs. Smith's dress shop. Remember when I asked my mom to buy that green dress for me and she did, and then I hardly ever wore it, and I felt terrible?"

"I haven't thought of that in years! You did feel guilty. And there's the old shoe shop. We definitely didn't like the smell of shoe leather in there. And look. The Episcopal Church by the bridge ...."

"And Vance Hardware. And there's my church," says Eddy.

Joan is nodding and smiling. "Remember when we loved to go into The Jewel Box and peek at the diamonds through the glass counters? We wanted to be rich so we could buy one, or at least buy *something*!"

"Really, Joanie? Did I want to buy diamonds too? I don't remember that." Eddy smiles at her friend. But how much will they remember of these days in the years to come? *Please don't let me forget. Even with the bad things like Jay dying, please don't let me forget.* And the train keeps circling the town. And the whistle blows every now and then.

"Now before you leave, look down into this little square building with the roof missing. See anything familiar?" Dr. Meyer is standing in the middle of the group, pointing to a spot. All three friends take turns leaning way over and trying to see down into the little building. Joan is last. "I see your dental chair!" Joan says loudly.

"There it is, the chair where I spend time making beautiful smiles!"

Joan looks at Eddy as if in disbelief, her eyebrows raised as if to say, is that what he's doing?

"This is unbelievable, sir," Roger says. "Must have taken a long time to make all this. You've got the smokestack from the furniture factory, and there's the mill, and there's the fire station, and ..."

The girls are pointing out all the little cars and trees and power poles and a pickup truck, and Dr. Meyer is letting them pick some of them up. Then he takes each item back from their hands and replaces it gently where it was before.

Mrs. Meyer comes down the stairs with a plate of sugar cookies, and again Eddy finds herself wondering whether her own mother would ever start making homemade cookies to serve to guests. The group gathers around Mrs. Meyer, and each of them takes a cookie.

Joan asks, "Mrs. Meyer, did you have to get used to hearing the train whistle?"

"Maybe at first, but that was a long, long time ago. We're pretty used to all this now, aren't we, Billy?"

"Yes, ma'am."

Eddy gets the feeling that Dr. and Mrs. Meyer have this routine down pat for whenever anyone comes to see the train. Billy too. A tour, a plate of cookies, Billy's part in it all … they all seem proud of this miniature town they've helped create.

The group slowly moves back upstairs and to the front door. Dr. Meyer is talking to Roger about whether he's going to keep on with his model train.

"Now that I've seen yours, I sure hope my dad and I can keep adding to ours."

"Then good luck, Roger." He shakes Roger's hand.

Mrs. Meyer takes her husband's arm. "Good luck to *all* of you."

Mrs. Meyer and Billy go back inside, and Dr. Meyer watches the three friends get in the car and pull away to head down the hill. He raises a hand in goodbye.

Roger looks into the rearview mirror at Eddy. "Well? Wasn't that something?"

Eddy smiles into his eyes. "It was. It really was. Thanks, Roger. Thanks, Joanie."

Joan's smile is the biggest as she looks at Roger and then back at Eddy. "Want to go to the Overlook and scream?"

Eddy looks out the window. "Not today. Not yet."

CHAPTER 35

When Eddy is dropped off at home, she finds her dad and mom planting a few geraniums in the garden beds in front of the boxwoods by the front door. With the woods out back, there's not enough sun for many summer plants in the backyard.

"Where's Jimmy?" she asks.

"Mowing a lawn down the street. He's going to have a nice little summer job." Mary looks up at Eddy when she says this and wipes her gloved hand across her forehead, leaving a dirt smudge behind. "Well? How was the outing?"

Harold stops digging for a minute and looks up. He shields his eyes from the bright sun, trying to see Eddy's face. And when she tells them with a little excitement about the surprise of finding a replica of the town, Harold and Mary seem genuinely pleased.

Eddy seems to be debating something in her head, so Mary asks, "Want to help with this planting?"

"Uh, no. But Dad, Mom … I'm thinking of going up to the hospital to see Buddy."

Both parents' faces shift to seriousness in an instant. Harold speaks first.

"Edna, do you think that's wise? That boy can't speak with his jaw wired."

"I've been thinking …. I don't know Buddy well, but he was Jay's best friend. I keep thinking about him lying up there in that bed hour after hour. I keep wondering, how can he stand it—what happened, that is."

Harold looks at Mary.

Mary is looking at Eddy. "Oh honey."

"Edna, I would be willing to drive up there with you," her father says, "but ..." Harold is rising to his feet when he says this. When he stands in front of Eddy, he seems to be searching for the right words. "But why put yourself—or him—through it?"

"I don't know exactly, but I keep having these thoughts of Buddy come into my head, and I swat them away. I want to swat him out of my mind. But I can't." Her parents wait. "If I just go up there and say I'm sorry for him, maybe that will clear my mind. That's all. I'll just say that."

So that's what the two of them decide to do: ride up to the hospital after supper. None of the family but Jimmy has plans for the Saturday night, not with Sunday and baccalaureate coming tomorrow and graduation on Monday. Jimmy is spending the night with Brad, and tonight's dinnertime conversation centers around Jimmy.

"What will y'all do over at Brad's tonight?" asks Harold.

"Nothing much. We have games of wiffle ball in the backyard till dark. Then we might watch *Adam-12* and mess around until *Mannix* comes on."

"You like those shows, eh?"

"Yeah."

"Yes, *sir*," Harold says to Jimmy.

"Yes, sir. Brad knows all about cars. The cops drive a Plymouth in *Adam-12*, and Mannix drives a Mercury something. Or maybe it's a Dodge. I forget. Brad is teaching me."

Eddy looks at her brother.

"I never knew you liked cars."

"Well, all the guys talk about them, so I guess I better pay more attention. I'm getting my license soon. And Dad, you like cars."

Harold smiles. "I always have. In my small town, cars were a big topic of conversation too. Mary, remember when I bought that car, a Cadillac, right after we were married?"

"How could I forget? It took a huge chunk of your paycheck. But you came to your senses and sold it within a couple of months, I think." They share a smile of remembrance.

"I think you like cars quite a lot, don't you Edna?" Harold asks.

"I like driving them. Don't know how they work though." The silence that follows for a moment is full of something rather than nothing, something a bit too close to what happened to Jay.

Mary takes up the return to speaking, talking of trivial things that bridge the deep silence. "How were my burgers tonight? I put more Worcestershire sauce in them than usual."

"I thought they were a bit tastier!" exclaims Harold, a bit overly enthusiastic.

"Ummm good," says Jimmy. "Gotta go now. See y'all tomorrow."

"Be home by church time," Harold says.

Jimmy looks at Eddy. Eddy raises her eyebrows in an understanding that siblings sometimes share when they're under the same discipline from parents. It's followed by a sigh of acceptance from Jimmy.

The trip up to the hospital on Magnolia Street takes no time. Sitting there large and imposing with its brick walls and two buildings, the hospital has seen better days. Eddy volunteered as a candy striper for a few months during her sophomore year in high school, and she didn't like it, wasn't good at it. The smells, the dark rooms, the poor people, the sick people—and she was supposed to be cheerful and deliver flowers and cards and help out the nurses. She stopped after a couple of months. Her mom was disappointed because she had volunteered in a hospital when she was in high school and liked it well enough. Sitting in the parking lot now, Harold turns off the car engine and looks over at Eddy.

"I don't know what we'll find. Are you sure about this? Are you ready?"

"No …. I don't know …. But I don't want to imagine him up here. Maybe if I actually see him up here then I can …"

Harold pats her arm. He's showered and put on nice pants and a white shirt and tie. Mary asked Eddy if she was going to dress up a bit to go to the hospital, and Eddy's look of generational angst at her mother's ways of thinking was evident. No, she was fine was all she said. So she has on pants, sandals, and a blouse—not tucked in.

When the woman at the front desk gives Harold the room number for Buddy Hall, he asks if Buddy has any visitors in his room. The family has just left, they're told. Harold and Eddy make their way up the elevator to the second floor and start down the hall. The waning sunlight from the window at the end of the hallway picks up the dreary gray colors of the walls, and everything looks dim. Sounds emanate from varying areas; TVs are on, casting wavering lights in some rooms. They pass a nurse heading somewhere. And then they arrive at Buddy's room. The door is slightly open. Harold tells Eddy that he'll stay outside the door for a few minutes so as not to surprise Buddy with a stranger. Eddy knocks and slowly pushes open the door.

"Buddy? It's me, Eddy."

The room is fairly dark, the window letting in the day's remaining light. The bed sits directly in front of Eddy, its headboard against the left, and there's a chair in the corner next to the window. Buddy's raised head rests on two pillows, and his right leg is hoisted up by a pulley of wires, his cast thick from the upper thigh to the toes. His toes stick out from the cast. There's a bar in the shape of a triangle for Buddy to use to pull himself up a bit in an elevated position like he's in now. The TV is on. Buddy's head slowly turns toward the door as Eddy stands there.

She lets the door drift closed behind her and takes a couple of steps to the right so that she can see Buddy more clearly, and so he doesn't have to turn his head so far to the right. His eyes open wider upon seeing her, and then they shut for a minute. When he opens them again, probably hoping that Eddy's not there, she thinks, she also registers how hollow they are. She wonders about the color of his eyes and tries to think if she ever noticed it the few times they were in each other's presence. But she can't see enough in this light. Eddy takes a breath.

"Buddy. I can't imagine how you feel ...." she starts. "I know you're sad—and angry." She waits.

A wire in Buddy's mouth suddenly picks up and reflects the light from the TV, but just for an instant.

"I'm ... I'm sad too. And angry. " Eddy hears voices from the hall. Her dad must be talking to someone. The door isn't shut all the way, and she figures her father has been listening.

"I know you can't speak, but I guess you're wondering why I've come. I don't know exactly." Buddy turns his head from her to look out the window. Eddy falters but then says, "I know he was your best friend. I'm so sorry."

All throughout the car ride to the hospital, she had practiced in her mind how she would say *I'm sorry for you*, giving a slight implication that the accident was Buddy's fault and he was now paying the price, but now she just stops at *I'm sorry*.

"I'm going now." And she steps over to the door. Buddy is still looking out the window. As she opens the door wide to see her father standing there, she thinks that he's about to come in and say something. But then, seeing how Buddy is turned away, her father must have decided not to enter, Eddy thinks. Eddy looks back at Buddy, and she can see his eyes from the side. They're shiny, swimming in the fading light from the window.

PART 6
JUNE 1969

CHAPTER 36

Eddy gets through Sunday morning at church. She gets through Dr. Stevens taking her hand as the family files out the door with everyone else and saying in a low voice, "Good to see you, Edna. If you need me, I'm here." She gets through the afternoon by going over to Joan's and sitting with Paul and Joan on the deck and playing a game of Flinch on the table outside. Mrs. Richards brings them a plate of oatmeal raisin cookies. They don't tell her they like chocolate chip better.

They laugh some as they each tell of the funny graduation gifts they've received. Joan now has some pettipants. Paul asks, "What in the world are they?" and the girls say, "Don't ask." Paul has received a book entitled *Apples of Gold*. Eddy says, "Paul, I got that one too." There are a billfold and white kid gloves, and cash (nothing funny about that, they decide) and pajamas, pajamas, pajamas for the girls. It feels good to laugh, and Eddy knows her friends are delighted that she's laughing a bit like her old self. Her old self. Is she a new self after Jay's death, she wonders?

She gets through the afternoon. She gets through baccalaureate that night, processing into the auditorium to "Pomp and Circumstance" and only coming onstage from her seat along with her fellow seniors to sing with the choir on "The King of Love My Shepherd Is" and "The Lord's Prayer." All the pastors in town seem to be there to participate. Then Eddy sits back down next to the other students whose last names start with W.

There's lots of praying, lots of words about dreams and goals—and God. Eddy feels mostly numb. She wonders if she's going crazy. She wonders if this state, this feeling that she's outside herself watching herself, will be permanent. She imagines herself floating up in the air, hovering like a human bird with arms outstretched and legs sort of dangling behind. She thinks about Jay hovering there beside her, his face looking toward her and smiling and then looking down at Eddy in her seat. The image is comical really. Eddy knows they're not disembodied spirits but the same bodies they have always been, just floating above all the things happening on earth. But Eddy feels more akin to that Eddy than the one sitting in the auditorium. Finally, baccalaureate is over and the seniors process out to the music of "The Grand March."

Her parents talk quietly on the ride home, and Eddy and Jimmy ride along silently. When they come into the house, Eddy says goodnight and goes to her room, curling up in a ball on her bed and thinking about the class motto that was printed on the baccalaureate bulletin, but instead of "The world in which you live is the world you make," she keeps mixing it up and thinking, "The world in which you live is the bed you make."

She whispers, "Jay, where are you really?" She wonders how it feels to be dead—really dead. Again she whispers, "Jay, where are you?" She thinks angrily about how she never got to know him. Not really. She thinks about going over to her record player and putting on "I'm So Lonesome I Could Cry" for the first time in a while just to make herself sadder. But she doesn't because the song runs through her mind anyway, in a loop that seems not to stop. The words repeat over and over: *I wonder where you are, I wonder where you are, I wonder where you are.* And lonesome means something at last.

CHAPTER 37

Graduation day dawns on Monday. Small towns love high school graduations. They have a festive feeling for most people. A red-letter day, especially for families with seniors. For Eddy, this day is just red. She normally likes Mondays because she likes their color. She used to think of Mondays as second chances. When she screwed up at the end of a week, she thought perhaps she would do better the next week, starting with Monday. Mondays have never been blue—Wednesdays are blue, like robin's eggs. But red Mondays burn hot with possibilities for Eddy. Of course, they usually cool somewhat by Tuesday, since Tuesdays are orange.

Eddy arises and sits at the kitchen table, looking out at the woods. She can hear the television in the den, evidence that it's Jimmy's first day of summer vacation. Her mother came into her room fairly early this morning with a cheery "Good morning—it's Graduation Day!" Mary picked up the graduation robe and said, "I'll iron your robe for you as a present! Why don't you put on something kinda nice …. Neighbors are bound to stop by."

As Eddy eats her Cheerios, sure enough, the doorbell rings. Mrs. Clifford is ushered in by Mary. "Hello Dear," she says cheerily. "Brought you a little something for graduation. Know you're excited that it's finally here." Eddy stands up. She likes Mr. and Mrs. Clifford. She'll make an effort. She opens the present. It's a pair of pink pajamas. "For next year at college, dear. We're going to miss seeing you so much. The neighborhood won't be the same."

"Thanks, Mrs. Clifford. And thank Mr. Clifford for me." Eddy thinks that a girl always needs four new pairs of pajamas to go off to college. *College.*

Next comes Hilda Garrison with a picture frame. Then Harold comes home for lunch, and everyone but Jimmy watches *Jeopardy!* in the den while eating sandwiches. Harold and Mary answer a couple of challenges correctly. Eddy answers none. Harold asks if Eddy thinks she'll come home for lunch when she starts her summer job at the grocery store. Eddy looks at her father. Her mouth is open slightly. She hasn't thought of her job in a week. She's supposed to start on Wednesday, or Thursday—she can't remember. She finally mumbles, "I don't know."

Harold doesn't push for more information. He just says he'll be home early to get ready for graduation. And he mentions that he and Mary are looking forward to hosting the after party at the Canteen that night. Again Eddy looks over at her parents. She really is losing her mind. She has forgotten all about her parents hosting. She's not even sure she'll go.

After lunch, Eddy goes upstairs and drags the phone into her room. She calls Joan.

"I don't think I can go to the after party, Joanie."

"Now Eddy, we'll get through it. My parents are hosting too. Lord help us all; there may be more parents there than seniors. Oh well, at least Thee Purity is playing."

"I don't know. You'll have Roger. Paul will have his friends, like Leonard. Even Johnny will have Sandra. So ..."

"Put on that paisley dress that you like, wear your graduation gown over it, and then take it off and go to the Canteen. We'll make it, and we'll try to have fun. I keep telling you, Roger and I are sad too. I mean, a classmate has *died*, and we knew him."

"Joanie ... do you believe in heaven?"

"Of course! Don't you?"

"What do you see? What does your heaven look like?"

"You mean, where do I see Jay? And my grandfather? And everyone who ever died?"

"Yeah."

"I don't know exactly. 'Up there' somewhere?"

"I just don't see anything, Joanie. Well, I had a feeling yesterday that Jay and I were floating over my head, both of us, both looking down at me during baccalaureate. Like an out-of-body experience. But he was beside me! And I was floating too. So that's not heaven. Where is heaven? Where is Jay?"

"Eddy, you're asking questions that I can't answer. Sure, religious folks talk about heaven, but they haven't been there. Why don't you ask your mom? She knows the Bible and all."

"I guess I could." There's a silence on the phone. "Joanie, I'm so sad. I can't explain it. I didn't know him that well, not yet. I feel like something has slipped out of my hands that I didn't have a hold on—not tight enough anyway. Now I'll never have it."

"I know, I know. Hang on, Eddy. There'll be better days ahead, I'm sure. Hang on. And while you're hanging, we'll go to the Canteen and listen to some music. And I'm going to wear the bracelet you gave me with our initials on the charms. And you better wear the jade earrings I gave you!" Both girls laugh at this command. "And Eddy? You gotta start playing your records again."

"See you tonight, Joanie Baloney."

Eddy hangs up the phone and sits there on the floor. She's just staring at nothing. Then she stands up to take the phone back to the stand in the hall. She hears her mom in her room, and Eddy decides to go in.

"Hey, Mom, can I talk to you for a minute?"

"Of course, darling. What is it?"

They both sit on the edge of Harold and Mary's bed. Eddy rubs her hand over the soft beige bedspread. When she rubs one way, the pattern is lighter. When she rubs the other way, the pattern and color darken.

The silence lasts a few minutes with Mary trying to see into Eddy's downturned face. Finally, Mary says, "Honey, I know you're sad. Of course you're sad. What do you want to ask me? You can ask anything, you know."

"I know. But I'm not sure how to think about things. It's like I'm in a fog. I can't get the fog to go away."

"That's sadness. For sure. That sadness won't go away just by asking it to. You're grieving for your friend. You're grieving for yourself, I imagine. Gosh, it's such hard work, all of that missing. But the sadness, or at least the sharpness of it, will lessen, I promise you. I *promise* you. And may I say, even if you don't want to hear it, that you *could* trust us, trust God, until it lessens."

Eddy looks at her mother. "What does God say about heaven? Where is it, if it even exists?"

Mary takes Eddy's hand. She thinks she sees what her daughter is asking. "Edna, I don't know any more about heaven than anyone else."

"But you read the Bible all the time."

"I don't know that the Bible says an awful lot about heaven. Oh, it's in there, but most of the Bible is about how to live now, not later. People do like to speculate though. Streets paved with gold, angels everywhere, and harps! As for me ..." Mary pauses so long that Eddy looks up at her mother, her eyes quizzical. "As for me, I'm going to trust in Jesus's words to that thief beside him on the cross: 'Today shalt thou be with me in paradise.' Whatever that means, that's what I choose to believe because Jesus is confident there is one—a paradise, a heaven. For many reasons, that line brings me comfort. Edna, you will have to decide for yourself what to believe. What comforts you about death."

Eddy looks back down at her lap. "Thanks, Mom." And they both stand up, and Eddy hugs Mary tightly. "Thanks." Mary's arms tighten around Eddy.

"Now let's go eat a bite of dinner and get ready for your graduation. And I've got to see if Jimmy has nice clothes to wear." Mary gives a slight roll of her eyes, and Eddy can't help but smile, thinking that her mother has actually rolled her eyes. Who would have imagined?

CHAPTER 38

The seniors, in their caps and gowns, have lined up in alphabetical order in the hall outside the auditorium doors as they practiced the last week of school. Eddy is near the end of the long snaking line and looks down at the new watch on her left wrist. At dinner, her parents and Jimmy gave her the watch with the band of varied-colored scarabs before coming to the graduation exercises. Eddy loves it, just loves it. Scarabs are popular; she has seen the bracelets on some of the girls at school, and now she has them on her watchband. She's rubbing her fingers over the rough lines of the blue and red and green scarabs, not knowing that they represent the ancient Egyptian belief in the cycles of life, death, and rebirth. She hears the school band start playing "Pomp and Circumstance." The line of seniors slowly moves toward the door and down the aisle. Row by row the seniors take their seats. After a few moments of silence while the last seniors get settled, the ceremony gets underway. First the Invocation by the Episcopal minister about how the Lord is watching over this place. Then Margaret Helms gives her salutatorian speech. Eddy thinks she does a good job speaking about the good teachers she's had and how she feels prepared for the future. That word *future*—Margaret is president of the Future Teachers of America, so it makes perfect sense for her.

Then Eddy has to make her way awkwardly through the row she's in to take the stage to sing with the choir. Two more religious pieces. After the choir leaves the stage and the seniors return to their seats, Janice Hines approaches the podium for her valedictorian speech. She starts a little softly, and Eddy strains to hear, but after a moment or two, Janice hits her stride, so to speak. Janice is good at math, and plans to pursue it in college. But she's also good in English. And every other subject. Janice takes the word *tomorrow* as her theme. Her first sentence is "Tomorrow will come, ready or not."

Over the podium's microphone, Janice's voice grows clearer and clearer, and Eddy feels rocked back and forth in the rhythms of her speech. Words about today and yesterday and other familiar times. Then Janice pauses before saying, "It's the future word, *will*, I want to talk about. Tomorrow *will* come. Are we ready? After we move our tassels today, will we have the *will* and the courage to face tomorrow? Surely we all have hopes and dreams. But will we start the future acting on those hopes and dreams, moving ourselves toward them? Don't put them in your back pocket, or your pocketbook (a little laughter is audible throughout the auditorium), and leave them there. Take them out and look at them, move them around in your head, act on them."

Janice goes on to be specific about her own dreams, about math and outer space and computers. She finishes with saying, "Okay world, here we come; will we be ready? Yes, we're ready! Thomasburg High School has prepared us to *be* ready. Be bold, Class of '69. Have the will to be bold!" And the clapping is louder than the usual polite clapping. Eddy claps hard too. She claps for her classmate who isn't a close friend, but who is nevertheless a person she has known for years. She claps for her classmate who at the end of her high school years has the highest average of anyone in the class and who has earned an academic scholarship to Roanoke College. She claps for her classmate who has a way with words.

Then the whole class stands and sings Penny's class song, "Try To Remember," and Eddy feels the sting of tears as she realizes Sneak Day seems forever ago. The girl she was on that day is not the girl sitting here now. Amid the clapping of the families at the end, the seniors sit back down while Mr. Dockett takes the podium to begin the awarding of diplomas. Mr. Arnold, the principal, takes his place by the table nearby in order to shake hands with each senior and give each one a diploma. Parents seem to be stirring a bit in their seats and getting their cameras ready. Mr. Dockett asks that families not clap too long for their senior so that the next name can be clearly heard when read.

And so it begins, this final process. Eddy is still sitting in her row with the other *W*'s and watching her classmates pass from right to left across the stage when she hears Mr. Dockett read, "Jay Palmer Nickles, diploma awarded posthumously." Even though their teachers have prepared the class that Jay's name will be called, even though Eddy has steeled herself for its coming, the moment of silence afterward when no one starts across the stage sounds like the sound Eddy hears when a conch shell is placed at the ear. That faraway ocean sound fills up the space so completely inside Eddy that it blots out the next name.

Mr. Dockett reads on. It's finally Eddy's time, and having heard "Edna Louise Walters" read out, she walks across the stage toward Mr. Arnold, but first looks at Mr. Dockett, who turns to her and smiles and gives her a friendly blink of his eyes as she passes by him. She's not displeased with his smile, a smile that says *I know you.* When Mr. Arnold shakes her hand and hands her the diploma, she sees the flash of the camera and then sees her father returning from the aisle to his seat as she walks to hers. Finally, Mr. Arnold makes the announcement that the seniors are to all stand and move their tassels from the right to the left sides of their caps. More applause, and then Mrs. Coble starts playing "The Alma Mater."

> *Dear Old Thomasburg*
> *Proudly we sing*
> *Of the glories thy name doth bring.*
> *Hallowed are thy halls*
> *Widespread thy fame;*
> *To thee we lift our voice*
> *Thy works proclaim.*

The class president begins the chant, and everyone joins in loudly: "We're hep, we're fine, we're the Class of '69!" Benediction, another

"Grand March" as the seniors file out less solemnly than they marched in. When the seniors make it through the exit doors to the hall outside, the whooping and hollering begin; the sounds of the young people celebrating are carried on the air back into the auditorium to their families. Out in the hall, Joan finds Eddy, Paul finds them, and together they take off their mortarboards and throw them into the air. *Let the family photographs begin*, Eddy thinks. Graduation is finished. High school is over. And slowly, with a slight heaviness in her body, she moves toward her family when she sees they've entered the fray, and she sees their arms waving to her. And Eddy smiles as she enters the embrace of those arms.

Joan was right. There are almost as many parents at the Canteen as there are seniors and their dates. In Thomasburg, the "Canteen" is a summer term for dances and music held at the gymnasium in the old Central High School that is now Central Middle School. On certain Saturday nights in summertime, the town sanctions dances there and lets bands perform. No one can really hurt that old gym floor any more than it already has been after years and years of use, and there are no plans or money in the town to replace it. It even doubles as a roller skating rink sometimes. But it's a warm old place to young people who don't have to take off their shoes like they do at the newer high school gym. And the town's council lets the music play loudly because there are hardly any homes near enough to mind. Most of the kids don't even know what that word *canteen* means. They don't care—they love going every summer to hear live music and see their friends.

This graduation party sees the students milling around in the nicer-than-usual clothes that were under their gowns at the ceremony. Thee Purity takes some time to finish setting up, and the parents set out drinks and food on the tables lining the wall farthest from the band. The doors to the gym are open, and the evening June air, cooling down a little from the warmer temperatures of the day, makes its way through the doors. The sunlight is fading over the tops of the surrounding mountains, hitting only the top ridgeline in the west as Eddy and her parents, along with Jimmy, park the car and walk toward the double gym doors at the back of the school Jimmy has attended up until a few days ago. They pass under the tall arched windows that gracefully adorn the auditorium of the old building. Jimmy glances up at the windows and says to Eddy, "I'm glad to be leaving this old school behind. It's a good thing you didn't come to that last assembly, Edna. It was boring."

Eddy turns toward her brother. Almost as if it has just dawned on her, she says, "Jimmy, I should have come. I *wish* I had come. I'm sorry. And you played your clarinet in the band, I bet. I should've been there." Eddy chalks up another regret in her long list of those feelings. She doesn't mind feeling the regret. It's better than not feeling anything at all.

"Aw, that's okay." And a look of brother-sister understanding passes between them, and Eddy thinks her brother looks older somehow.

As she steps into the Canteen and stands for a few minutes looking around, Eddy remembers how much she used to like "this old school," Central. How she remembers the oiled wooden floors in the hallways, the tall windows, the grand entrance with columns, and the gym where the light pours in from the high windows. Eddy feels a strange warm, tender feeling for the dark wooden bleachers and the scuffed-up floor where she once played on a recreational basketball team named The Seven Gunners. Seven girls who "gunned" the basketball over and over toward those high baskets; few of those shots found their way *through* the basket, however. She smiles in remembrance of those not-so-much innocent days but days when the whole world seemed young because she was young.

Now Eddy looks for her friends. There are so many small groups standing around, although there are also people moving from spot to spot. Eddy notices how Diane and Carol, the cheerleaders, still cheerful, still light of foot, almost dance between groups. The class president, Sheila McNeill, seems stately and reserved as she talks with classmates. Johnny and the rest of the football players, along with some other guys who play sports, are laughing about something. Johnny sees Eddy, and there's a half-smile on his lips, and she's glad to see that he may have forgiven her. Almost on cue, Sandra looks in the direction Johnny is looking and sees Eddy. Sandra may not be as warmly disposed toward Eddy, for she quickly turns back to the other girls in her little enclave, some of them the girlfriends of these popular guys.

The Black students are standing in a group of their own. The choir too. But certain students, like Diane and Sheila and Gwen and Daniella, Penny, and Andrew are also walking between groups, the amoeba-like shape of each group shifting subtly. Watching the crowd from afar, Eddy likes this, these movements of her classmates. She's startled when she hears Jay's words in her head: *You judging, Eddy?* Her mouth is open as she remembers those words, spoken at another dance. But this time Jay isn't hovering nearby. He's actually *in* her head.

"Hey, Jay," she whispers. If her parents had been looking over at her, they would have seen a slight smile. "I'm not judging—just looking. See? Can you see?" And it comes to her that Jay is now in that "undiscover'd country" Hamlet contemplated. The one no one on earth knows yet.

And then Joan comes skipping over to grab Eddy's hand and pull her farther into the gym. "C'mon Eddy. Music is about to start!" They join Roger and Paul and Leonard and a couple of others in front of the bleachers. Sheila McNeill moves to one of the microphones in front of the band. She says, "This may be the last time I get to stand in front of you as your class president. So welcome, everyone—let's have fun, class of '69!" Some more whooping and hollering follow that. Thee Purity members all look at Mark, who begins counting down "a one and a two and a three," and then comes the intro. Steve on trumpet plays those opening notes from Duke Ellington's "Satin Doll," the intro Joey taught her to recognize. Eddy knows it now. Well, knows that it's the beginning of their set of songs. The seniors just stand there for a minute. Then ... then come the opening notes from Steve's trumpet again, but this time, the drums and the guitars chime in too, and Alan steps up to the mic and calls out for "Dancing in the Street."

At that, couples start heading for the middle of the floor. The trumpet is loud; the band is loud. As the singing begins, Eddy is still standing next to Joan, and when Joan moves with Roger to the edge of the group that's dancing, she turns to Eddy and motions for her to join. Eddy shakes her head, but Joan comes rushing back over to her and starts pulling her to the floor. "Not this time, kiddo. We're dancing every dance with our arms over our heads."

Joan grabs Penny's hand on the way back to the middle of the floor, and the three of them join the dancers, and no one can tell who's dancing with whom. Gwen and Daniella and Johnny and Sandra and Paul and Leonard and Jimbo and Sheila and Betty … it's a free-for-all with arms flying and feet shuffling on the old gym floor. And when Alan sings out the names of cities where people are dancing in the streets, cities like Chicago, New Orleans, and New York City, Joey shouts out, "And in Thomasburg!" And the Canteen rings with the seniors' cheers. More students join in the dancing because, as the song says, all you need is music. Eddy looks over at the refreshment table, and she can see the smiles on her parents' faces. Their relief actually. And for Eddy? It's Martha and the Vandellas, this time channeled through Alan and Joey and Thee Purity. And it's pretty damn good.

On the way home, Harold and Mary are chitchatting up a storm. Even Jimmy mentions a couple of things he witnessed, like boys smoking outside the gym and someone trying to take the band's tambourine at one point but getting caught by Joey. Mary turns to look at Eddy in the back seat.

"Wasn't that nice when Joey said that the next song was for Eddy Walters. What was it?"

"That was 'House of the Rising Sun,'" offers Harold, looking in the rearview mirror.

"Why did he dedicate that to you, Edna?" Mary is still looking back at Eddy. "It sounded like a kinda sad song."

"At first I didn't know why he said that, but then I remembered that even though The Animals made it a hit, Bob Dylan also sang it. Joey knows I like Bob Dylan."

"Well, it sure was nice of him to say that. I hope you were pleased." Mary has turned back around to face the front.

"It was sort of a joke—Joey doesn't particularly like Bob Dylan, but I guess he likes that song well enough for the band to play it."

"Edna," her father starts. "Edna, was the night all right? The graduation and all of it?"

"Yeah, Dad." Eddy rubs her fingers over the scarabs on her watch. "Yeah. It was all right."

"We're proud of you, Edna. For all of it."

Eddy looks into her father's eyes. She's about to ask what he means by "all of it." But she decides not to ask. She's pretty sure she knows what he means.

CHAPTER 39

And so the rest of Eddy's life begins. She starts work at the Shop and Save that week, training to learn the checkout procedure. She isn't that good at it; she goes too fast and makes mistakes, so Mr. Ratcliffe often has her doing other tasks around the store like bringing out extra items from the back, restocking the paper bags at checkout, boxing up the groceries called in by older people who can't come in themselves and have to have boys deliver them. That's her favorite job, with not much talking or interacting with people. Just boxing up items.

Joan is working at a furniture company for the summer, helping with filing and stuffing envelopes, etc. She hates it, but she does it. And Paul helps his father in his construction business, doing odd jobs and running errands. Joan and Paul and Eddy decide to meet at the Overlook one Saturday. Eddy almost protests, knowing Joan is trying to "get her back out there," but she decides to let her win. And Eddy takes her stone from Jay with her, thinking that she might throw it when they all yell together from the top of the cliffs. The three friends stand on the edge of the rock and bend their bodies toward the "abyss" that holds the railroad tracks, the caves below, and the far mountains. They scream. And their screams echo through the still air for a few moments. And then they turn to one another and laugh as only friends can do when they're young.

But Eddy finds that she can't part with Jay's stone. She decides then and there that she will carry it with her to college in the fall. She has one of those sharp pangs in her chest when she remembers again that she never gave him one damn thing, not one gift like a stone or a pin or a record album. But she did give him her kisses, and her scream is a bit primal for all she will miss. And it crosses Eddy's mind to wonder if Jay, wherever he is, carries something of her with him. Like the feel of her hand or the look in her eyes or the touch of her lips. She squeezes the streaked quartz in her palm.

The days in that summer of '69 pass. One Saturday night in June, Harold comes to the bottom of the steps and yells up to Eddy. "Edna, come down quickly. There's something on TV you'll want to see." When she enters the den and stands in front of the screen, she hears Johnny Cash and his guest, Bob Dylan, singing "Girl from the North Country" together. The two singers sit side by side, their guitars strumming and their voices taking turns on the tune, sometimes harmonizing. They're not pure. Just mesmerizing. Eddy stands there till it's over, holding her breath. Dylan's words are about a boy caring about a girl he's not with, a boy who cares enough to hope she has a warm coat against the cold, howling winds.

Harold says, "I was just checking on programs and found this new Johnny Cash Show. And there was your favorite, Bob Dylan, singing with him. Isn't that something?" Eddy smiles at her dad.

"Yeah, that's something," she says. "So it comes on on Saturdays? I'll have to tune in again sometime. Maybe I'll start liking country music more someday," she says to her dad. "Maybe."

And when Joan and Eddy go to the movies to see *Romeo and Juliet*, Eddy can't stop crying at the end; she realizes that those two lovely young people have the most beautiful lines, given to them by Shakespeare to say. Words to break her heart when she hears them. And her heart is broken for them, and for Jay and herself, who, like Romeo and Juliet, didn't have very long together.

Oh, then, dear saint, let lips do what hands do.

She also knows that the music that swells during the death scene is meant to pull at her heart, but her tears still remain unstoppable. Joan puts her hand on her arm to comfort her. But the force of her tears, like a breach in a dam, scares Eddy a little, even though she knows they come from somewhere deep within her and have to do with Jay. Joan and Eddy sit in the theater alone until all the patrons have left. Finally, when the manager starts sweeping in the rows behind them, the friends leave and walk out into the Thomasburg night.

Roger and Joan and Eddy and Paul and Leonard meet at the lake sometimes on the weekends. Sometimes they meet at each other's houses as they've always done. At Paul's one Saturday, he shows them the new album *Tommy* by The Who, and Eddy and Joan join him in listening and analyzing the whole rock opera, as it's called. Eddy likes it immensely. This album is a planned whole with a story. She immediately thinks of Simon and Garfunkel's soundtrack for the movie *The Graduate* and how new and different that choice felt when she heard all that music from the same band thematically related. She suddenly realizes she hasn't played that album in a long time. *Why not?* she wonders. As the friends listen to The Who through Paul's really good speakers that make the music crisp and clear, Eddy recognizes that to hear music, really hear it, she needs a good system like Paul's; she decides to save her money to buy one.

The town's young people go to the Canteen, swim at the lake, walk the streets of the town, and sit in the theater for the latest movies, and as the summer days of June fade, so do Eddy's sobs that seem to come out of nowhere and make her catch her breath; the stabs of pain are not as sharp. Jimmy still annoys her ("Jimmy, you're tracking grass clippings in on your shoes! Stop it! Mom, do something!). Her parents keep on being the same Harold and Mary, going to church, playing bridge, watching Eddy a bit too closely. Eddy hears that Buddy finally got out of the hospital and went home. She and Paul are sitting in a booth at Kenny's after work on a purple Thursday when Eddy overhears someone in the booth behind them talking about how changed Buddy will be for the rest of his life. *Now there's an understatement*, thinks Eddy.

CHAPTER 40

Summer seems surreal in some way. Eddy moves sometimes as if in a dream, again as though she's watching herself. She doesn't feel like Jay is there though. He's not there when she loads up boxes of groceries or helps out at the cash register at the Shop and Save. He isn't there when she watches TV with her parents, just as he wasn't there that time she saw Bob Dylan and Johnny Cash on *The Johnny Cash Show*. He's not there when she and her mother listen to her dad read about the Stonewall Riots in the paper. On June 28th, New York City police raided the Stonewall Inn in Greenwich Village, a bar known to be a popular place for homosexuals, and violent demonstrations followed the raids.

He's not there when she sits in the den reading a magazine and hears her dad in the living room at his desk humming along to Frank Sinatra, who's singing about a girl with moonlight in her eyes. Eddy gives her attention to the song for a few minutes and finds she likes the plaintive song about a time that was "once upon a time." Jay's not there when she sits in the sand at the edge of Claytor Lake, listening to the jukebox. He's not there at Kenny's or the movies, or for her dad's decision to sell the Mustang. But she remembers. She lies on her bed and goes over and over the times she was with him, creating a sort of timeline of events that she doesn't want to forget. His thumb caressing her hands, his arm on her locker and around her waist, his lips on hers. The cave. And the daffodils. Always the daffodils. She hasn't played "I'm So Lonesome I Could Cry" yet. Not yet.

On July 20th, Eddy sits with her parents in the den while Apollo 11 lands Neil Armstrong, Buzz Aldrin, and Michael Collins on the moon. Jimmy and Brad are playing a kids' game called Hats Off on the floor. Harold tells them that they may play but they *must* be quiet. He has to remind them more than once. Mary seems entranced, and even Eddy feels a little of what that first step and those halting words sent back to Earth for all people to hear mean for the world. A step nobody on this Earth has ever taken before. She realizes nobody will ever be "the first" again.

In August, when newspapers and television cover the music festival that would become known as Woodstock, Joan and Paul and Eddy can't get enough. They discuss whether they would have liked to have been there amid all the mud and music—Paul yes, the girls no. But oh, the music! Eddy and Paul particularly can't stop contemplating the sheer number of musicians playing and the songs they chose. When the news outlets cover Hendrix playing a raucous guitar rendition of "The Star Spangled Banner" amid great controversy, they hardly know what to think about it. In his red headband, his long fingers on his left hand picking the strings of his guitar, Hendrix makes the music of the national anthem wail and reverberate through the air. Is he brave? Is he foolish? Is he irreverent? Is he true to himself? The friends pick up magazines like *Seventeen* and *Rolling Stone* and *16*, immersing themselves in all things Woodstock.

Eddy does save her money throughout the summer, and in late August she buys a turntable and speakers on sale at Roses. Even though she knows she needs to save money for college and not depend on her dad for everything, he says he thinks the deal is a good one, and she should buy it. One thing she does know: It will be hard to decide which records to take to VPI in the fall. She keeps adding to her notebook that lists her records and starts underlining the ones she can't leave behind until she realizes that she's underlined most of them.

Eddy doesn't see as much of Roger these days since he and Joan double-date with another couple now and then. But Eddy will forever be grateful to him for "the list." He arrives at Joan's on a warm August night when

Eddy is there, and the three of them sit on the deck and eat cookies. Roger has started compiling a list of songs with lines about trains in them. "We can keep adding to it as we find more songs. What do you think?"

"Roger! You're brilliant!" Joanie yells as she looks over the list. "Eddy, isn't he wonderful?"

"Just brilliant." Eddy nods. And she means it. And then the three of them relive a few moments they recall of that morning in Dr. Meyer's basement and then look at the list and try to come up with more songs with lines about trains. Roger's mom has suggested a couple: "Chattanooga Choo Choo," "The Wreck of the Ole '97," and "On the Atchison, Topeka and the Sante Fe." None of the young people have ever heard of them. Johnny Cash's "Folsom Prison Blues" is on there. "The Midnight Special" is on the list along with "500 Miles."

"Put 'This Train is Bound for Glory' on there," Eddy says. She knows that one from her Peter, Paul and Mary album. And "Freight Train." Joan comes up with "King of the Road" by Roger Miller, and they laugh and sing the line about knowing every engineer on all of the trains and all their children and their names. And Eddy thinks of "People Get Ready." She knows the first line about people getting ready because the train is coming. But she can't remember any lines after that one. The three friends silently try to come up with more. Suddenly Joan shouts, "How about 'I've Been Working on the Railroad'?" And all three of them start singing that old childhood favorite. Eddy comes up with Gordon Lightfoot's "Early Morning Rain" and of course, "I'm So Lonesome I Could I Cry." Both songs have trains in them. Then she asks, "Does the train whistle at the end of the *Pet Sounds* album by the Beach Boys count?" They all wonder, but can't decide, so Roger puts it on there anyway.

"Hey Eddy, is it all right ... I mean, is it okay to talk about our time at the caves and the train going by? I don't want you to be sad," Roger asks this haltingly.

Eddy pauses at the sweet phrasing Roger uses. "Of course we can talk about it," she says sincerely. "That's an exciting highlight of my life. I never want to forget that and the way Jay protected me. How you protected Joanie."

"Well, it was certainly a highlight for me." Roger smiles as he says this and looks kind of adoringly at Joan.

"For me too!" Joan says laughingly.

"I can talk about Jay a bit easier now with you two. And I don't want to forget. We had some good times, didn't we?" The question is met with smiles and hangs in the air between friends. Eddy looks over the deck to the alley below and knows how much she will miss these deck times at Joan's.

When Eddy gets ready to leave to go home, Roger insists that she take the list and keep adding to it. The paper is a smudged mess of Roger's scribbling, but Eddy thinks it one of the best gifts she's ever been given. She promises to type up the list for each of them. It's a lovely summer evening in the mountains, and Eddy feels a breeze with a freshness about it, a coolness that makes her think a change of seasons is coming. The friends make plans to go to their last Canteen that coming Saturday. But beyond that, they don't speak of plans for the future at all.

CHaPTeR 41

It's the second week of September, and Eddy sits in Books, Strings and Things with her college roommate, Sandy, and Paul. Eddy feels like she's pretending to be grown up as she sips a cup of coffee, a drink she's trying to learn to like so that she can stay up late when she's studying. Her courses are a wide range of introductory courses, like English, a higher algebra, a science, and an elective called Music History. She has to take PE and pass a swim test. "A swim test?" She yelled to Joan over the telephone line when they spoke soon after school started.

"Calm down, Eddy. Every college has that requirement."

"Joanie, do you remember how much I hate to be told to calm down?" Eddy says this slowly and in measured tones.

"Yep, I remember. Do you remember hearing me say 'Lighten up'?"

And with that, the friends laugh.

Eddy looks at her coffee cup sitting before her. Everybody at college seems to drink coffee. And smoke cigarettes or pot. And drink beer and wine. She hasn't branched out much yet into any of the slightly taboo and new social activities. Both she and Sandy are taking it slowly. For now, Eddy's looking around.

And as she looks around this store, sees the shelves all around her packed with so many books and then into the next room with the records, old and new, she hurts a little, remembering that time she was here with Jay; she hurts for Jay and everything he's missing. It crosses her mind to ask, *Where are you, Jay?* as she does so often in her mind, but she's getting better at not expecting an answer. Remembering will have to do, and she's resolved to bring him into the present with her memories. But oh how she absolutely hates that it's *life* that he's missing.

Eddy turns her eyes back to her friends as they sit at this little table in Books, Strings and Things. Paul and Sandy are talking about ordinary events. More ordinary events are happening all around their table. There's a hum of everyday sounds that fills the air. Chairs are being pulled out from the tables. Two friends are saying hello as they pass in the store. A person drops a book she's pulled out from a shelf, and Eddy watches as she tries to put it back, running her finger along the book spines, trying to find where it belongs and finally shelving it. Eddy is reminded of her days in the high school library when she shelved books. A song is playing over the store's sound system, and for the moment, Eddy doesn't try to figure it out. She just wants to be—be still and take it all in, as if by listening and looking enough, she could take in enough for two persons.

Yes, Jay, I'm still watching. Not judging, just paying attention and trying to see what's in front of me. I'm not looking too far ahead. I know there are not-so-good things like war and violence and death out there. But I also know there are other things, good things. Like the beauty of daffodils. And the touch of a hand. And friends who laugh with you but also cry with you. Jay, the clouds seem to be clearing, and I think I can see better now. I can't see you, Jay, but I'm carrying the memory of you with me. Carry me with you wherever you are, okay? Why, if you're in the full light, you may actually see everything! Eddy smiles at this thought.

Then she suddenly hears David Bowie's "A Space Oddity" come over the sound system. *Oh if I could give you this music, Jay. A late present. Ground control to Jay. Ground control to Jay.* She smiles as she thinks about her parody of the song. But then she thinks maybe he hears his own music up there, or out there, or wherever he is.

Sandy is saying her name, and it finally breaks through her reverie.

"What?" says Eddy. "What did you say?"

Paul laughs. "Sandy, have you noticed that your roommate is often somewhere else? Lost somewhere? Joan and I often wondered where she was off to, but she always comes back to us—eventually. Just bring the conversation back to music."

Sandy smiles. "Good to know, Paul. What I said, Eddy, is that now that we've finished our drinks, let's go see what new records are in."

"Perfect. I'm with you. And you know what? I'm going to buy the Bowie record for us. And we'll play this record so loudly that it will reach all the way to …"

But their chairs scraping the floor as they stand up drown out the last of Eddy's words.

acknowledgments

I have been so lucky to have had access to the knowledge of others in the writing of this book. After completing a rough draft, these friends agreed to be first readers: Mike Maxey, Debbie Columbus, Becky Rizzo, Belinda Scanlon, Debbie Barber, and Tom Vass. Their feedback and friendship gave me the courage to send the book out to Warren Publishing. After being accepted there, I had the incalculable help of President of Warren Publishing Mindy Kuhn, Vice President and Editor-in-Chief Amy Ashby, along with editors Amy Klein and Danielle Lange, and Marketing Director Lacey Cope, to bring this book to fruition. With their good spirits and know-how, they have led me through the processes of the publishing world to reach this point.

The process of writing this novel was a joy each morning, as I was curious to see what the characters would do next and what would happen in their lives. I learned a lot from these fictional people who are nevertheless composites and blendings of humans I have met along my own path.

My two sons Daniel and Christopher Sarjeant, along with their families, have encouraged me in many ways, and my love for them will be steadfast all the days of my life.

And to my husband Dale, I have to say that his words to me when he finished the book will stay in my heart forever. He said, "I cried." And if you are reading this book, you will understand.

SONGS AND ALBUMS IN EDDY'S NOTEBOOK:

1963
- "Sugar Shack" by Jimmy Gilmer
- "He's So Fine" by Chiffons
- "Heat Wave" by Martha and the Vandellas
- "Sukiyaki" by Kyu Sakamoto
- "My Boyfriend's Back" by The Angels
- "Surf City" by Jan and Dean
- "Louie Louie" by Kingsmen
- "Sally Go 'Round the Roses" by The Jaynettes
- "It's My Party" by Lesley Gore
- "The End of the World" by Skeeter Davis
- "I Can't Stay Mad At You" by Skeeter Davis
- "Surfer Girl" by Beach Boys
- "Foolish Little Girl" by The Shirells
- "Wipe Out" by The Surfaris
- "Monkey Time" by Major Lance
- "Surfin' Bird" by The Trashmen
- "Be My Baby" by The Ronettes
- "I Want To Hold Your Hand" by The Beatles

1964
- "Can't Buy Me Love" by The Beatles
- "Pretty Woman" by Roy Orbison
- "House of the Rising Sun" by The Animals
- "Dancing In the Streets" by Martha and the Vandellas
- "Walking in the Rain" by The Ronettes

1965
- "Hung On You" by The Righteous Brothers
- "Action" by Freddy Cannon
- "Unchained Melody" by The Righteous Brothers
- "Tracks Of My Tears" by Smokey Robinson
- "In My Life" by The Beatles

- "Drive My Car" by The Beatles
- "(I Can't Get No) Satisfaction" by The Rolling Stones
- "Eve of Destruction" by Barry McGuire
- "Tell Her No" by The Zombies
- "You Were On My Mind" by We Five
- "Rescue Me" by Fontella Bass
- "She's About a Mover" by Sir Douglas Quintet
- "Don't Let Me Be Misunderstood" by The Animals
- "Are You a Boy Or Are You a Girl" by The Barbarians
- "Land of 1000 Dances" by Cannibal & the Headhunters
- "California Dreamin'" by The Mamas and The Papas

1966
- "Someone to Love" by The Great Society
- "And Your Bird Can Sing" by The Beatles
- "Homeward Bound" by Simon and Garfunkel
- "Good Lovin'" by The Young Rascals
- "Monday, Monday" by The Mamas and The Papas
- "Wild Thing" by The Troggs
- "Summer in the City" by The Lovin' Spoonful
- "Little Girl" by Syndicate of Sound
- "Hold On, I'm comin'" by Sam and Dave
- "Black is Black" by Los Bravos
- "Sunny" by Bobby Hebb
- "See You in September" by The Happenings
- "I'm Your Puppet" by James and Bobby Purify
- "Mellow Yellow" by Donovan
- "Sunshine Superman" by Donovan
- "Knock On Wood" by Eddie Floyd
- "Mustang Sally" by Wilson Pickett
- "Cherish" by The Association
- "Last Train to Clarksville" by The Monkees
- "I Saw Her Again" by The Mamas and The Papas
- "Eight Miles High" by The Byrds
- "Gloria" by The Shadows of Knight
- "I'm So Lonesome I Could Cry" by B.J. Thomas & The Triumphs
- "I'm A Believer" by The Monkees

1967
- "Stand By Me" by Bill Withers
- "Surrealistic Pillow" by Jefferson Airplane
- "Don't You Care" by" The Buckinghams
- "I think We're Alone Now" by Tommy James & The Shondells
- "Brown Eyed Girl" by Van Morrison
- "I'm A Man" by The Spencer Davis Group
- "Alfie" by Dionne Warwick
- "More Love" by Smokey Robinson
- "All Along the Watchtower" by Bob Dylan

1968
- 2001 A Space Odyssey Soundtrack
- "I Heard It Through the Grapevine" by Marvin Gay
- "Hurdy Gurdy Man" by Donovan
- "For Once in My Life" by Stevie Wonder
- "Atlantis" by Donovan
- "Crimson and Clover" by Tommy James & The Shondells
- "I Started a Joke" by The Bee Gees
- "All Along the Watchtower" by Jimi Hendrix

1969
- Aquarius - Fifth Dimension
- It's Your Thing - The Isley Brothers
- Across the Universe - The Beatles
- Sweet Cherry Wine - Tommy James and the Shondells

TRAIN SONGS FROM ROGER WITH HELP FROM JOAN AND EDDY AND OTHERS

- "This Train is Bound For Glory"
  by Sister Rosetta Tharp; also Peter, Paul and Mary
- "Freight Train" by Peter, Paul and Mary
- "Freight Train Blues" by Bob Dylan
- "I'm So Lonesome I Could Cry" by Hank Williams; also B.J. Thomas
- "Early Morning Rain" by Gordon Lightfoot
- "500 Miles" by Peter, Paul and Mary
- "Life is Like a Mountain Railroad" by Michael Wayne Avery
- "Chattanooga Choo Choo" by The Andrews Sisters
- "Sentimental Journey" by Doris Day
- "The 3:10 To Yuma" by Frankie Laine
- "Orange Blossom Special" by Bill Monroe
- "Wreck of the Old '97" by Johnny Cash
- "John Henry Was a Steel Drivin' Man" by
  The Stanley Brothers; also Tennessee Ernie Ford
- "Take the 'A' Train" by Duke Ellington
- "People Get Ready" by Curtis Mayfield and The Impressions
- "Night Train" by James Brown & The Famous Flames
- "Green, Green Grass of Home" by Porter Wagoner; also Tom Jones
- "House of the Rising Sun" by Bob Dylan; also The Animals
- "King of the Road" by Roger Miller
- "Wabash Cannonball" by Roy Acuff and His Smokey Mountain Boys
- "City of New Orleans" by Steve Goodman; also Arlo Guthrie
- "Folsom Prison Blues" by Johnny Cash
- "In the Middle of the House" by Rusty Draper
- "M.T.A." by The Kingston Trio
- "Last Train to Clarksville" by The Monkees
- "Slow Train" by The Staple Singers
- "I've Been Working On the Railroad" by various artists
- "Shuffle Off To Buffalo" by various artists
- "Mystery Train" by Elvis Presley